ANTHOLOGY OF SHORT STORIES
BY
YOUNG AMERICANS®

2007 EDITION
VOLUME II

Published by Anthology of Poetry, Inc.

Printed in the United States of America

To submit short stories
for consideration in the year 2008 edition of the
Anthology of Short Stories by Young Americans®,
send to: poetry@anthologyofpoetry.com or

      Anthology of Poetry, Inc.
      PO Box 698
      Asheboro, NC 27204-0698

Authors responsible
for originality of short stories submitted.

The Anthology of Poetry, Inc.
307 East Salisbury • P.O. Box 698
Asheboro, NC   27204-0698

Paperback ISBN: 978-1-883931-69-8
Hardback ISBN: 978-1-883931-68-1

Anthology of Short Stories by Young Americans®
is a registered trademark of
Anthology of Poetry, Inc.

www.anthologyofpoetry.com

There is an old expression that says "the proof is in the pudding". When it comes to learning, the proof is in the "putting" down of words on paper. Each year, students from all over the country, ages five to eighteen, submit short stories that reflect the totality of their life experiences, their learning experiences, the nurturing of their families, and the quality of their educators. This year we have been privileged to receive some of the best compositions ever! The stories selected for the 2007 edition of the *Anthology of Short Stories by Young Americans*® are proof of the authors' dedication and the inspiration of those who facilitate their learning on a daily basis. While all authors, both the novice and the fluent, express their individuality, their works will always reflect the influence of those who helped shape their identities.

We hope you will share our delight at the depth of creativity these young authors have shown. Like wildflowers in a field extending to a horizon of brightest blue, each story is as unique and colorful as the wildest of the perfumed flowers are sweet or spicy. Each story is like an explosion of the inner spirit of each child who shares their individual fragrance with us.

As you read each story, try to imagine each child who sits poised over his or her work struggling to find the perfect turn of a phrase; the one thought that will perfectly spice the story so that you may share in their experience. The scent of their "flower" must be precisely described so that you can sense exactly what they are trying to share whether it be as pleasing as a rose in morning bloom or as sad as the day lily closing its beautiful flower never to open again. As we journeyed with these authors through meadows of both laughter and tears, we were deeply touched. We hope that you too experience their joy and sorrow as you explore the prosaic fields that follow. Our hope is that the spirit and fragrance of each child will leave a memorable imprint on you and that you will be profoundly amazed at what America's youth has accomplished. Bravo!

                                                                    The Editors

Registry of Authors

HERO'S ESCAPE

Long, long ago, a meteorite struck Earth. Two hundred years later, twenty-three kids and two adults found out that they had super powers. The next day, twenty-four of them went to Hampden Meadows School. Here are the students who went to this school: Michael, Kellan, David, Reid, Rachel, Nash, Samantha, Nate, Teddy, Lizzie, Samuel, Daniel, Stephen, Joe, Elizabeth, Mason, Amanda, Rebecca, Caroline, Lauren, Jia, Emma, Andrew, and Mrs. Bailey.

Before they were able to use their powers; they had to ace the Super Hero Quiz. All of them did ace the test. Michael, Nash, Samuel, Mason, and Jia can all read minds. Kellan, Samantha, Daniel, Amanda, and Emma can build things super fast. David, Nate, Stephen, and Rebecca can shoot fire out of their hands. Reid, Joe, Teddy, Caroline, and Andrew can run super fast. Rachel, Lauren, Lizzie, and Elizabeth can go invisible for a month. Mrs. Bailey is super strong.

But Dr. Demerit, a bad guy, can go invisible for a month.

A couple minutes later the chalkboard opened up and Mrs. Migeul said, "Mrs. Bailey and class, an evil-doer is on the loose. Try to defeat him."

Then Mrs. Bailey replied, "Strong One, out! Kids, this is a big job. We need five groups. READ GROUP! BUILD GROUP! FIRE GROUP! SPEED GROUP! And INVISO GROUP! LET'S GO! Speed group, stop the rotation of the earth and take red spray paint, once you get the spray paint, spray the earth to turn Dr. Demerit red," she commanded. "Inviso group, go around town and see what's happening. Build group, do you think you can build me a glass helicopter?"

The build group huddled and finally said, "Okay, but we'll need a fire and sand. Fire group, we need it from you. You think you can do that?"

The fire group said, "YES!"

Then Mrs. Bailey said, "Sorry for interrupting, but Read group, read the mind of Dr. Demerit and see what he's thinking. YOU ALL GOT THAT?"

The students all yelled, "YES!"

"THEN LET'S MOVE IT!" she said. They all did their job. Finally they found him. Dr. Demerit was robbing the national bank.

Then he turned around and said, "You will never catch me!"

Then Mrs. B. ordered speed group to make Dr. D. dizzy. Read group actually made a message in Morse code that said, "Let's go, Mrs. Bailey. Go get Dr. D. and throw him in jail!" which she did.

Then she yelled out, "That is for messin' with the Bailey Bombers!"

Andrew W. Kuhn
Age: 10

THE TROUBLESOME BIRTHDAY PRESENT

Sports didn't work for Benny Karkay; just plain and simple. He tried baseball, soccer, hockey, and basketball; they just didn't work. The most activity he did lately was moving his thumb on the television remote.

It drives him crazy when his dad, Mr. Karkay, asks him to go outside and "be a boy"; to climb trees and fences, to get dirty and muddy. Benny never understood this.

His mom, Mrs. Karkay, got him a skateboard before she left for a business trip. He took it outside and started going down the declining driveway. When he got to the bottom, he had quite a few bumps and bruises.

Dad got him a scooter before they moved to Tallahassee. He tried it out not knowing the outcome would be a scraped knee and a broken wrist.

So as you see, Benny tried many activities, but none could be as disastrous as the last time he tried a new activity.

Dad kept begging Benny to put down his new Game Boy he got from his grandparents for his birthday. Dad wanted Benny to come outside with the usual "be a boy" lecture—even on his birthday.

Finally Benny gave in to three minutes of fresh air, no more.

Benny walked out to see a blue and black, sparkling four-wheeler, with a shiny, gleaming, white helmet on the seat. But there was one problem: it was way too big for him.

Not to show disappointment, he ran to his dad gave him a hug and then ran inside to his mom who was watching through the window. He hugged her and said, "Thank you" repeatedly.

He then looked through the window and saw Dad motion him back outside.

When he got back outside he looked at his mom in the window again; she was gone. Suddenly, the garage door opened and he saw his mom with another four-wheeler; this one looking his size. It was dazzling red with an orange helmet.

Immediately it dawned on him: the blue and black one was for his dad and the red one for himself. He went through the whole thank-you article again and immediately wanted to go ride.

His mom said to go for a short while because she knew that a hurricane was supposed to roll in shortly.

Benny leapt on it and put the helmet on. He was really excited. Dad showed him how to operate the ATV. Dad got on his and soon they were in the midst of the woods.

The wind picked up and the leaves seemed like a tornado whirling around quicker and quicker. But Benny wasn't nervous because his dad knew his way around.

Suddenly his dad's ATV hit a rock and Dad was thrown into the winds with no trail. Benny flipped the stop switch on his ATV and got off to run to his dad.

He found his dad lying on the ground with a gash on his head bleeding tremendously. He was conscious, just lying there, weak and suffering.

Benny was really scared. It was raining, hard. Lightning and thunder were making an earthquake in the sky. And it was dark out. He was hungry but that was the least of this thoughts right now.

He started to cry. Benny lay there all night holding his dad crying and listening to the howls of the wind. He later fell asleep.

When he woke up it was the next morning he was a little relieved because the sun was shining some so he could see a little more than last night. It was still raining pretty hard.

Benny stood up and started walking. He soon came across a hut-like tree house on the ground. It looked secure so Benny went inside the dry, small shelter. Inside there was a blanket, a lamp, and some crackers. He ate one and, as stale as it was, it tasted like a hot-fudge sundae. There was also a gallon of dirty water, but he took a sip.

Benny wanted to try to drag his dad out of the freezing rain and into the shelter. When he stepped out he saw a stream running next to the hut. He ran to the water gallon and brought it to his dad to wake him up. He poured it on his dad's face. That woke him up.

Benny filled him in on what was happening on the way to the hut. Dad had two crackers and finished up the water and decided to lie down because he was tired. When Dad turned, he had a huge wound in the back of his neck.

Benny went out to the stream to refill the jug. When he bent down, he saw a black Lab in the reflection of the water. He stood up and looked at the collar and saw the dog's name was Jenna. He laughed and played with Jenna. When his dad woke up about four hours later, Benny asked if they could keep Jenna. Dad said they could keep her 'til they got home.

They then ate some crackers sparingly and drank some water. It was getting dark out and they were tired. Benny thought he saw a light, so he ran outside, only to realize it was a star. Benny fell asleep that night gazing at the stars and petting Jenna. The rain slowed down the next day and the sun was shining.

Jenna wouldn't stop sniffing Benny. Benny told her to stop, and, finally, she stopped. She started sniffing the ground. She mazed through the trees. The farther she went, the fewer trees there were. He started seeing grass. Benny looked up and saw the place where he got his birthday present just three days before—his own backyard!

Benny ran to the back door, pounding on it quicker and quicker with each knock. Mom opened the door and they hugged each other. Mom started to cry. It took a few minutes for them both to notice that Dad wasn't there. Benny introduced Jenna, who led them back to Dad. Dad and Mom were thrilled to be together again. In fact, the whole family was happy.

Later that day Dad went to Tallahassee State Hospital. They said it was lucky that the wound in the back of his neck stopped bleeding.

After some time, they went to the local animal shelter. Jenna was a Seeing Eye dog in training at the shelter. Then the whole Karkay family went out to eat. They were happy to be together.

That night, before Benny went to bed, he grabbed a pen and a sticky note and wrote:

Note to self: ask for a cell phone for my birthday.

Patrick Rogers
Age: 11

"We have decided to form into squads to find food. As you know that we have a lack of food. We need to find food or else many of us will die. Many of us have died already and we will worship them for saving food for us," announced Narth, the king of ants. "Each squad must contain at least one chipmunk and one ant. Whichever squad finds food for all of us first, will earn a little surprise. Perhaps a big surprise. Now gang up together and pack up and get ready to go."

"Yes, Majesty," every ant and chipmunk replied. Honor, an ant, was wandering around to see if he knew any chipmunks. He suddenly bumped into a chipmunk.

"HEY! WATCH IT!" screamed the unharmed chipmunk over all the noise.

"Sorry, I'm just looking for a partner," Honor murmured.

"Oh, so am I. What's your name? Mine is Sparrok," said Sparrok.

"I'm Honor. Would you like to be my partner?" replied Honor more confident this time.

"Uh, sure," answered Sparrok as if he were to think before that.

"All right, let's go. We've packed everything and packed our food to eat," said Honor. So the now friends set off together to find food.

"Hey, I found some berries!" said Sparrok to Honor.

"You did? Where?" answered Honor.

"Over near the dried grass," replied Sparrok. Honor went over to take a look at the berry bush that Sparrok had found.

"I don't think that's enough for over ten thousand ants and ten thousand chipmunks, but it's off to a good start," said Honor. The two friends worked for over an hour trying to get all the berries off. Sparrok would climb the bush and throw down the berries and Honor would catch them and place them carefully in their food sack. The two made a campsite and stayed there for the rest of the night.

"What do you think the surprise is?" asked Honor.

"Huh? What surprise?" answered Sparrok.

"You know the one Narth mentioned. The one if you collect enough food," replied Honor.

"Oh, that one, I really don't know. What about you?" said Sparrok scratching his head.

"Me neither," answered Honor quietly, "let's go to bed."

"All right," said Sparrok.

The next morning, they set off together to collect more food. They did not know something bad was about to happen to them. "La la la," sang Honor.

"Halt," shouted a voice. Both Honor and Sparrok froze. Out stepped three ants and three chipmunks. "Those-e are-e the-e c-collo-on-n-y's b-best b-ullies-s," stammered Honor.

"Those chipmunks are the strongest ones in our colony," Sparrok said quietly. "What do you w-ant?" stammered Sparrok this time.

"What do we want? We want all your food," said the gang boss meanly.

"O-OK," stammered Honor. "Here," as he gave them all the food he and Sparrok have collected. The three ants and three chipmunks guffawed meanly at Honor and Sparrok.

"We're never going to be able to collect enough food to feed all the ants and chipmunks. Do you ever wonder who's going to win the surprise?" asked Honor.

"Hey don't be that discouraged, we could suddenly get lucky and still have enough food," said Sparrok strongly.

"Oh yeah sure, like I'm going to say 'open sesame' in front of the big oak tree and it will open . . ." said Honor rolling his eyes. CRACK! Went the giant oak tree in front of them as it opened up. "Uh . . . heh . . . heh . . ." said Honor backing away.

"Enter if you dare, leave if you don't," said the Giant oak tree mysteriously.

"S-should w-we?" Honor asked in a tiny voice.

"I think we shouldn't act like scaredy-cats," answered Sparrok sarcastically.

"Oh fine," replied Honor. "You go first then."

"Fine, with me," answered Sparrok confidently, as he stepped into the tree. Honor followed Sparrok into the tree.

"Wow," whispered Honor.

"I see you have made it to the good side," boomed a mysterious voice. Out stepped a tree spirit, (Tree spirit: a spirit that lives in trees most likely.) "Since you went in the good side, you will be able to make a wish and I will grant it for you."

"Really?" Sparrok asked suspiciously.

"Really, swear to the tree spirit god," answered the tree spirit.

"Well, we wish that we would have enough food for all the ants and chipmunks and make it back safely without being mugged or something," replied Honor.

Then the tree spirit did some strange gestures and said, "Granted."

Sparrok and Honor make it back safely with all the food just as the tree spirit said.

"All right, now I present the surprise to Honor and Sparrok. In honor of their hard work, I will give my place of king to Honor, and the king of chipmunks will give king to Sparrok!" shouted the king of ants.

"YEAH!" shouted all the other ants and chipmunks. All except the six ant and chipmunk bullies were happy.

Sparrok and Honor smiled at each other and then secretly winked at each other.

Teddy Ni
Age: 10

5

THE NIGHT AT BLACK HOTEL

I was awake at night listening to my radio. On the radio, I heard that a prize would be given to the lucky caller who tells the talk-show hosts the name of the celebrity on the recording. The DJs played the recording. I thought for a minute, then decided to call. "They're probably not going to pick up my call, anyway," I said to myself.

Just as I was about to hang the phone up, I heard a voice. The voice said, "Hi. You are our lucky caller. Can you tell us what celebrity was on that recording?" I almost screamed, but stopped, realizing I wasn't being professional and most importantly, I didn't want to wake anyone up in my house.

I said, "The celebrity was Simon Cowell." They didn't answer. I decided to hang up, but then, again, I heard a voice.

They said "Congratulations! You have earned a night at Black Hotel."

I jumped for joy for about a minute. Then I quickly said, "Thank you. Bye."

When morning came around, I told my parents. I convinced them we would have a great night and it would give us some family bonding time. They finally gave some thought to it. I begged and pleaded. Then, something abnormal happened. They gave in! "Tonight we are sleeping at Black Hotel," I said, as I was waking my little brother up!

He yelled, "What are you talking about? We can't go there. It's a very eerie place and I know that we shouldn't go!" I told him how he was being a baby, so we made a deal. If something goes wrong, I would do his chores for a month. If it goes fine, he does my chores for a month. We shook on it and started packing our bags.

We stopped by the radio station to pick our tickets up and then headed to Black Hotel. I was watching my brother, Johni, stare in horror. Let's just say it's not what any of us imagined it to be like. It looked like a run-down, old, grimy, disgusting piece of building placed in the middle of nowhere. We rang the cobwebbed doorbell. An old man, slightly looking like a butler, came to the door. He showed us around and then brought us to our rooms. Mom and Dad shared a room, so I thought I would have my own room. But I was wrong. I was to share my room with Johni.

We finally got to our room. We walked in, seeing that there was no TV, no radio, and no computer. What were we to do? There was absolutely nothing that interested me in any way. "This must be a mistake!" I said to the butler.

He answered with his voice in a moan saying, "No mistake. You will enjoy your stay at Black Hotel." I was definitely starting to get freaked out. This was turning into a catastrophe. My chance for no chores for one month was slowly decreasing. My brother was saying he wanted to leave. I started questioning.

"You want to send us into the dark at this time of night?" Mom and Dad said we would stay 'til morning and leave right when the sun came up. But I knew I could make this trip better and increase the chance of no chores for a month.

It was getting dark out, so dark, books were not able to read. There was no electricity, so I knew we would have to use candlelight. I looked outside. There was an onslaught of rain coming quickly down the window. It was also starting to thunder and lightning. At the same second I heard thunder and lightning, I heard a loud shriek coming from across the hallway. The shriek pervaded the whole hotel and it slowly echoed again and again.

I got Johni and we quickly swerved around the corner into the hallway. Johni ran as fast as he could, and I could not catch up. I finally caught up to him and made him stop. "What are you doing, Johni?" I asked.

"What do you mean?" he replied.

"You just started to run away from me down the hall. You don't know what could be down there. Why did you run?"

"What are you talking about? I didn't run," he answered. He was definitely starting to creep me out. He didn't give any incentive and he didn't tell me he was just kidding. All he did was stare at me like I was crazy. I ordered him to stay by my side no matter what. He was not to leave my sight.

We continued down the hall. Again, we heard the loud shriek a little further down the hallway. The shriek was such an intense shriek, it sounded like a shriek in a horror movie. Still, we continued down the hall. A big drip of sweat came down my forehead. I was so nervous I could barely move. As we came to the middle of the hallway, there she was. The maid was lying on the ground bleeding. The maid who was to clean our rooms was just about dead. We didn't know what to do.

We decided to go get our mom and dad. We went to their room, but there was nothing. Not even clothes, food, drinks, books, money, and the most horrible part: there were no parents. We were now panicking. We were all alone in this horrible place. We were so scared, not knowing where our parents were. There were no people in this hotel except the butler who had already gone home and the maid who was shrieking in pain in the hallway. But we knew there was one person left in the hotel other than us. That person was the murderer.

My brother knew that it would be a miracle to get out of this place alive. He had a tear rolling down the side of his cheek. We both knew we needed to be quiet so the murderer couldn't hear us. We snuck off to the side corner in our room. We heard creaks coming up the stairs. Our room was right above the three flights of stairs, so I told Johni we needed to go somewhere else. We quietly ran across the hall to the secret staircase, which I'm guessing the murderer didn't know about. As he was going up, we were going down. The door was right in front of us when we heard a voice saying, "Don't you dare move an inch." I told Johni we should run quickly out the door. We did. The murderer was running down the flights of stairs to get us. We were running with all our might trying to get to the police station. We could see him right behind us. We never stopped. We ran straight out the door and into the police station about one second before he was going to grab us. We ran behind the policemen, and the murderer walked right through the door. The chief of police ran up to the murderer, and had his powerful police gun with him and said, "Don't move. You're under arrest." The chief got the murderer in handcuffs.

The whole police crew told us how we were brave and how we did the right thing. They also said Mimerfleemer J. Doohman (the murderer) was on the F.B.I.'s most wanted list.

The chief of police asked us why we looked very sad. We told him that we think our mom and dad died because we did not see them in the hotel anymore. Then he asked us if our mom and dad's names are Joan and Jiff Micron. We answered, "Yes, that is them," thinking the police were going to tell us that they were reported dead last night.

"Well, have we got a surprise for you. They are here," the chief said. Johni and I screamed and hugged the police.

"Where are they? I don't see them," I said. He brought us into this room and there they were; my mom and dad. Mom and Dad explained to us how they thought we were already either dead or at the police station because when we went to see the maid is when they checked our room and, at the time, we brought our stuff just in case we had to run out of the place. This was a life-teaching adventure for me. It told me how important family is. It showed me that you should be thankful for your family and not just take them for granted. I also learned never to call the radio for anymore prizes.

A week later I went to school. I was talking to my friend Lynn. Suddenly, she said, "Guess what?"

I asked, "What?"

"I won a contest on the radio and this weekend I am spending a night at Black Hotel."

Kelly A. Freitas
Age: 12

"Timmy!" shouted Ann Marie. "Come here, now!" she yelled louder.

"One second!" said Timmy. "I've got to get Jinks out of the tree."

"Oh, that little cat!" scolded Ann Marie. Jinks was a jet-black cat, as big as a large notebook. She was a skinny cat with a long tail.

"Hiss!" growled Jinks.

"Jinks, please come down," said Timmy's younger sister, Molly, in a soft voice. Jinks jumped right down and landed on the ground.

"How did you do that?" asked Timmy in amazement.

"It's called being nice!" said Molly in a bratty voice.

"Timmy!" shouted Ann Marie. Ann Marie was Timmy's mother.

"Coming!" yelled Timmy.

"Your father needs you to take out the trash so he can back in the driveway." Timmy headed out to take out the trash when he bumped into Jinks.

"Hey, girl," said Timmy.

"Meow!" cried Jinks in a frightened voice. She seemed alarmed about something. Timmy was not alarmed until he heard a loud scream. Timmy turned around fast and Jinks ran around the corner and scratched Timmy.

"What?" asked Timmy sort of worried. Jinks' meow was desperate. She walked at a speed Timmy could follow. Jinks went into the backyard at a quicker speed. She led Timmy to the junk pit in their backyard. He looked in to see Molly lying in the pit, injured and afraid. "Molly!" screamed Timmy, jumping into the pit. He grabbed Molly and pulled her out of the pit. He picked her up and ran at top speed to the house. Jinks followed. "Mom!" yelled Timmy. "Help!" Ann Marie rushed out the door to see what had happened.

"Get the phone!" shouted Ann Marie. "Call 911!" Timmy rushed into the house and grabbed his cell phone. A minute later, the ambulance arrived, along with the police and firemen. Molly was rushed to the hospital and got better soon. All thanks to Jinks, Molly McConnal is alive!

Hannah Tremblay
Age: 8

THE JOURNEY

Hello! My name is Athena Rabbitt. My brother, Loki, and I got separated at birth. My mom and dad got catnapped so now I am going on a journey to find my brother, mother, and father. Today, I am going on my journey to find my brother, so we can find our parents and be a big, happy family again.

I am ten months old. My brother is a turtle and he is seven years old. I met a porcupine on the way to find my brother, Loki. I asked if I could have a piggy-back ride. I got on his back and—well, I get stuck by all his quills. Then my brother Loki appeared.

Athena are you OK?

Yes, I'm fine, thanks.

Come along Lokadoke.

Where did you get that name from?

Mom and Dad of course. We have to go save them. They are still missing.

I just have to get some stuff.

Like what?

Well food I just left at the lake.

What kind of food is it?

It's fish.

As we were going along we met a wolf.

What is your name?

Athena don't ask him that, said Loki.

Don't worry about me, the wolf said. I am three-quarters wolf and a quarter dog.

My name is Loki and this is my sister Athena.

Why are you in the woods, asked the wolf.

We are looking for our parents. They were catnapped.

Well my owners didn't like me, said the wolf.

Why didn't they like you? Athena asked.

They found out that I was mostly wolf and they threw me out in the woods.

Are you doing okay in the woods? Athena asked.

I'm fine, said the wolf. I love living in the woods.

By the way what is your name?

My name is Scruffy.

Athena it's time to go and it was nice to meet you, Loki said.

You don't have to be so rude Loki, Athena said.

I'm sorry but I just want to get back to our journey.

Maybe Scruffy can help us with our plan to get Mom and Dad back?

I thought you would never ask. Of course he can.

Thank you so much Loki.

You're welcome Scruffy.

This is the plan. Now Scruffy you are going to jump over the fence and run in front of the people and bark. Then me and Athena will jump over the fence and grab my mom and dad. We will go back over and start to meow. That is when Scruffy will come back over and grab us all by our necks and run.

So when we did that we went right to the house. Loki, Mom, Dad, and myself just kept thanking Scruffy so much for saving us.

You're welcome everybody, he said.

After that Loki, Athena, their mom, and dad lived in the woods with Scruffy because he had no family and no friends.

Madison Rabbitt
Age: 8

THE DREAM

I was at home eating food while playing video games. I was thinking of how I would be starting middle school in September. I was really not looking forward to going, but the more I thought about it, the more I wanted to go.

That night as I was playing with my toys, my dad called me to bring him his toolbox. I helped him fix his Corvette. After helping my dad, I went to bed and started thinking of what the new school would be like.

I woke up and got ready for the new school. There was a limo outside waiting for me. I rode the limo to school. I was the most popular kid in school. I had a math quiz and got a one hundred. My next class was woodshop. I made a clock and a cabinet. I went to lunch and ate pizza. After lunch, I went to gym. In gym I climbed a rope and rang the bell. I did twenty push-ups and twenty chin-ups. The class was cheering me on.

The end of the day came fast. My limo was ready to pick me up. Inside the limo on my way home, I watched the Yankees win the World Series.

As the limo was going up the driveway to my mansion, I WOKE UP!!!

Dylan Harrington
Age: 11

POWER OF THE SEA

Pat, Pat, Pat. The waves lapped against the sides of the Sophia Christina as the crew prepared her for her next voyage. I was a passenger on board and was coming for my job as a photographer. We were sailing from San Francisco to the Hawaiian Islands, and I knew that I could get some great shots on the way and at our destination. I gazed out at the endless expanse of deep, blue water, specks of foam frothing at the tips of seaweed-flecked waves clattering down onto the seawater-soaked sand.

"C'mon!" shouted a sweat-drenched figure from aboard the boat. He gestured for me to come onboard the ship. We were sleeping on the vessel that night so I could get a feel of the boat. It was going to be a long trip.

I woke to the soft rocking of the boat in the water and looking up out of my petite room, I saw the five crewmen on deck readying the vessel for launch. I squinted my eyes, blinded by the bright, morning sun. Light flooded in around the outlines of the dark figures, straining their muscles against the halyards. Pure white sails unfurled and sped up the masts like an eagle spreading its wings.

"Ready to launch!" screeched one of the men, Rob I believe, to a worker on the docks. The man doubled over and released us from our bonds, then hurled the thick ropes onto the deck and we tacked out of the harbor.

We were on our way! This would be the furthest distance that I had ever sailed. From San Francisco to Hawaii was nearly two thousand miles! With my camera strapped around my neck, I jogged up the steps onto the deck when "Splash", a long and thin shape hurtled out of the blue mass of water, shattering the surface into thousands of brilliant, shining water crystals, sending them spraying into the cool breeze and in seconds it was gone.

"There's your first dolphin!" said Rob, the friendliest of the sailors. The others that I knew were Jack, John, and Jake. Their parents named them all with the same initials (They were brothers).

"I didn't think we would see any dolphins this close!" I stated, alarmed, but hoping we would see more so I could try and get some pictures of them.

"Close?" bellowed Jake from the rigging. "Look back!" Gradually pivoting backwards, I realized we were not close at all.

"Oh!" I squealed, hardly able to believe my eyes. San Francisco was but a cloud in the distance.

"She's fast in a good wind," Rob replied, and boy did I now know.

Boom! Boom! Crack! Boom! Thunder drums rolled their tune overhead, and it started to pour cats and dogs. Luckily, though, the thunder and lightning was not near our boat. Suddenly, with a huge gust of wind, gargantuan waves began rolling in one by one. The vessel rocked back and forth, knocking me off my feet. Jack looked down at my pale, white face. "Don't worry, the keel will keep us upright," he roared over the gale-force winds, though I could hardly hear his efforts of comfort. The deck was slippery with rain and seawater. All at once something came flying through the air towards me and I knew no more.

I came back to consciousness lying on a soft mattress with some blurry faces leaning over me. As my vision improved, I realized it was the three brothers with Rob. "He's comin' around," Jake uttered, gazing into my eyes.

"What happened?" I questioned, suddenly realizing the crazy pain in my forehead, and reaching up I found an egg planted squat in the middle of my bangs.

"You were hit in the head by a piece of driftwood that flew through the air in those storm winds." John placed an ice pack on the lump, and a cool feeling flooded the bruise with relief. I walked out onto the deck, clasping the icepack to my head. Thump! The ice pack dropped from my grasp, landing with a thud on the wooden deck, and my jaw sank down to my knees at what I saw. It was a rogue wave.

"Get up here!" I screamed at the men below deck, my feet rooted to the spot. The four men leapt up on deck but were stopped in their tracks by the deep blue wall of water.

"Get inside!" they shouted simultaneously. We sprinted down the steps when Whoom! The massive wave shattered the masts, crushing everything on deck. Water rushed into the rooms and we all grabbed onto something. I held onto the remains of a splintering door and held on for dear life. I felt myself rocketed upside down and hurled against the sides of the ship. My knee was crushed against a chair. I cried out in agony. I peered down at my leg and couldn't help but notice the disfigured kneecap. I was jolted onto what remained of the Sophia Christina's decrepit deck. The force of the wave toppled the gargantuan ship, rolling it into a chaotic, tumbling spiral. I was heaved overboard along with the crippled door I had clutched to my chest in a grip the jaws of life couldn't break it out of. I was drenched to the bone in the freezing saltwater.

"Aaaaaahhhhhh!" I screamed, as I sped down the face of the massive force of nature, lying down on the door as if it were a Boogie Board. I turned away from the tube of the tidal wave and I zipped across it. I looked ahead and saw the wave was dying down, and that in about fifty yards in front of me I could be free from the grasps of the horrible thing. I pushed my weight forward and Whoosh! I shot out of the tube as fast as a rocket launching from Earth. I glided through the water, free from the wave, and let out a long breath of air in relief. That's when the crewmen popped into my mind. Memories of the four men I had sailed on this accursed voyage with drifted into the smoke rings of my mind. I wanted to scream, but not a sound could escape my chapped lips. "No!" I squealed, as a dark, looming shape floated into my field of view. I paddled furiously toward the wave and as I got closer I saw through the misty-green, sprouts shooting up out of the thing. The fog was so thick I could have chopped it up and served it for dinner. Then I realized it was not a wave at all, but a beach! I kicked crazily with my leg, launching myself out of the cold water onto the white sands. I lay down, kissing the ground in thankfulness, and sifting the soft sand through my blistering fingers. I dragged myself down the beach, howling in pain as my leg trailed behind me. I finally lost all strength and dropped down onto the sand. Suddenly, as though an angel had called my name, came a voice out of the fog.

"Aloha!" said the angel. I was in Hawaii.

Halyards are the ropes on a sailboat for pulling up the sails.
Tacking is a sailing technique used in certain wind conditions.

Brien Bradley
Age: 11

MAISY'S MAGICAL LIFE

I am Maisy and I have a magical life. My family and I live in a big house! I love the people that take care of me. There's Mom, Dad, Paige, Nathan, and Molly who love and spoil me a lot. My favorite activity is skating on the pond behind our house when it's frozen. I sleep on the couch and sometimes on my big, green couch. I recently turned five on February 18.

I eat anything I can get my paws on. When I get jealous and/or playful, I act silly and go under my mom and through her legs. I open my eyes really wide and smile. When I need to blow my nose, I sneeze. It's so great. They call me Really Lazy Maisy.

Molly Angell Comstock
Age: 9

FRIENDS IN THE END

Between these two people lies a sickening rivalry. The two people are Roy West of the Pacers, and Vince Anthony of the Bucks. This 1996 season was a super competitive one. Two people, and only one position left on the all-star ballot. To Roy's enormous disappointment, Vince made the team. That made the grudge between the two even more important. Eventually, after another week, the news would be out.

Rapid rumors began after the all-star break. The rumors were Vince Anthony would be traded. Three days later, Vince was on the Pacers bench waiting to be put in the game. Roy was furious about this trade. "Why don't the coaches dislike him?" Roy asked himself that many times on that first evening. Vince made a gigantic impact on the team because at one point they had an eleven-game winning streak. A few days after the Pacers lost for the first time in eleven games, Roy asked to have his locker moved away from Vince's.

Next month after losing a game, Roy and Vince had a fight. Roy provoked Vince by saying, "On that last shot, it looked like you were aiming for a person in the stands!" Until the coaches broke up the fight, it went back and forth. That fight caused the downfall of the team. Within time, the Pacers were at the bottom of the ladder, also known as last place. The coaches kept Roy away from Vince, for what seemed like a year. Because of this, they barely conversed with each other. If they did talk to each other, it would only be criticism about what someone didn't do, or should have done.

At home after a game, Roy realized something important. If we want to win, we need to work together, thought Roy. The next day, there Roy was, in front of Vince, apologizing. Vince gladly accepted the apology. Now the team could focus on actually playing basketball.

They ended up winning their division. In the finals, they ended up facing Vince's old team, the Milwaukee Bucks. The Pacers won in four games. Roy and Vince were co most valuable players for the playoffs. Vince won the NBA's regular season most valuable player. This time, Roy accepted the fact that Vince was better than him.

Christopher Celona
Age: 10

THE ALMOST-PERFECT CRIME

"Artifacts from the AMTA--Stolen!" That was the headline on the front page of the Seattle Times on March 12, 1997. Many treasures had been stolen from the American Museum of Treasured Artifacts in Seattle, Washington. I'm Agent James Lowell of the FBI and I was assigned to the case the next day. I flew to Seattle from FBI headquarters in D.C. and immediately began to assess the crime.

When I arrived at the museum, the local police chief met me at the door. He told me all the details of the case. I was most surprised when he told me that no alarms had gone off. He also told me that they had no suspects, no fingerprints, and no DNA. It seemed as if the artifacts had disappeared into thin air. I walked into the museum and began to search the crime scene for any clues. When I got to the exhibit where the stolen artifacts were previously displayed, I saw no point of forced entry; no broken windows, no broken items, and no signs of an intruder on the security camera tapes. It seemed that whoever committed this robbery was very good at what he or she did. I decided to go and find the security guards who were on duty and interrogate them.

When I spoke to them, they said that they had all doors and windows under surveillance. The guards also said that there was a secret entrance to the exhibit which housed the stolen artifacts. They said that the secret entrance was in the museum's vault to which only employees had the password. The guards gave me a list of the employees who worked that day. The employees were Jon Cox, William Jacobson, Marcus Brown, Jamie Smith, and Mary Warren. Those people were now my main list of suspects.

I went to my hotel that night and accessed the FBI database from my laptop. I did a background check on all five suspects. None of them had any history of criminal behavior. However, Marcus Brown and Jamie Smith both had financial problems. The artifacts were worth hundreds of thousands of dollars. Those two suspects had a good motive to commit this crime. I decided to pay them a visit the next day.

First on my list was Jamie Smith. Her house was only few blocks away from the museum. That would give her an easy escape. She also had a big van that would make it easy for her to carry all the artifacts. I rang the doorbell and she answered the door. She said that she would rather talk outside because her house was "dirty." I agreed and began questioning her. She denied stealing anything and was very defensive about it. Her behavior told me that she either knew more than she was telling or that she committed the crime. However, I still had to visit Marcus Brown the next day.

I knocked on Marcus Brown's door and he let me in. We began to talk over coffee. When I asked him about the crime, he too denied any wrong-doing. He implicated Jamie Smith because he supposedly overhead Jamie saying that she didn't get paid enough. She said that she was going to do something to get her message through. This was a very interesting piece of information. I decided to go back to the museum and investigate some more.

Upon arriving, I used my laptop to access the museum database. I accessed two documents that caused the case to make a sharp U-turn. The first had a list of employees who had the vault password. Jamie Smith's name wasn't on it! I also saw a document that showed who had opened the vault the day of the robbery. Marcus Brown was the last one to open it. Now I had to believe that Marcus Brown committed the crime. It was an almost-perfect crime. He left no evidence and made up a motive to implicate Jamie as the culprit. Now came the hard part. I had to catch Marcus Brown, recover the stolen artifacts, and get Brown a nice, long jail sentence. I live for cases like this. Tomorrow, I would start the next phase of the case: catching the perpetrator.

It was March 16 when I went to the local storage facility. I wanted to see if Brown had rented space. He did, but I would need a warrant to search it. When I did, I wouldn't let him know that I suspected that he committed the crime. I would try to arrest him when he least expected it.

The next morning, I went to the Seattle Police Department to get a search warrant for Marcus Brown's storage container. I showed them the evidence that led me to believe that Mr. Brown committed the crime, and they agreed to get me one. They said it would be available that night for me to pick up.

Later that night, I went to the SPD and picked up the search warrant. I went to the storage facility, showed them the warrant, and went to Brown's container. I opened it and there were all of the stolen artifacts! I took pictures, but left them where they were because they were very fragile. Then, I went back to my hotel to get some rest.

The next day, I followed Marcus Brown to work. I was planning on arresting him that day. I went to his office, showed him my badge, and arrested him. There was no struggle. I brought him to the SPD and showed them the pictures from his storage container. Finally, the person who stole the artifacts from the AMTA was in police custody.

Three weeks later, Marcus Brown went to court. I had taken the artifacts from his storage container and returned them to the museum the week before. I was there in the courtroom to show the jury the evidence and give them my report. Mr. Brown was charged with robbery and trespassing and was sentenced to fifteen years of jail time. Local people called me a hero in that case, but for me, it was all in a day's work. Case closed.

Eric Borges
Age: 12

I'LL BE HOME FOR CHRISTMAS

Alyssa sat on her window seat staring aimlessly out of the window. A golden-yellow taxi pulled up in front of her house and honked the horn. Alyssa's father rushed out of the house, luggage in hand. He stuffed his suitcase in the trunk and climbed into the back seat. As the taxi drove away, Alyssa's father waved from the cab and mouthed out the words, "I'll be home for Christmas." Alyssa waved back as a few tears glimmered as they rolled down her rosy cheeks. Her dad had been promising her that for months. She picked up her diary and pen off her rug and began to write.

December 1, 2006

Dear Diary,

Today has to be the worst day of my life. My dad just left for Iraq. I am so horribly sad, I can't take it! I'm not just sad, I'm horrified for my dad.

"Alyssa, time for dinner," her mother quietly declared from the bottom of the stairs.
"Coming . . ." Alyssa mumbled. She looked outside one more time and a flash of lightning struck the sky. She picked up her diary and wrote one more thing before going downstairs.

Dear Diary,

I'm right. Today is the worst day of my life.

As Alyssa slid into her seat at the kitchen table, she could tell by her mother's rosy-red face that she had been crying too. Alyssa's eyes filled up with tears again. She wiped them away with her napkin, but they immediately filled up once more. To keep her mind off her dad, she began to fiddle with her meatloaf.
"Alyssa," her mother whispered. Alyssa knew her mom hated it when she played with her food. Alyssa took a little bite of her meatloaf. She almost never ate the meatloaf her mom made. But that day was different.

December 16, 2007

Dear Diary,

It's been only fifteen days since Dad's been gone. I still haven't gotten over it yet, and I don't think I ever will. It's been so strange without him around . . . I just can't stand it!!

Alyssa glanced out the window at the smoky-gray clouds. One silent snowflake sailed to the road. A couple more followed. Soon, blankets of white were floating and melting on the pavement below. Alyssa thought of those snowflakes as soldiers. One goes to the war and more follow. Before you know it you have a whole troop. The troop soon reaches that dangerous road below and only a few survive. Alyssa squeezed her eyes shut to stop the tears from coming.

"Please let my dad be in that small group that survives," she whispered.

One afternoon at dinner, Alyssa was worried. Her mother's eyes were red like the day her father left.

"Alyssa." Her mother frowned, staring at the chicken in her plate. Alyssa knew something had to be wrong.

"Alyssa," her mother repeated, "there's been a bombing . . ."

"No," Alyssa whispered. "No," she whimpered again. Tears fiercely stung her eyes.

"Your father . . ." Her mom could hardly hold back the tears and neither could Alyssa. Rivers of tears ran down their rosy cheeks.

"This can't be happening!!!" Alyssa cried. "This has to be a dream!!" she screamed.

"It's not a dream, Alyssa," her mom whispered.

Alyssa pushed her chair back from the table and ran up to her room, crying like never before. She dug under her pillow for her diary.

December 20, 2006

Dear Diary,

THIS CAN'T BE HAPPENING!!! NO!!! I CAN'T BELIEVE THIS!!!

Alyssa's diary and pen fell to the rug. She couldn't write anymore. It made her too sad. She buried her face in her pillow and sadly fell asleep, crying silently all through the night.

December 25, 2006
(WORST CHRISTMAS EVER!!!)

Dear Diary,

Things are getting worse than ever!! First, my dad left for the war!! Then his area got bombed!!! He didn't keep his promise!! Now that was bad enough! But now my mom brought home a man named Mr. McKay that she hardly introduced me to!! All she told me was his name and that he's having Christmas dinner with us.

I wish I could rewind my life so that I can convince my dad never to go!!! If only I could!!!

"Alyssa, time for dinner!!!" her mom called from downstairs. Alyssa's anger built up inside of her until she burst. Bang!!! Her diary flew through the air and smashed against her wall. The covers broke in two and all her thoughts and memories flew through the air.

"No!" Alyssa demanded. "I'm not going downstairs to eat with you and your new boyfriend!"

A look of shock swept across Mr. McKay's face.

"B-b-b-boyfriend??" Mr. McKay stuttered.

"Alyssa!!!" her mom screamed. She stormed up the stairs and burst into Alyssa's room. Alyssa was laying on her bed with her face in her pillow.

"Alyssa," her mom whispered, "there are a few things we have to discuss."

She sat down on Alyssa's bed. Alyssa flipped herself over and stared at the ceiling.

"I'm listening," she mumbled.

"First of all," her mom began, "Mr. McKay is not my boyfriend."

"He's not?" Alyssa asked, still staring up at the ceiling.

"No, he's not," her mom declared. "He's my boss. He lost his wife in the war. He had no one to spend Christmas with so I invited him over." Alyssa sat up and looked at her feet.

"So how about we go downstairs and have our Christmas dinner now?" Alyssa's mom suggested.

Alyssa smiled weakly. "Sure."

As Alyssa jumped to her feet, the ring of the doorbell sounded through the house.

"I'll get it!" Alyssa cried as she scurried down the stairs.

When Alyssa opened the door, the sight in front of her almost blew her over.

"I'm home," the man whispered.

"DAD!!!" Alyssa exclaimed, as she jumped into his arms. "You're home!!!"

Alyssa's mom stood there in amazement. "But how?" she stuttered.

Alyssa's dad sat down on the couch as he began his explanation. "There was a bombing in Iraq. But it was about five hundred miles away from the area I was in. They thought I was in that area when I really wasn't," he explained. "Now," he continued, "I have something for you." He poked Alyssa on the nose. He handed her a new diary with pink fur all over it.

Alyssa's smile reached ear to ear.

After dinner, Alyssa ran to her room to write in her brand-new diary.

December 25, 2006

Dear Diary,

Everything is great!!! Absolutely great!!! My dad is back and tonight we ate dinner as a family again (plus Mr. McKay). The best part of it all is that my dad kept his promise. He was home for Christmas.

Love, Alyssa

Kristen Fontaine
Age: 11

My name is Gablowhan and I like candy. I keep it in the room in the attic. I like candy so much. I am the keeper.

Valexja Johnson
Age: 6

COPY BOTS

One day, a famous person named Harold Razor was holding a science fair in a mansion that he owned. Many people entered, but only two were super competitive. They were Tom Press and Bob Hanks. They got into a disagreement on who would win and they became enemies.

The next day, they woke up with the same evil idea to copy each other. So they went to the science fair staring at each other, waiting for one of them to start building.

Then Tom started building and Bob copied him. Then Bob continued and Tom copied him. They kept copying each other until they finished with the same robot. Then Harold Razor saw them and said, "These two robots are copy bots." So they were both disqualified. Finally they forgave each other and became friends.

Matthew Duggan
Age: 9

ZINGOZ

A little zingo was walking down the street in Zingoz World. Her name is Beauty. Her name is Beauty because she is the most beautiful zingo in town. She is raindrop-shaped and is blue. Out of nowhere she heard Thump, Thump. Everyone in Zingoz town heard it. Some zingoz ran, yelling, "Run for your zingo life!" but some of them were just standing there in amazement of what they heard. They heard it again.

Thump, Thump.

"What is it?" Beauty asked herself.

One of the zingoz came and yelled, "It is a human walking near us but it won't hit us." All of the zingoz went back to work and Beauty went back to planting flowers in the garden. Suddenly, a big hand came a picked her up. She started yelling as loud as she could, but she was so far from the ground that none of the zingoz heard her. She found out that it was the same human that was walking near them. The human was a five-year-old girl and her name is Katie. She took Beauty home and showed her to her family. Katie kept the zingo and put her in a cage and would play with her every day. She named her Kate. After about a week, the other zingoz were searching high and low for Beauty. While the other zingoz were sad and not having a good time, Beauty and Katie were having a blast having tea parties and playing hide-and-seek. Beauty won every time. Beauty started to forget about Zingoz World. She was having so much fun with Katie. One day, Beauty got lost in Katie's backyard. The grass was really short so Beauty was lucky there was no dog around. Katie's backyard is a huge place. It was four acres of land. Beauty was scared for a long time and then got used to the backyard. She had to sleep there because she couldn't find the way to get in. The next day she searched for an hour. She was starving. She found a little bit of food and ate some grass. She would eat anything right now. After she ate a little bit, she started to look around again. For about two hours she looked and then took a break. A bird almost took her away. After about another two hours she finally found a way out into the front yard. She ran straight for a while and turned right. She could smell the food they eat in Zingoz World. She knew she was close to the Zingoz World!

She ran full speed ahead and took the wrong turn! After she ran about a half an hour she couldn't smell the food anymore. She was mad when she found out that she took the wrong turn. She tried to find her way back and finally got on the right track. She could smell what she smelled about forty-five minutes ago. Beauty could just taste the food that she smelled. Finally she got back to Zingoz World. She was behind a tree and looked at the town. All the zingoz had droopy faces. One of the zingoz saw her behind the tree and yelled, "Everybody, she's back!" Since they hadn't seen her in about three months and joked that she was back, no one got excited and came running to her, they just kept working and didn't even look where she was standing.

Then they looked and said hi and kept on working. After one minute, they looked backed at Beauty and ran straight for her. After a little while, they celebrated because she got back. The cook made a cake that said "Welcome Back Beauty". They put music on as loud as possible and danced. Remember, if you ever see a tiny raindrop-shaped creature running in your backyard, you have started a zingoz adventure!

Coralie Wilcox
Age: 8

SNOWBOARDING

Snowboarding is not easy, even though it looks it. It takes a lot of skill to try to snowboard. Just to turn takes a lot of thinking on what to do. I tried to snowboard at Yawgoo Valley. I went on the ski lift with my dad. It was hard to keep my board up. It hurt a lot. I did very well for a beginner. At Yawgoo Valley, you have to wear a special kind of boot to fit in the snowboards that Yawgoo Valley has. You have to get one size bigger than your shoe. If you need extra space, rent a locker for only four dollars. There also is a rope to slide up to the top of the hill. Snowboarding is a fun sport to do!

Christopher Wright
Age: 8

The dead leaves rustled as a wolf stepped on them. The wind whistled and made the branches in the trees sway. As little mice heard the wolf and the wind, they scurried from log to log. The wolf got ready to chase. His jaws snapped as he chased after a helpless mouse. He made one determined leap and caught the mouse. Clenched tightly in his jaws, he shook it back and forth until he sensed it was dead. Prancing slightly, he carried his prize to where his mate was waiting. His mate was stretched out on a log napping. She jerked her head up as she knew something or someone was approaching. The male dropped his prize on the dusty ground. His mate lazily got up off the decayed log she was napping on, nuzzled the male in thanks, clenched the mouse in her jaws, and roughly chewed and swallowed.

For on and off moments you could see a full moon in between the swaying trees. As soon as the male's mate was done eating, she lazily walked back to her log and drifted off. The male walked off again and repeated the hunt, except this time kept the prize for himself.

The ground was soft and moist against the male's paws as dirt flew up in the air from behind him. He was digging a burrow for his mate who could not dig because she was going to have a litter of pups in a few days. The male was daydreaming about how he earned his name: Rouse. Rouse had earned it a good time after he was born by his mother because he was a great killer and played sly tricks on other small animals. Rouse's mate, Octavia, simply called him over and asked what he cherished as names for their newborns. Octavia then mentioned a name she dreamed of naming a wonderful girl wolf which was Vantasia. Rouse told his mate that he fancied the names Sly and Springer. Octavia grunted a low, soft bark. She figured if there were three surviving wolves, the two mates could name them that. Octavia let out a soft howl. The sun was just rising and Octavia was in her new den on a bed of soft, pulled-up grass sprawled around on the floor of the moist, safe den. She just gave birth to a handsome male newborn. In the end, she had five pups, but not all survived. One was born dead, the other crippled. Octavia purposely let that one be. Though she felt bad, she knew the pup wouldn't survive. Rouse returned to the den carrying three chipmunks in his mouth. Octavia motioned towards the three living pups. Rouse barked a soft bark in surprise. The pups whimpered softly and nestled closer together in Octavia's fur. Rouse dropped one of the chipmunks by Octavia's paws. Octavia took it and ate it hungrily. Darkness swept over the den a few hours later.

Octavia stirred as Rouse got up and walked out of the den. Across the dead leaves, he slowly crept, making as little noise as a hare scurrying across the leaves, instead of a hungry wolf. Rouse's ears pricked up alarmingly. Someone was here. Rouse froze in his tracks with one paw in the air. Something struck Rouse's leg and sent a searing pain towards it. Rouse fell to the ground whimpering. It struck again throbbing in the back of his neck. He was in great pain—pain that was almost blinding him. He quickly realized what had struck him—a coyote. The coyote had won. Rouse put his head on the ground, let out a howl, and his breathing eventually ceased.

Octavia heard the howl and pricked up her ears alarmingly. She quickly knew it was Rouse's cry of pain. She dreaded leaving her newborns, only she wanted to be at her mate's side. She covered them up with dry grass and nosed them closer together. Octavia softly padded to where Rouse lay. Once she got there, she realized what had happened. Rouse lay there motionless. Octavia had seen many living and dead things in her life and now her beloved mate was among the dead. When she saw this, it hit her like a cold stone. Rouse was gone and now she would have to fight for herself and babies alone. No more comforting, brave Rouse. No Rouse to sometimes surprise her by bringing home meat. At this moment, Octavia realized that she was alone.

Five Months Later

Vantasia's head got pushed against the damp ground, sending little puddles of water to splash up, as Springer and Sly playfully wrestled her down. After a few moments of resting there, she finally regained her strength and got up. She placed her muddy paws on Sly's tiny chest and pushed him down. A cold raindrop hit Sly on his cheek and sent a chilled shiver down his spine. Vantasia, Springer, and Sly were pressed, heads together, in their den, shivering. A gentle sprinkle of rain turned into a great thunder and storm. Octavia had gone off hunting and still hadn't returned, causing her three babies to be famished. Suddenly, as fast as a strike of lightning, the soft earth that had been a safe den collapsed on them from the pressure of rain and wind. The babies panicked and scurried from under the dirt into the whistling winds. The babies stood there dumbfounded for minutes, hours. As daylight broke, their mother, Octavia, still hadn't returned.

Almost everything around where the family used to play happily vanished. Because of the destructive storm, all of the familiar surroundings vanished.

Springer motioned for his littermates to creep into the woods. The babies, mainly following Springer, ventured off, not knowing what they would come to. Lucky for them, their mother had taught them how to hunt for themselves in case they were ever alone, such as right now.

The babies would venture days and nights not knowing where or what happened to their cherished mother. Little did they know that their question would be answered sooner than they were expecting. This is what happened to the not-so-fortunate babies: Just as they normally did, they ventured out trying to find a new place to settle, when they came across a limp animal sprawled out with a bloody hind leg across the path blocking their way. A huge swoosh of fear came across the babies. Their mother also was dead!

For days more, they ventured through the wreckage of the storm. Finally the wreckage started to thin out and the now almost-year-old wolves found a comfortable and warm cave which turned into their home forever. They were little survivors.

Once they were all grown up they realized how they survived—their cherished mother and father, whom they never knew had taught them everything they knew and Sly, Springer, and Vantasia were all happy that their wonderful parents were in a safe and happy place.

Jane Schiavone
Age: 9

THE UNWANTED

Chapter One: The Old Apartment

Inside an old deserted apartment building, voices could be heard in the middle of the night. There seemed to be two young male voices in one of the apartment rooms. One man was sitting in a chair and the other was standing. The first voice asked, his voice shaking, "Master, how could we demolish all the evidence?"

The second voice replied, "You'll have to steal the records file and burn it. In the meanwhile, I'll be hunting down the few witnesses who can still fight."

The first voice asked with a quiver, "Um . . . master? How would I find the folder? Where would I look?"

The second voice hissed, "Just keep a lookout for my signal. You'll be working with another person, just in case one of you gets taken down." The first man shuddered and looked around the room they were in. There was not much in the room. There was a table on one side which was placed next to a wardrobe. Then there was the chair the other man was sitting in. There were four doors in the room and a small window by the first man. There were light curtains on the window so an occasional breeze would enter through the window.

The first man hesitantly asked, "Um, Master, who will you be hunting?"

The second voice replied, "Who I am looking for doesn't concern you, but if you must know, the first person I want is Charlie Brenid. My sources can locate exactly where he is which will help me plenty." A cold breeze entered through the window.

The first voice asked, "Why do you want to kill him?"

The second voice said, "There are some things people should know and then there are things people should not know. Let me put this as simple as possible. If you don't do what I want right now then I'll kill you also." There was a dangerous glare in his eyes which meant he was upset. Only the moonlight lit the room. The second voice commanded, "Now go and find that folder!"

The first voice said, "Yes, Master," and left the room in the blink of an eye.

The glare in his eye was still there which not only meant he was mad, but he was scheming. Only a fool would mess with him.

Chapter Two: Wanted

Charlie Brenid woke up to the noise of other children in the halls playing games and racing with each other. Charlie was sent to a foster home to live ever since his parents were found dead. His parents died eleven years before, when he was only one. No one knew who killed his parents or how they were killed. Charlie was often left out and didn't have any friends. None of the children, younger or older, ever wanted to even talk to him. But he didn't care. He didn't need friends though, at least friends from here. He had never been adopted at all and spent all of those eleven years at the foster home. He had aunts and uncles who visited him often but would never take him in as their own. It would be just too much trouble. From their visits he learned he had an older brother somewhere out there. No one knew his whereabouts. He never even showed up at their parents' funeral. Charlie never remembered his parents. He never even saw a picture of them. He somehow felt his brother, who his aunts and uncles said his name was Lee, was related to his parents' death. Charlie promised himself to one day find his brother and find out how his parents really died. The foster home manager Mrs. Priddle told him that his parents died in a deadly car crash but he knew that wasn't true. He didn't know how he knew, he just did.

He got up and went to go take a shower, got dressed, and ate his breakfast. He lay down on his bed just to think about his life. One of the foster kids stopped outside his door. It was a boy he'd never seen before. He had brown hair and black eyes. He told Charlie, "Mrs. Priddle wants to talk to you," and the boy left immediately. What did Mrs. Priddle want with him? Charlie got up from his bed and headed down to Mrs. Priddle's office.

Chapter Three: Special News

He knocked on her door and a voice from inside called out, "Come in," so Charlie entered. In Mrs. Priddle's office there was a giant window and miles away could be seen. There was a desk at which Mrs. Priddle was sitting. A couple of chairs for visitors to sit in were there and a few plants. She was on the phone talking away. She noticed Charlie and beckoned for him to sit down. Mrs. Priddle got off the phone and crossed her arms on the desk. She started, "Charlie, I have some very special news for you." She paused. "One of your uncles agreed to adopt you." Charlie gasped, filled with shock. Mrs. Priddle continued, "He'll be here by four this afternoon, so get ready and pack your bags."

Charlie asked, "Who will I be staying with?"

Mrs. Priddle answered, "You'll be staying with your aunt Heather and uncle William. Remember he's coming at four." Charlie had heard of his uncle William and aunt Heather but he had never met them. They've ignored the fact that he was in the foster home even though they were at his parents' funeral. He left the office and let out a sigh. He knew that they had a son and a daughter, but he didn't know their names. He also knew his uncle was short tempered, but that was it. He went to his room and got out a suitcase. There wasn't much to pack—only clothes and few other things he had. He was not looking forward to staying at his aunt and uncle's house, but it had to be better than where he was now.

By lunchtime everyone seemed to know that Charlie was leaving. They kept bombarding him with questions only because he was leaving. Had he not been leaving they would have just ignored him completely. He answered almost all of the questions he was asked and by the time he got to his room he was already tired of talking.

Chapter Four: A New Arrival

He was ready to go by the time it was four. He was waiting for his uncle William in the main entrance of the foster home. Charlie had been told to look presentable for when his uncle came to pick him up. At ten minutes past four Charlie saw someone who looked like his uncle walking to enter the building. The man was not so tall and had a mustache. The man walked right past him and stopped at Mrs. Priddle's office. He knocked on the door and entered. At about 4:20 the man came out of the office and stopped facing Charlie. Mrs. Priddle came out also and walked up to Charlie.

She announced, "Charlie, this is your uncle William. He's going to be taking care of you from now on, okay?" Charlie nodded. His uncle seemed to be wearing a forced smile and looked at Mrs. Priddle.

He said to her, "Well, we'll be on our way. Bye." Charlie and his uncle walked out of the building and headed towards his uncle's car. As soon as they closed the car doors Uncle William started talking.

"All right, listen up. I'm going to tell you the rules we have in my house. No asking questions, I will not tolerate disrespect from you . . ." Charlie looked out the backseat window and wondered. He did not know where they were headed to, but did think of asking. He could hear his uncle talking to him but did not bother listening. He wondered what the family was like. He wondered if they were all short tempered like his uncle. The last thing he heard his uncle say was "And never touch anything in the house except for your things while we are out. By we, I mean your cousins, your aunt, and myself." He at last pulled into the driveway and parked the car. Charlie grabbed his suitcase and took it out with him. Uncle William was already opening the door.

As soon as he entered he could be heard saying, "He's here." Charlie entered the house and looked around. He put his suitcase down next to him. He saw his aunt Heather and his two cousins, a boy and a girl, sitting on a maroon couch.

Uncle William started, "Boy, here is your aunt Heather." Aunt Heather looked somewhat tall and had brown hair. She wore glasses and was wearing a blue skirt with a blue shirt to match. Charlie assumed that her favorite color was blue. She was even wearing blue slippers. Uncle William continued, "Here are your cousins Dylan and Lillian." Charlie knew from that day onward his life would change.

Obiora Ofokansi
Age: 12

MAGICAL DRAWINGS

Once upon a time, there was a little girl who loved to draw and her name was Annabella. She was very talented. She created the most beautiful drawings I have ever seen. Every year she won first place at the state art fair.

Annabella had a special room in her house where she hung up all her drawings. She hung them up by category; portraits on one wall, characters on another, wildlife on another, and still-life on another.

One day after returning from a family vacation to Disney World, Annabella went to her art room to hang up her latest masterpiece, when she noticed her drawings were out of order. She thought she was seeing things, so she went upstairs to bed to get a good night's sleep. When she woke up the next morning, she noticed the drawings were still out of order, so she put them each back into their proper place wondering what had happened. All day she kept thinking about it.

That evening, while Annabella was sleeping, she woke up suddenly at the sound of some strange noises coming from the art room. She got out of bed to see what it was. To her surprise, she saw the people, animals, characters, and scenery from her drawings alive and in real-life form. She could not believe her eyes! As soon as the drawing realized someone was there, they froze and jumped back to their places on the wall. Annabella thought to herself, I must be dreaming, and she fainted. When she woke up, she was still lying in the middle of her art room. She thought, my dream couldn't have been true—could it?

That night, she decided to tell her mom what she had seen. To make sure her daughter wasn't going crazy, she agreed to sleep with Annabella to check out this situation. That night while Annabella and her mom were pretending to sleep, they suddenly heard some noise. They quietly tiptoed out of her room and peeked through the art-room door. To their surprise, the artwork was alive just as Annabella had explained. The sceneries and still-lifes were so beautiful and the wildlife and characters were alive and walking around. It was unbelievable. From then on, every time Annabella created a new drawing, she would spy with her mom to see it come alive! They discovered that her drawings were magical. Every piece of artwork that Annabella created came to life secretly. This made her famous and she was forever known as the Artist of Magical Drawings.

Kendra Cimaglia
Age: 10

ZINK

Prologue

Ikka bent down low with a kill inside her beak. Her brood, Pip, stood up tall to receive the food. A sudden noise of a bird in the distress flooded the niche with a screeching. Ikka's feathers bristled with alarm. Pip hissed in fright. His mother relaxed. No matter. Ever since her young one, Zink, had been captured by those detestable human beings to see how different species of birds were doing in the wild, she hadn't cared about anyone or anything, except her sons. Catha, the eldest of them, did not help in finding victuals, which was inconvenient, as Pop was still too little to hunt. She frowned, and felt that somewhere deep inside her, like a buried treasure, something that she had known and was gone, was rushing back to her and she would have it. Soon.

"Numbers 19-B, 26-C, and 45-D to report to lab," came over the loudspeaker.

"Drat," I muttered. Robin came over.

"Hi, Zink."

I shrugged as an answer.

"What's the matter?" she asked, concerned. I told her she'd never guess.

I said, "I want to fly home."

"Oh, yeah?" Robin snapped. "Go try it, then."

"Okay." I wondered if she was serious. "Bye," I called.

"Bye. Oh for Pete's sake," she cried, laughing.

"What?"

"You can't go alone," she retorted.

"Why?"

"I dunno."

"Then you get Gaya and Julian to come with us." I was joking, but I guess Robin thought I was for real.

"Sure." Off she went. I smiled just about as much as a raptor can smile, and more.

We needed to prepare. So that night (unfortunately), Robin decided to be all ready (and crafty) as a thief. Snatching bits of this and that from the kitchens (the humans who ran the lab had left the door open by some carelessness or mistake which made it laughably easy for Robin to nudge it ajar). She did well in getting provisions for the journey. We had expertly planned for the Great Escape to be on the day of the next Tuesday (from my navagational instincts).

Everyone helped get set. Gaya drew up a map, I explored a route to the outside we had found only the previous weekend, and Julian helped raid the icebox. We were satisfied.

I woke to the sound of my best friend screeching at me.

"Get up!" I did, and shot up like a soldier, banging her on the head. Robin was very cool towards me during the first period of air traveling, but she got nicer as we neared the Hushya, a great desert (using Gaya's accurate map of course). I began wondering how we ever survived without it.

On we flew looking (I thought) like tiny toy ships bobbing in the water.

I felt like the place I had been brought up in was close. I remembered memories that had been destroyed: me and my sullen older brother Catha (Pip hadn't been born yet) fighting for minnows in a little pond, teaming with carp.

Robin brought me back to reality. "Earth to Zink," she said, poking me.

I groaned. "Thanks a lot."

She ignored me. "Hey, if you weren't so preoccupied, you'd be able to see that there's a bird on port side."

"Really?" The bird was approaching us. "Uh-oh," I breathed.

"Hello," Robin said nervously. (I hid behind her.) "Do you know the way to the crevasses?" He did not reply.

"Maybe he isn't familiar with what we're talking about," I suggested, peeking at him. I realized what he was going to do a second before it actually happened.

I tried to prevent it.

He struck Gaya. She gasped, eyes widening. I uttered a scream of rage and dove at him. He dodged. I came closer—an error, because a second later his talons raked my face. Suddenly I was falling into blackness and death.

My eyes snapped open like photos out of a camera.

What the heck, I thought.

I was in a hollow.

A bird sailed in casually. "Hey," he said. I started. It was Julian!

"What're you and what am I doing here?!* I demanded crossly.

Gaya came in too. "Zink," she said quietly. "Do you remember—uh—the fight? I looked, horrified. She had a pale scar, on her forehead. It disfigured her face.

"Um, I think so," I stammered.

"Well, after you fell, Julian swooped and caught you before you fell. Then you became delirious."

"What?!" I shrieked, certain I had heard wrong.

"Delirious," Gaya repeated louder.

"You've been up here five days, delirious."

"And—" she paused, suspending me.

"What?"

"Zink, let me introduce you to your mother who rescued you."

I sat in stunned silence. One side of my mind yelled: They're definitely lying to you. The other side shouted: C'mon. You're facing facts. It's true.

"It's not fake," said Robin coming in and breaking the stillness.

I glared at her as if she were crazy.

I looked my so-called parent over.

A body built for flying. A razor-sharp beak. Broad chest.

That red-tailed hawk was my ma.

Yeah.

Epilogue

I stayed on with my mom. As it comes out, like butter on a churn, Robin and Julian decided to remain with me. I am teaching Pip to fly ("Pip, you have to get those wing beats straight. Watch Julian soar.") Work—but a lot of fun. Recently I got a news broadcast from a messenger osprey. It seems that four birds escaped from their cage in a laboratory. Ha.

Caroline Tien
Age: 9

WORRY WART

The lights were flashing behind me, and the siren was sounding. I looked in my rearview mirror and saw the ambulance coming up fast. I quickly pulled to the right to get out of its way. As the flashing lights and loud siren sped past I couldn't help but get the chills. It happened every time I saw an ambulance. The thought of them scared me. I always wondered who was in them and why? Did I know them? I thought about it for a second and then kept driving.

My destination was Pizza Hut. I was meeting my friends there for lunch. I was so hungry. When my stomach growled it seemed louder than the ambulance that had just passed me. I finally arrived, grabbed my purse, and put my phone on silent. I hated it when I was in a restaurant and it rang out loud. I ran inside and luckily for me they already had the pizza ordered. I sat down and began to tell them about how I saw an ambulance and couldn't help but think about the worst when I saw it. They just looked at me funny and told me I worry too much. I do, I thought to myself. The littlest thing gets me thinking and it's never good when I think too much.

We were all done eating and I thought I was going to explode. I got back into my car and looked at my phone. I had one missed call from my mom. She left a voicemail but I called her as soon as I could instead of checking it. She answered and I said, "What is it? Is everything OK?" She replied by telling me everything was fine but I needed to come to the hospital right away. My cousin had gone into labor. The ambulance I saw earlier had her in it. Her husband wasn't home to give her a ride. She didn't think to call anyone else so she called 911. She told me the rest of the story and gave a little chuckle at the end. As I was on my way to the hospital, my heart was beating one hundred miles per hour. I was so excited that she was finally having her baby. I ran to the waiting room. When I got there, there was the whole family. I told them about how I saw the ambulance and how worried I got. They just laughed. I guess not everything was as bad as I expected it to be.

Miranda B. Lundin
Age: 17

MY LUNAR ADVENTURE

Whoosh! We shot into space in our rocket ship. Stars were everywhere. Shooting stars, shining stars, and soaring stars. It was amazing. There were meteors everywhere. I was terrified.

One afternoon, my mom and I went to the museum on 93 Railroad Drive. It was full of space things. I saw an arch that said, "children 8 years or older." When we walked in, there was a huge crowd around a spaceship. I heard a man say, "There are no children in the crowd. There are just adults." I was scared to go into the crowd.

A man on the ceiling hollered, "I see a child!" Everyone stared at me.

A man near a microphone said, "We have a winner!" I was so puzzled I almost fainted. I was chosen to be the first child astronaut ever to go into space to the moon.

After I was chosen, I started packing right away because space is so interesting to me. My friend, Maria, was hoping she could come too, so she packed in my suitcase. In a week we would be going into space. As we were packing, I came across a jar of ravioli. It smelled funny, but I packed it anyway. "Honey," my mom yelled, "go get us some canned food to eat on the trip."

"Okay," I answered. So I went to Stop and Shop.

The next week, we were ready to launch. The man said my mom would drive, Maria would control the map, and I would fill the gas and make sure the flames lit up so we would stay in the air. "Ready to launch in five, four, three, two, one . . ." Whoosh! We shot up into the air. We were flying!

As we were soaring through space, we saw constellations . . . Leo, Zeus, Scorpius, and Conis Major. Next, we saw a field of stars. They were beautiful. Then I heard a rumble. A meteor shower had begun! Soon we reached the moon, escaping the meteor shower. It was very dark on the moon. It looked nothing like Earth. We had to stay on the moon for one day. Soon it was late. We had to hop back to the ship to sleep. That night, I dreamed we met an alien on the moon. It scared me a bit but I knew it was only a dream. Or was it? Soon we returned to Earth with some rocks from the moon. I saw something on the spaceship. It can't be . . . can it? I wondered. But it was a tiny, green alien on the spaceship. Just like the one in my dream.

Adriana Saccoccio
Age: 8

SHARDS

My father worked the late shift at a grocery in Northampton, punching in amounts for England's nocturnal wanderers. He bought all our food at the grocery, and saved all the money he could. The money was part of something larger, a sign along the road to the Promised Land that was prosperity in England. The English grocery was below my father, who reluctantly traded in his pride, his store, for new dreams for his family and four plane tickets to London. Flying above the ghats as our city drifted away, we were false royalty, off to settle down in a new kingdom.

Our kingdom's rolling hills turned out to be once sparkling white, but now jaundiced linoleum that would cling to the bottom of my father's shoes when he walked in at 9:30, thirty minutes before his shift began, to assiduously clean the entire store. The afternoon clerk, a sallow man in his thirties, would silently watch my father, bewildered by the foreigner's interest in everything, even the roach traps.

This meant that the floor was already clean as I slaved over it, a punishment for bad marks. Then two young men came in and dragged England's dirt from their boots all over my floor. My father gave me a look and pointedly glanced towards the newly soiled spot, but remained silent. They walked through the aisles, pulling down bags of chips and putting them in a basket. One grabbed a pack of ales and brought it to the counter. My father, elevated behind the counter, peered down at their assortment of purchases. Meticulously, he typed in each price, careful not to miss a pence on the old machine. When he reached the ale, he paused, and almost reluctantly asked, "Sir, could I please see a form of identification?"

The young man half-heartedly patted his jean's pocket. He turned to his friend and murmured for an ID. The friend looked blank, stuck his hands in his pockets and came up empty.

"Sir, I'm sorry," my father said. "I would sell it, but I need identification."

"Do you think you could do it just this once?" the youth asked.

"I don't want any trouble, sir. I'm sorry, but I can't sell you this."

And with that, the man shoved the mess of snacks across the counter, until they went toppling over, along with the few small, religious idols of Ganesha my father kept there. The ale bottles shattered and the liquid crept over the tiles behind the counter, soaking the plastic bags and my father's tired loafers. For a moment, he stood silent, as if contemplating simply leaving the mess. But then he slowly folded, taking a washcloth with him, and I heard nothing but the clink of ceramic pieces against the floor as he soaked up the bitter spirits. I stood still and silent, watching my father's bowed back. Then, as the men left, I looked down, suddenly keen to follow the path of the mop's thick tendrils.

I finished the floor and began tidying the shelves where the men had left a trail of misplaced items and empty spaces. Erasing their traces, I walked over with a new pack of ales from the back, and I put them in the refrigerator. From where I was standing, I saw my father crouched over on his knees, his hands wet from the paper towel with which he was drying the spilled liquids. As I walked into the cold, I noticed that from the corner of my eye, my father was suddenly very small. He almost couldn't fit behind the counter in Bombay, but in the grocery, he was hidden completely.

That night, I awoke and walked to the communal kitchen on our floor. Seeing a light in the doorway, I paused and looked inside. Crumpled in a worn, plastic chair by the table was my father. In one hand he held the bottle that had escaped quick death on the linoleum. His lips were wet from his tears and the ale that had crept into his mouth for the first time. In his other hand, he held the tube of glue my younger brother used to craft masterpieces of macaroni. My father's project was proving harder than a simple frame, and although he had all the adhesive he needed, he could not stick the pieces together to remake the broken Ganesha.

Tarit Rao-Chakravorti
Age: 16

WHAT ABOUT SCHOOLWORK?
A Student's Point Of View

In school, if you don't listen, you will not learn what your teachers want you to learn. They will ask you if you know what she said because teachers know when you are not listening in class. Even if you are bored, you still have to pay attention in class. If you want to be smart, listen in class when the teacher is talking to the class. Sometimes teachers will wait for you to be quiet, but sometimes they make you stay in for recess. Sometimes she will wait and wait and wait for you to stop talking for about two minutes or more. If this happens, your parents will be really mad at you and you will probably get grounded or have to do chores for a month or two months or three months or more! It is important to be a good student in school because you will get a good report card and you won't get in trouble or stay in for recess and you will be smart too!

Michaela Simanski
Age: 9

STALKING GEORGE LUCAS

At 1:38 a.m., the plane Jim-Bob and his parents were on landed at the airport in Nicasio, California. Despite the fact that it was scorching outside, Jim-Bob didn't notice the heat. His parents said that they were going to spend their vacation visiting the Nicasio Reservoir and other local landmarks, but he had other plans. As the plane touched down onto the tarmac, Jim-Bob put the finishing touches on his scheme to slip past the security at nearby Skywalker Ranch, get into the office of his hero George Lucas (creator of the Star Wars movies), and finally meet him in person. If the plan worked, he would be able to meet George, get a few things autographed, and disappear without a trace. If it didn't, he and his family might not be allowed back in California. But, those are the risks you have to take if you want to meet a famous director.

Now, Jim-Bob wasn't a person who ordinarily broke the law, he just had a huge obsession with Star Wars. He was twelve years old, a little on the small side, and had short, brown hair. Most of his spare time was spent going to movie theaters, watching movies, and researching movies. One of his life-long dreams was to meet George Lucas, so prior to this trip he read as much as he could about him, reading through six biographies. He felt that it was finally time to meet his idol, and with his master plan he knew he would be able to do so at last.

His parents were checking in to the Dykstraflex Hotel, so Jim-Bob decided to go over the plan. First, he had to ask to take a walk around town while his parents were seeing the nearby reservoir, and head to Skywalker Ranch. Though George doesn't live at the ranch, Jim-Bob knew that he was working there and he just might have a chance of seeing him. Originally, Jim-Bob had planned to get one of the windows open, and if that didn't work he had taught himself how to pick locks. However, after he realized that was illegal, he decided to pack a backpack with some camouflage clothes to sneak past the guards. Finally, if he could run fast enough, he might be able to get to Mr. Lucas' office and get him to call off the security. It was Monday, and Jim-Bob's family was staying for another week, so he was preparing to try the plan on Saturday. For the time being, Jim-Bob tried to enjoy his vacation. He brought his notebook containing the floor plan of Skywalker Ranch (something easily found on the Internet) everywhere, so it wouldn't fall into the wrong hands. When he was having dinner with his parents at Rancho Nicasio, they decided to figure out what that notebook was all about. "Uh, Jim-Bob?" his dad asked.

"What is it?" he replied

"Well, we noticed that you've been carrying that notebook around with you everywhere for the past few days. Are you drawing sketches of the places we've visited?"

"Not exactly," Jim-Bob responded. "It's for, a, uh . . . a project."

"Okay, then," his mom stated, "as long as it doesn't hurt anybody or involve you breaking into a famous director's workplace, it's fine with me."

"Erm, you see, the thing about that is . . ." Just then, the waiter came with their food, excusing Jim-Bob from explaining his "project."

The days went by on the family vacation, and before long it was Saturday morning. Once the family set off to the Nicasio Reservoir, it was finally time to put his plan into action. Jim-Bob asked his parents if he could take a walk around town and, after much persuading, they agreed. So far, so good. As he sneaked up to Skywalker Ranch, he quickly scanned the area and saw that two guards were standing in front of the gate. Suddenly, Jim-Bob realized that there were probably security cameras constantly watching the house. He quickly ducked into the bushes and took the camouflage clothes out of his backpack. Slipping them over his regular clothes, he crawled out of the bushes and inched towards the front. Once the guards had turned their backs, he climbed over the fence as swiftly as he could. Success!

"Hey, Kid! Stop! Get back here!"

Oh no, the guards had seen him! Jim-Bob raced to the front door and tried the doorknob. Much to his surprise, the door swung open and the guards were still a good distance behind him. There were two more guards chasing him now, but he had wisely memorized the floor plan and was able to dash to George's office. The guards were catching up now, but it was too late to stop him. He had reached the office. As his heart raced he flung the door open and saw . . . nothing. The office was completely empty. About a half hour later, he had arrived back at the Reservoir. The guards had let him off easy, realizing that he was more of a nuisance than a problem, and just threw him out of the Ranch. Although he was relieved that he was not more severely punished, he was disappointed that his plan was thwarted. Since he had been gone for a while, Jim-Bob decided to stop at a diner to use the bathroom before heading back to his parents. Inside the men's room of Biff's Greasy Paradise, he was washing his hands when he heard, "Hey, can I borrow some soap? The dispenser at this sink is all out."

When he looked over at the person who had asked this, he couldn't believe his eyes. It was . . . no, it was impossible.

"Are you George Lucas?"

"Well, yes. Now about that soap . . ."

Jim-Bob struck a deal with George Lucas. George could have some soap if he autographed a few things for Jim-Bob. Mr. Lucas accepted and signed the pictures Jim-Bob was carrying in his backpack. Mission accomplished.

Erik Nikander
Age: 13

THE GARDEN OF HOPE

I hope I get a bike for Christmas this year, pondered Ronan. The kind that you pedal with your hands is the kind I want.

It was a regular, boring day in the Great Depression. As usual, everyone was almost starving, being only fed a minor breakfast. Supper at the orphanage was always the main meal, and Ronan could not wait. He was diagnosed with muscular dystrophy. Ronan was a twelve-year-old orphan who was dreadfully skinny, with red hair and a twirly nose. He was sitting on the table playing his guitar. Joey was seated next to him, singing "Jingle Bells" at the top of his lungs. His curly, black hair fell over his chubby face. Joey was a little shorter than Ronan, but that entire loss was made up in girth.

Ronan halted his playing and weighed himself into his wheelchair. Rolling over to the window, he looked out at a pitiful garden. Actually, the whole scene was pitiful! The sun was blocked by a group of bully clouds. Under that, in the small side yard was the minuscule garden. Weeds took over the celery. The sun never seemed to get near the spinach plants, but it always found its way to the poor, shriveled-up tomatoes. The only thing that grew well was the carrots. All the kids were sick and tired of them since they were forced to eat the carrots so often. They called it the Garden of Hope because all they ate came from there. The leftovers were sold for the meat the orphans ate.

Soon, the teachers came in from the den where they, all the kids believed, were planning the Christmas presents. All the children, especially Ronan and Joey, thought they would all come out of there with mysterious smiles on their faces. Mrs. Tinno went up on the balcony and blew her whistle for silence.

"Children, I don't know how to break this to you, but we will not be having a Christmas feast this year . . ." Her voice broke. "Also, Mrs. Ralph's family is moving south, so we had to find a new secretary. She is doing this for no money so please be kind to her. Ronan, did you hear me?"

Ronan and Joey were born troublemakers and proud of it.

"Yes, Ma'am," he answered. Just then, the door flew open and in walked the meanest ogre this world has ever seen.

"This is Mrs. Gemochica," said Mrs. Tinno. Her smile seemed to have flown south with the birds, but it was not coming back. Her hair was pulled back into a tight bun.

"Hi!" Ronan broke the silence.

"Hello, Ma'am," she demanded that he repeat.

"I am a sir, not a ma'am," Ronan told her. Oh, she was fuming.

As days went by, kids kept coming up to Ronan asking him to get rid of Mrs. Gemochica.

"What am I supposed to do? I used my itching powder in her socks, gum in her hair, glue on the doorknob and in her toothpaste. What else?" Ronan was out of ideas.

Everyone knew that Mrs. Demon, as the kids called her, was part of the NHQ (New Hotels Quickly). They wanted the orphanage to sell the old building to them. The only thing Mrs. Gemochica did was make sure the garden was not cared for. That meant there was a lot less food to eat. Even Joey was getting skinny.

Finally, Ronan devised a plan. It was a weak one, but a plan it was. He called together an assembly of kids and told them the plan. "We can do this because we are a family!" They planned it for the next rainy day.

Luckily, the next day it was pouring. Joey walked into the rain. Someone told Mrs. Gemochica, who went flying out the door after him. The door closed behind her. Joey ran to the back door and locked it. It was the next morning when she was let back in. Nobody had told the teachers about the plan so they did not know. Mrs. Gemochica was so mad that she left without packing her bags.

About a week later, a basket filled with thousands of seeds was found on the doorstep. The card signed: Mrs. Demon. Ronan knew the only reason they got her to change her mind was because they showed her that they were a family.

Amelia O'Rourke
Age: 11

I am a pet dog, Jay Z. I can do a flip. I can chase a car. I can climb a truck. I can kick a ball. I can run really fast.

Jamal Correy
Age: 7

GROUNDED IN SPACE

Twelve-year-old Billy MacDonald looked like his father. He was very tall for his age with pale skin, baby blue eyes, and light brown hair. Unlike his father, a strict, tall man with similar features, Billy had lots of freckles and two dimples; one on each side of his mouth. The two were having dinner; steak and potatoes. The steak was burnt and the potatoes were lumpy. On this particular night it was quiet, the lights were dim, and there were lots of stars in the sky. Billy looked up from his dinner and saw that it was 5:35 p.m. and through the thick silence, the phone rang. It was a loud, obnoxious-sounding ring. Billy jumped at the sound of the ringing phone. Billy's father answered the phone. The call was for Billy. It was Billy's best friend, Josh Haines. Josh was a short boy with blond hair and brown eyes. He was calling Billy to go to the movies. Billy looked at his dad, worried to ask as he was nervous his dad would say no, but his dad said yes under one condition. Billy had to be home no later than 9 p.m.! No time to argue, Billy agreed.

Billy finished his dinner, ran up the stairs, took a quick shower, brushed his teeth and hair, and got dressed. He ran down the just in time as the doorbell rang. It was Josh with his dad, a rather large man wearing sweatpants and an old T-shirt untucked. Billy's dad gave him some money, said to spend it wisely and reiterated that he had to be home by 9 p.m. Billy nodded, as if to accept his father's terms for allowing him to go to the movies, and off the two boys ran, down the front stairs, down the front walkway, and into the backseat of Josh's father's car.

It was a just after 6 p.m. when Mr. Haines dropped the two boys off at the movie theater. Josh's dad told them to call when they were ready to come home. Josh's dad was much more laid back than Billy's dad. Billy and Josh nodded their heads and went into the theater, purchased two tickets, and bought a large bucket of popcorn.

The movie ended at 8:30 p.m. and Billy and Josh decided to take the rest of their money and play in the arcade. Forgetting the time, the two boys played well past Billy's 9 p.m. curfew. Worried when the two boys did not come home, Mr. MacDonald called Josh's house, but there was no answer. He decided to go to the theater to see if the boys were still there. Happy to see that the boys were okay, Mr. MacDonald suddenly turned angry. He went up to his son and started yelling. He asked why they did not come home when he specifically told them to be home no later than 9 p.m. The two boys, not knowing what to say, hung their heads down low and shrugged their shoulders. The two got in Billy's dad's car. It was a silent ride home. The air felt thick, as if something was about to burst, but no one said anything. Josh got dropped off and Billy's dad drove off quickly. It was then that Billy's dad started to yell. Billy and his dad yelled all the way home; Billy trying to defend why he should be allowed to stay out later and his dad defending that he trusted Billy to do as he was told. When they arrived home, Billy jumped out of the car, slammed the door and ran up to his room where he slammed that door too.

Upset with his dad, Billy decided to run away. It was just after midnight. He grabbed his backpack, filled it with some goodies and some clothes, opened his window, went down the fire escape, and ran across his lawn. Not knowing where he would go, he ran faster and faster until he stopped, out of breath, by a railroad track. He looked up at the sky, where there were so many stars, more than he had ever noticed before. Then, a bright light appeared. Billy could not see anything as the light blinded him. When the light disappeared, Billy disappeared too.

When Billy's eyes adjusted to the light, he realized he was not by the railroad anymore. He was on a spaceship orbiting Earth. It was large and metallic with lots of buttons and flashing lights everywhere. Nervous, he ran to a window and started to cry. He wanted to go home and wished he had never run away. Billy was tapped on the shoulder by a tall man wearing a dark suit. He had a beard, but a nice smile. Billy started to shake, but the man spoke to calm him down. The man explained that he was the commander of the Outer-Space Surveillance Group (OSG) and had been watching Billy and his dad argue. When Billy ran away, he decided to pick him up to help him see what he was doing was wrong. Running away would not fix anything, but instead would hurt the ones that loved him most.

Billy tried to tell the commander his point of view, but the commander looked at Billy and with a straight face said that he was only twelve and that twelve year olds needed to listen to their parents because they know what's best. Billy, for the first time, kind of understood what the commander was trying to say. Billy decided he wanted to go home. The commander said that he would take him home in thirty days because they were orbiting Earth and he could not get him back any sooner. Nervous, Billy started to explain that his dad would be scared when he was not in his bed when morning came. The commander said that Billy should have thought of his dad before he decided to run away. The commander turned and walked away, leaving Billy to be by himself. Billy sat on the floor and closed his eyes. He wished he had never run away and said a prayer that if he could get home fast, he would never yell or hurt his father again.

At that, Billy opened his eyes and found that he was in his room under his blanket. His dad came in and asked if he was okay because he heard a big thump. Billy looked at his dad and gave him a great big hug. His father asked what that was all about, but Billy just kept hugging him and said nothing. His father told Billy to go back to bed and that they would talk in the morning. Billy smiled at his dad, looked him in the eye, and said I understand why you have rules and I will try to obey them from now on. His father looked at him, smiled, and closed the door behind him. Billy sat in his bed, looked out the window, and saw a bright light go off into the sky. He realized that he had a secret and was grateful for it.

Brianna O'Donnell
Age: 12

SURVIVING THE AFTERMATH

During World War II, Hitler and his Nazi army had taken over most of Europe. Now, German and Italian forces were planning to attack southern France, the last part of France controlled by the Allied forces. A teenage boy named Durand Hurst and his friend, Pauline Guerin, lived peacefully in Laure, a large city in southern France.

It was a cold November night and Durand was reading a book on his bed. Durand was a smart boy who liked to read. He had brown eyes and short black hair. He was a kind, quiet person who feared being drafted by the army. Durand thought the war was silly and he did not want to be a part of it.

Just as he was reading the last sentence on a page of his book, a soft knock on the door stopped him. It was Pauline. Pauline lived next door in the same, large apartment building. Durand's mother opened the door and greeted Pauline.

"Hello Mrs. Hurst. My apartment is being repaired because of an oven fire. Would it be okay if I sleep here tonight?" asked Pauline. Pauline was a brave teenage girl with brown hair and blue eyes. Her hair was long and curly and she had pale skin. She liked to talk and Durand liked to listen. She also thought the war was a bad idea. She also had a fear of fire.

"Hello Pauline," said Durand, "You can sle . . ." Durand couldn't finish his sentence because of an alarm outside. Air-raid sirens and search lights turned on all over the city. Someone knocked on the door.

"The Nazis are bombing the town!" called out someone from the other side of the door. Durand, Pauline, and Durand's mother ran into the hallway. They heard small explosions outside. Their neighbors were running around and screaming. Everyone quickly went downstairs.

"We have to stay calm and not panic!" Mrs. Hurst yelled over the explosions. Pauline looked out the window and it looked very chaotic. Planes filled the sky and many buildings were on fire or already destroyed. There was a loud explosion above them and suddenly smoke was everywhere.

Fire blocked the entrance, so they were trapped. Rapid gunfire and screaming were heard outside. Durand fainted and fell to the ground. Pauline thought he was dead and ran away. She escaped through a broken window. It was a long, chaotic night.

The following morning Durand woke up. He looked around and could see only debris and a bunch of ruins that used to be buildings. He shouted, "Hello. Is anyone out there?" There was no response but the howling wind. Everything was so different. The apartment that used to be above him was gone, and his mother and Pauline were missing. Durand started walking around town to find someone.

Meanwhile, Pauline sought refuge in Domall, a nearby village. Domall was surrounded by a large forest, so the Nazi army couldn't find it. Durand's mother was there, but she was badly wounded. They both prayed that Durand would be safe. Many others from Laure were there, but there was no sign of Durand.

"My lady, anyone who was left behind could've been shot by the Nazis," suggested a tall man with a broken arm.

"Don't say that!" retorted Pauline in a loud, angry voice as she jumped to her feet. Everyone stared at her. Pauline just looked back at them. "There just has to be survivors back there!" retorted Pauline.

"Calm down. We can't go back there or we'll get shot. Just pray that everything is okay," said a woman nearby. Pauline took a deep breath and sat back down.

"Durand is a smart boy. He can survive," said Mrs. Durand.

Durand was already in the town center. Still, everything around him was a mess. Durand wondered how he could have survived all of this last night. Suddenly, Durand's thoughts were interrupted by a loud mechanical rumble from behind. Durand looked back and found that this was incredibly bad news! A tank with a Nazi insignia was aiming its large cannon right at him. Durand ran behind a building and around a large pile of debris. He heard explosions and knew that the tank was firing at him.

It was a cold afternoon and most people were inside. Pauline was talking to an off-duty French soldier. As they were talking, a tall tree fell down near a small house. Then, more trees fell down, and large, gray-colored trucks appeared behind the trees. There was an Italian flag on one of the trucks. Armed soldiers hopped out of the truck.

"It's the enemy! We're being invaded!" cried the French soldier. A shot was heard and Pauline ducked under a bush. Then, she quickly crawled underneath a stilted house. More gunshots were heard. Pauline closed her eyes, hoping not to see anyone getting killed. There were screams and a bunch of rattling around her. Some people, including Mrs. Hurst, hid underneath the building with Pauline. French soldiers started yelling and fighting back against the Italian troops.

"Keep quiet, everyone," whispered a man who was also hiding with them. The battle was over, and the Italians had won.

"If you see any survivors, kill them!" ordered the commanding officer of the Italian army. Pauline and the other people were still lying prone underneath the building.

"We can't stay here forever," whispered a lady.

"Well, what are we going to do?" asked Pauline. Two large boots appeared right in front of Mrs. Hurst. A tired Italian soldier was leaning against the building they were hiding under.

"I think I have a plan, but it's very risky," said Mrs. Hurst. "See that soldier right in front of us? This is what we're going to do."

Durand was now hiding in the top of a half-destroyed church steeple. The tank had lost him. As he looked through a broken window, he saw a child running across the road. Two German soldiers were nearby, and Durand heard a gunshot. He looked away and heard a faint scream. He put his hands over his face and took a deep breath. Durand slept in the church steeple for the night.

The next morning, Durand was awakened by a loud rumbling sound. He looked down and saw another tank with soldiers surrounding it. Durand turned around and saw a soldier standing in front of him. Durand moved back.

"Don't worry, I'm not going to hurt you," said the soldier, "we're here to rescue the survivors." The soldier spoke French so Durand understood what he said. "Come with us." Durand got up and followed.

It was early in the morning and the Italian soldiers were still sleeping. However, Pauline, Mrs. Hurst, and the others were already awake. Everyone got out from under the house.

"Quickly, disarm the soldiers while they're still sleeping," whispered Mrs. Hurst. Everyone did as they were told. Then, they quietly escaped the village. About two miles away, they reached a small dirt road. Everyone heard a rumbling sound nearby and looked where it was coming from.

"Look it's another tank!" someone yelled. Everyone hid back in the woods. The tank moved slowly down the road. Pauline spotted another tank on the other side of the road. Suddenly, there was a loud explosion and the two tanks started firing at each other. The tank that Pauline spotted was an Allied tank. The other tank obviously was a German tank. The firing continued. Finally, the German tank was obliterated. The Allied tank drove closer and Pauline saw a familiar-looking person hopping off the tank. Pauline figured out who it was.

"Durand!" she yelled, and ran up to him. Durand came up and gave Pauline a big hug. "I thought you were . . ." Pauline couldn't finish her sentence.

"Me too. I thought you were gone," interrupted Durand. Mrs. Hurst came up and hugged Durand.

"Mom, I'm so glad you're alive!" said Durand, excitedly. Everyone greeted each other and looked relieved. Then, a large truck went by. There was a sound of yelling from behind. It was the Italian soldiers! Luckily, they didn't have any weapons.

"Everyone, get in! It's still not safe here!" yelled a man from inside the truck, "I'll take you to the closest refugee camp." The people got in, and they drove away. Plus, the tank followed behind to escort.

Durand was very happy to see his family and friends again after all the terrors and lonely days by himself. Eventually, France was liberated by the Allied Forces and the war was over. They moved back to Laure City and built new homes. Pauline hopes that war never haunts her country again.

Chris Amarello
Age: 14

I'M HERE FOR YOU

"La la la!" Bethany sang into the radio when she was riding down a country road. Bethany was talking to her friend about her eighteenth birthday. Bethany heard the news that the storm was coming, but she thought she could make it to her grandmother's house in time.

She started to talk when she heard a big pop in the road. Her car was beginning to move slower. She got out of the car. When she opened the door, the snow finally came in. Bethany couldn't see anything.

Bethany walked forward; then she stepped on glass. She thought that was what caused the noise. She tripped over the sidewalk and started falling down a hill. Bethany didn't know what was happening; she was scared. She started to slow down, and then she stopped.

The snow was up to her knees now. Bethany tried to find the hill and climb back up, but everything was white. Bethany started walking trying to find the hill.

She couldn't feel her fingers. She was in so much pain. The worse thing of all was that her coat was in the car. She gave up walking and tried to build a shelter. When she finished, it collapsed. Bethany started to walk further. She bumped into a tree so hard she got a concussion.

Three hours later she woke up. Her whole body was frozen. She was desperate to find warmth. She could only crawl with her arms because her legs wouldn't move. She was dehydrated, hungry, and cold. Bad thoughts began to creep into her head: What if I have hypothermia? What if I die?

Bethany saw a faint light in the distance. Her grandmother opened the door and rushed out to rescue her. She dragged Bethany to the car.

In the car Bethany's grandma gave her five blankets. When she got to the hospital, she was treated for hypothermia.

Soon her parents got there, and they were upset. They asked her how she was feeling and gave her a stuffed animal.

Two days later her parents got a heartbreaking call. The news was that their daughter had died. Even though the parents were upset, they were proud that she was brave enough to keep looking for help.

Bethany's mom looked at the picture of her daughter and said, "If you were here, I would tell you that I am here for you."

Jennifer Rose Calnan
Age: 9

THE MISSION

"Brrring" went the phone as I scrambled to the floor to answer it.

"Hey," screeched the voice on the phone. I soon recognized the voice. It was my new friend CJ. After two weeks of visiting my uncle Geoff in London I couldn't believe I made a friend so quickly. CJ showed me his autographed World Cup soccer champs cards and I showed off my Super Bowl jersey football card collection. CJ seemed to think his cards were worth 500 British pounds but I didn't have the heart to tell him my autographed collection was worth more. Who in the world would be interested in soccer trading cards, I thought to myself. Our opinions in sports were different but one thing we did have in common was Alex Rider, the 007 teenager that was the main character in Anthony Horowitz's action-packed books. I hung up the phone, tiptoed down the steps to avoid my uncle Geoff as he watched the news. I felt like James Bond in the middle of one of his great missions. As quiet as a snake I slithered out the door and as sly as a fox I met CJ in front of Kensington Palace. From there we hopped on the tube to Knightsbridge. CJ, in my opinion, was a city kid. He went on the subways as much as I rode my bike back home in Rhode Island. As we hopped on the tube and glanced out the window we saw crowds of people become a blur as the underground train zoomed away.

The first thing I noticed when we got off the tube was a grand palace. I rubbed my eyes as if I was imagining what I saw. It looked like I was back in the United States in Las Vegas with all its bright lights. "Where are you taking me?" I questioned.

"Shopping," he said with excitement.

Under my breath I whispered, "Oh I think he has more in common with my mom."

"Trust me on this one. You'll like it," said CJ.

As I walked in, I thought I was inside an Egyptian pyramid. Golden pharaohs and Egyptian statues were everywhere. Gold balconies had opera singers singing as we weaved through the crowds and up the Egyptian staircase to the third floor. "Wow!" I yelled as we approached the third floor. I could hardly believe my eyes! Magicians dressed in top coats giving magic shows, a carousel filled with kids spinning like a top, and mountains of toys filled every nook and cranny like Santa's workshop. The best thing about this place was there was a duplicate copy of every toy opened for children to fiddle around with. Opened toys to experiment with all day long without anyone ever saying: "Please don't touch that . . . will you be purchasing that today . . . is there a parent with you?" The third floor was just a place for kids to have fun. As I was strolling through the store, out of the corner of my eye I saw my prey. It was Anthony Horowitz, my all-time favorite author. I gazed at him for minutes without saying a world.

"Come on," he whispered. "Let's get out of here before your uncle sends the police looking for you."

"Look!" I said with excitement. He soon spotted Anthony Horowitz. He stared with his mouth wide open in disbelief. He almost looked like a dog when it sees a bone. We sat there for minutes and gazed and gazed.

"Well," CJ said with disappointment, "it's time to leave. Maybe tomorrow we can come back. I don't want your uncle to start getting worried."

I quickly said, "Trust me. As long as he has his TV and his computer it will be almost as if I was never even in London."

Just then I spotted what looked like an animal chute in the corner of the toy department. As I opened the chute and peered down I screamed, "AWESOME!"

"What is it?" CJ questioned.

"I know exactly what it is," I said. "It is the jungle gym tubes we have in McDonald's in America," I whispered. "They are so much fun! There are twists and turns going in every direction. It is kind of like a maze, but you are in a tube."

"Let's check it out," CJ said excitedly.

"Let's," I screeched. We zoomed over to the door and hopped in one after another and went sliding down the tubes.

"Weeeee!" CJ yelled.

We soon landed with a soft thump. I soon noticed that we weren't in a pool of balls; we were in a pool of toys! "Where are we?" I questioned.

"I don't know. You tell me. You're the person who came up with the brilliant idea," said CJ.

We figured that the only way to get back up to Harrods was if we climbed up the slide. We soon started trudging up the slide, both looking like the Hunchback of Notre Dame as we bent down. As we reached the third floor, the first thing we noticed was that the store was pitch black. It was almost as if we were playing a game of manhunt. The power must have went out, I thought. I soon remembered the magician was using a flashlight for one of his magic tricks. I shuffled my hands around trying to find the flashlight. I looked like my papa when he is looking for his glasses. I soon found what seemed to be priceless . . . a lighting device from the magic show. With a simple press of my thumb I heard a quiet click. The first thing that clicked into my mind was that there was nobody there. It was a ghost town. "What happened here?" CJ questioned.

"It looks like the store is closed," I said in disbelief.

"This is not good," CJ said. I quickly shined my flashlight over at the crepe shop. "Or not," CJ said under his breath.

We scrambled off the floor and in the blink of an eye we were both standing in front of the crepe shop with a bit of drool spilling out of the corner of our mouths. We ate crepes until our bellies couldn't hold much more.

After minutes of eating crepes, we shined the flashlight up at the ceiling and put our hands over the flashlight to make it look like the shadow of a spider. But when we looked up to see the shadow, something else caught our eye; a man hanging from the ceiling with a rope attached to his belt. It looked almost as if it were Spider-Man. But we were no dummies. It was a robber!

Like a spider scurrying down its line from its web, the robber eyed its prey. There sitting in a clear display case was a doughnut-like circle that could fit on a finger and sparkled like the twinkling night sky. It was Princess Diana's engagement ring! CJ and I quickly huddled up like a football team and discussed our plan to stop the robber. Thinking like the Anthony Horowitz books, CJ skirted to the magician's desk and grabbed the lighting device used at the magic show. I zoomed over to the Egyptian sarcophagus. Next we waited silently as the robber quietly cut a circle in the glass case just big enough to fit his fist through. Mission accomplished; at least that is what he thought. Smiling with success, the robber dashed to the exit with his precious diamond ring. With a simple click of the thumb on the lighting device, a door with an exit sign appeared. It was an illusion. As I was standing there quietly, holding the sarcophagus open the robber sprinted right through what he thought was the exit and landed inside the sarcophagus with a thump. I quickly slammed the door shut and locked it. "Mission success," I shouted. CJ scrambled over to where I was standing and we both leapt for joy. After the police came and took the robber away, we got the biggest surprise of all. The owner of Harrods told us that Anthony Horowitz wanted to personally meet us and write a book about our mission. After reading all of those Anthony Horowitz books, I never thought I would stumble across a mission myself, especially when I found out that the British Intelligence, MI6 wanted me to join their team as the next Alex Rider.

Andrew Widdifield
Age: 10

THE EBONY LIGHTHOUSE

"Are you ready yet?" said Mom.

"Yeah," said Laura. She was a shy nine-year-old.

"OK, be good. I know you three don't like Aunt Adeline, but we'll be doing other things at Pemiquid, Maine too."

"I love living at Littleton, New Hampshire, I love going to Maine, but I don't like Aunt Adeline," said James. Aunt Adeline was the mother's sister. She sat around at home all day and did nothing. She was short, lazy, and round.

"Well, I'm going to go to the lighthouse at sunset," said Kathleen. Kathleen and James were Laura's big brother and sister. Kathleen was ten and very brave. James was eleven and very smart for his age.

"Is it even open in June?" asked Laura.

"Yeah, and it's filled with ghosts of the people that have drowned on the ships that have sunk," explained Kathleen.

"Time to go, kids" said their mom. They traveled the five hours it took to get to Maine.

"OK, we're here. It's only six o'clock."

"Welcome, everyone! I'm so happy to see you. I'll cook supper and you can go play," said Aunt Adeline.

"Come on, let's go to the lighthouse," said Kathleen quietly.

"Kathleen, wait!" James and Laura cried. They ran to catch her, and then they continued on to the lighthouse.

"OK, we're here, and WOW! Look at that ship. It's gigantic," said Laura.

"It's also a cargo ship," said James.

"Look! The lighthouse light is not on!" cried Kathleen.

"Let's go!" Kathleen, James, and Laura swiftly cantered up the lighthouse stairs.

"The light bulb isn't there, but I found it!" exclaimed Laura.

"Over there that man has all the light bulbs," shouted James.

"I'll call for help," said Kathleen. Thankfully, she had her new cell phone with her and called 911. After a few minutes the police arrived.

"You are under arrest for the felony of shutting off the light," said a solemn officer. "Thank you, kids, for solving the mystery of the lighthouse."

The children were glad to help. They had a great vacation even though they had to stay with their Aunt Adeline.

Sara Taylor
Age: 11

THE BUILDING

"Rain, it's amazing, isn't it? It can do some massive damage, but it can also save lives. I wonder, if someone could stop time when it is raining, what would it be like? Could you just touch it with a finger and move it? Or would it just splash on your hand?"

"Sit down, Stanley. There is no need to stand. Don't think so hard, either. Just relax. You're on vacation," Stanley's grandmother commented. Two out of his three cousins laughed at him. The third cousin was thinking the same thing as Stan.

It was a warm, summer night, with the moon sheltered by the cloud-covered sky. It was rainy, of course, that's what brought up the conversation of rain. The young boy, Stan (who started the discussion), was spending the week with his grandparents and three cousins. The cousins laughed whenever Stan mentioned things like: if you could stop time . . . except for one; a boy two years older than the nine-year-old Stan. His name was Tom. For some reason, Stan and Tom would sometimes think about the same things at the same time.

Around midnight, the four cousins decided to get in bed. The moonlight shone through the living room windows where they slept. It was an old house, probably around seventy years old, so it made a lot of sounds. The youngest cousin, who was six, was afraid of the dark. Of course, being older boys, they all made up stories to scare the youngster. Stan started to fall asleep listening to the stories. He started to arrive in a dream. In the dream, he was outside with his cousins. Stan and Tom were walking and they found a road. He knew where he was, but he never knew there was a road there. The road was a peaceful path, with birds singing, crickets chirping, and other peaceful noises. The great oak trees only let a little bit of the sun in, making the path not too dark, but not too light.

The boys came to a group of ruined buildings. The buildings were all covered in different drawings. Some were of rain, fire, and sundials. An altar was in the center of the buildings. Tom and Stan marveled at its ancient beauty. They both got closer to the altar. It started to glow a bright blue light. They got closer to investigate. It looked as if someone could walk through. They got even closer and then . . ."Hey, Stan, wake up! Stan! Stan!"

Stan opened his eyes. Still half asleep, the light poured into his dark brown eyes. Once his vision focused, he saw his cousins getting ready to go outside. The smell of bacon flooded into his nose. "Aren't you coming?" the cousin said again.

"Sure, um, hold on." Stan grabbed a piece of bacon and went outside, fighting the temptation to flop on the couch. After a few minutes out in the July sun, Stan started to come to his senses. His eyes were finally wide open and the crust surrounding them was gone. He was up at bat now, and he was ready to smash the ball across the state. Bam! He smashed the ball into the woods. That ball wasn't even worth running the bases for. Everyone knew it was a home run. Now came the hard part—finding the ball.

Stan and Tom went searching together to try to find the ball. They found a path. It seemed familiar to both of them. After walking a while, they knew what this path led to. They also knew that the other boy knew also. This path led them to an old, broken-down building, with drawings on the side. The two boys got closer to the paintings. One was of rain; others were of sundials and fire. One was a painting of two people thinking the same thing, which somehow, the boys knew was important. They got closer to the ancient buildings, and then, just like the two boys thought, an altar, surrounded by the buildings, started to glow bright blue. The trees started to shake and clouds started to appear over them. They started to feel something that they had never felt before. They started to lose their bodies. Parts of them vaporized, and the particles traveled into the blue. After all of them were gone, their souls also went into the portal.

Stan and Tom found themselves lying on the ground, stunned. The drawing on the wall of two figures sharing the same thoughts stuck out in their minds. They realized now, why no one else had ever seen the building. Only people who share magnificent thoughts saw it—people like Stan and Tom.

They didn't feel like getting up. Going through the portal took a lot of strength out of them. They heard a sound come crashing through the wooded area. This sound was familiar to Stan and Tom. "It's starting to rain, Stan. Let's find shelter," Tom suggested. Then Stan got an idea. He looked back into his memory and saw something.

"Wait. One of those drawings on the buildings was of rain, right?" Stan asked.

"Yeah."

"Another was of something thinking, right?"

". . . Yeah."

"Well, I was just thinking of rain before it started, so maybe . . ." he was interrupted.

"Don't be so silly. You can't just think of something and it'll happen. This place may be weird, but that will never happen. Watch. I'll think of fire . . ." Tom stopped talking.

In the middle of his sentence, a lick of flames burst out of the trees. Tom stood, puzzled. That thought soon came to an end when the whole forest was up in flames. Neither of the boys spoke, they just thought. As the thoughts came, so did the rain. It splashed onto the fire, extinguishing it within a matter of minutes. Amongst the rain, the two boys saw something glowing bright blue. They got closer and noticed what it was. It was the same altar as before. They knew they had to leave. They got ready to go. Tom walked in first. He was gone in an instant. Stan turned around. It was still raining out. He thought one last thing for now. Just as he thought of it, the rain didn't move.

Stan poked one finger at it and said, "Oh, so that's what happens."

Nicholas Louis Kaschak
Age: 13

ANNA'S ZOO STORY

Chapter One

"Aaahhh," I screamed. "Where are my car keys?" I screamed again. "How could I lose them on a day like this? Oh, there they are," I said. As I walked out of the kitchen, I looked at the clock. It was 8:05 a.m. It took me half an hour to get to the zoo. I had to be there by 9:00. As I was about to walk out the door, my daughter Maddy came down and asked if she could come with me. I said, "Yes, of course you can."

When we got to the zoo, we saw that all the animals were out of cages. "Who did this?" Maddy said. "The horses, the cattle, the . . ." Before she could even finish, her eyes were already up and over to the left.

"Oh, no!" we both said.

"Luke!" I said. "Did you do this?"

"Uhhh," said Luke, "OK, fine, I did it!"

"Luke, how could you do this to us?" I asked.

"Well, because you locked me in a cage," Luke said.

As soon as we were about to run to bring back all the animals, Luke ran after us saying, "Stop! Wait! I want to do it. I deserve to do it. I deserve to because I let them out!"

"OK," we both said.

So off Luke went after all the animals.

Chapter Two

After Luke was done, his best friend Jake came over to the zoo. Jake was thirty-nine inches tall and ten years old. He was just about Luke's age and height. Jake said, "Do you want to come to my house and play Spider-Man?"

"OK, sure," said Luke.

So off they went. Jake lived about three miles away from the zoo. Jake had a sister. Her name was Mary Ann. Jake came over daily while Mary Ann was at school. Mary Ann went to Belview High School and Middle School. Mary Ann was thirteen years old. Mary Ann said to me, "I go to Belview High School and Middle School."

"Oh how cool is that? My daughter goes to the same school. What class are you in?" I asked.

"I'm in Mrs. Candy's class," said Mary Ann.

"My daughter is in her class, too. Her name is Maddy."

"Oh, I'm so sorry, but I have to go now."

"Oh, that's okay. I will talk to you later. Bye!"

So Mary Ann went home with Jake and Luke. Maddy and I had to go home and do dishes and wash clothes.

Chapter Three

After we were all done, Maddy had to go to her aunt's house to babysit. Her aunt's name was Allison. Allison was just about my age. Allison had a little girl named Cassidy. Cassidy was sixteen months old. She could only say "mama". When Maddy got home, it was about 9:30 at night. Maddy had school tomorrow so she had to get to bed. So the next morning, the bus came over to pick up Maddy, but when she got on the bus, nobody was on. "Why isn't anyone on the bus?" she asked the bus driver.

"I don't know, maybe they are all sick," she said.

When she got to school, everyone was there. "They must have gotten picked up," she said very softly, but loud enough so everyone could hear it.

"Yep, we did," everyone said.

"I was the only one on bus five. Mrs. Scowler drove that bus," I said.

"I think Mrs. Scowler got her name because she scowls a lot," said Cindy. Cindy was Maddy's other best friend.

They were in seventh grade. Today Mrs. Candy was out sick, so they had a substitute teacher. Surprisingly it was Mrs. Scowler. "Oh no," cried Maddy. Maddy thought that if she pretended to be sick, she may not have to be with her. So Maddy went over to Mrs. Scowler and said, "I don't feel good, can I go see the nurse?"

She said, "Yes."

Maddy had mumbled under her breath. "Now I wonder if the nurse will fall for it."

She could go home because her mom was home. You could only go home if there was an adult there.

Chapter Four

The next day, Maddy went to school saying, "Same old locker, same old teacher."

Then Cindy, Lexie, Ann Marie, and Lori came over to Maddy's locker and said, "Guess what, guess what?"

"What, what?" Maddy asked.

"Tomorrow we are going on a field trip to the Boston Museum!"

"It's going to be a blast!" said Lexie. Maddy fell to the ground in excitement, laughing so hard that she started to choke.

"But how are we going to get there?" asked Maddy.

"Mrs. Candy said we could take a limo down. She also said there will be a hot tub in it!"

Lori said, "I asked her if we could take one of our limos down and guess what she said? She said yes!" All five girls were jumping with excitement.

"Our limo also has a huge, big, flat-screen TV," said Ann Marie. "Yes but what about our popcorn-maker? Are we going to keep that in there too?" asked Ann Marie.

"Maybe not," said Maddy.

"There might not be enough room in the limo for twenty-five kids," said Lexie.

Lexie wanted to know whose limo we were going to take.

"We are going to take mine, Lexie's, Maddy's, and Ann Marie's."

"OK," said Lexie.

All five girls were laughing and jumping about because they were so excited about going.

Then one of the non-rich girls in the class said, "Hey, what is going on?" Her name was Mary Anne.

"Nothing," said Cindy.

"OK," said Mary Anne.

Chapter Five

The next day they were on their way to the museum and one of the limos broke down, so they had to switch limos with Lexie. Now it was really crowded, so they made room.

Then when they got to the Boston Museum, they had so many places to go they just could not decide where to go first. They decided they were going to go see all the famous statues of people.

After they saw the whole museum, they went to the big, ten thousand million year dinosaur. They learned that it lived ten thousand million years ago.

"For that long, the bones have gotten all rusty," said the tour guide.

"These bones are very old, so please don't touch them," said Mrs. Candy.

"All right," said the class in a big sigh.

"Thank you," said Mrs. Candy.

After they saw all that they wanted to see, they also mentioned that it was getting too late so they wanted to stay at a hotel. The hotel they chose was called The Snowy Blizzard. They had an advertisement on television for it. The advertisement said: "The Snowy Blizzard Hotel! Come here when it is a snowy blizzard, we have everything you need!"

"Wow, what an advertisement," said Mrs. Candy.

"Yeah, really," they all said sarcastically.

Chapter Six

The next day, they all went home. When Maddy came home, she was all excited. I mean she was talking so fast I could not even understand her. I told her to calm down, so she did. She said how she got to see everything in the museum, and how she stayed at the Snowy Blizzard, and . . . she could not even finish because she was already fast asleep.

Kara Lounsbury
Age: 9

GUARDIAN ANGEL

When people look up at the sky and see nothing but the bright sunshine, and the large, round clouds, they wish they could fly and live in those beautiful clouds where there are no worries or cares. Well, for a girl named Amy, this happened. Amy is a freshman at the High School of St. Ann's. She has just moved from her hometown in Maine. She does not have many friends because they think of her as an outcast, because of her dreams. She often dreams of being a mermaid, or becoming the first female president. She felt alone, until one day . . .

As the warm, bright sun was shining down on her head, she noticed that someone was following her. At first, she thought it was one of the neighborhood kids out to bully her again so she paid no attention to it. But, as she continued to walk, she noticed that each time she would turn around the mysterious person would get closer and closer. Being as scared as she was, she ran behind a pile of dirt in an old construction site. This is where she felt safe. As soon as she was feeling prepared to leave, she heard a voice so soft and gentle say, "Amy, Amy, do not be afraid. I am here to be your companion, as well as your protector."

Amy was very frightened, but managed to stutter out, "Who . . . Who are you?"

The voice responded, "I am your guardian angel, Abigail."

"Well, how did you find me?"

"I did not find you, you found me. You found me when you asked the stars above to send someone who will care for and love you just the way you are. I am that someone who loves you no matter what."

When Amy heard this, it made her feel special and cared for. Even her mom and dad did not care like this. After two good hours of conversation, Abigail said, "About that one dream where you wished you could fly and live in the sky? Well, now is your chance."

"What do you mean?" responded a confused Amy.

"I mean that I am going to take you away from this hurt and pain you feel to a place called Freedom Palace, where you can be free from hurt and pain and be free from worries."

"Oh, wow!! That sounds wonderful! But," Amy said.

"But what?" responded Abigail.

"My parents will worry."

"Oh, no, they will not. I know you love them, but they are always too busy to spend quality time with you, which you deserve. And besides, you will be back in two weeks."

"Well, you are right, I do need to find the true me."

No more than three seconds after Amy had finished her sentence, Abigail stretched out two gorgeous wings. They were the color of the whitest rose, and felt as soft as silk.

Abigail said, "Well, hop on, we are leaving."

Amy did not waste one second. Amy loved the way Abigail moved. She moved as gracefully as dolphins jumping in and out of the water.

As they reached the gates of Freedom Palace, Amy felt a warm sensation rush over her body. Abigail told her that her body was being cleansed from all of the bad and the new spirit of happiness was entering her body.

Once inside the gate, she was greeted with open arms from all of the other angels. They showed her to her own personal cloud. The cloud had a nice king-size bed, beautiful furniture, and a nice bathtub. She was in amazement. She didn't know that when she said she wanted to live on a cloud that it would be that elaborate!

From across the way, she heard Abigail calling her. She quickly went over to see what was up. "Amy, there is one big surprise I would like you to know about."

"Well what is it?" Amy responded, practically jumping from excitement.

"I would like to present you with your very own pair of wings."

She handed Amy a beautiful shade of pink wings that felt like the hands of a baby.

"These are absolutely beautiful! Thank you!" Amy put them on and away she flew. She knew from then on things in her life would only get better, instead of worse. She flew at the speed of lightning.

Two weeks came very fast, and the day came when she had to return to Earth. She was very disappointed and wanted to stay forever. Abigail told her that this experience made her a stronger person. Now, when children pick on her, she has the power to ignore them and be the bigger person. Abigail would be there for her day and night no matter what.

As she was saying good-bye to all of her new angel friends, she felt a little discouraged because she knew it was time to give back her beautiful wings. Abigail told her that they will always be in a special place, so when she returned they would always be there.

When they arrived back on Earth, Amy felt like a brand-new person. She felt that nothing or no one could bring her down. As Amy was saying good-bye to her new-found friend, tears of joy ran down her cheeks. Abigail said that she shouldn't cry because she would always be there. If she looked up, there she would stand. Before Abigail left, she handed Amy a pin that looked like her pink wings.

On the wings there was a message that read,

Dear Amy,

With these wings you are invincible. No one can tell you you're not worth anything because you are. You are worth so much. I am here and I know someday soon you will realize that other people are too. If you need me, just make a wish on a star and I will be here. But remember, I am always in your heart.

Love,
Abigail.

By the time Amy finished reading the pin, Abigail had gone, leaving Amy a new person and feeling a new sense of self.

Although Amy could not stay in her magical world, she would always remember how it impacted her life. It made her realize that she was someone very special, and she had people who do care. Whenever she has doubts or wishes she was someone else, she holds on to that pin and looks at the stars and realizes there is someone who is always watching over her; it is none other than her guardian angel.

Sarah Morrell
Age: 14

WILLEY

I love dogs. Do you? Soon I will have my own dog if I earn him or her. I hope I get a little dog, but I can't get a dog yet. My mom gave me a fish first. I fed him and gave him new water for a week or two. I thought he was boring at first, but after a couple days he got funny and my mom said I did so good I could get a bird. She was blue and green and I fed her bird food mostly. But she got an egg in her belly, so I gave her more water. She had an egg and we had to sell her and my mom said I did so good she said I could have a cat and if I do good I could have a dog. But I have a cat. He is black, brown, and white. He has a big tail. I fed him and gave him water. I loved and cared for him and my mom let me get a dog! We went to the pet store and we looked and looked for a good dog and we found just the right dog and we got him some toys and a cage for him. On the way home we were finding a name for him. I wanted to call him Chomper, but we could not, so we named him Willey. At first I was scared of Willey, but after a few days I was not. I love him very, very, very much. I will never forget when I got Willey.

Amber Wallgren
Age: 8

A VACATION IN NEW YORK

It was the last day of school and everyone was eager to get out of school. When school was over I ran home and prepared for my trip to New York. I have black hair, brown eyes. I am four feet, ten inches, and I am twelve years old. I have never been to New York and I was extremely excited about the trip, until my parents told me that it took four and a half hours to drive to New York. I quickly packed my clothes and went into the bus. The bus started moving and I was incredibly thrilled. I was excited for the first hour of the bus ride, but I was dreadfully bored after riding the bus for a few hours. When the bus finally stopped, it was nighttime. Consequently, my family and I got off the bus and walked toward the hotel.

The next day I was eager to go sightseeing, but my family wasn't awake yet. I wanted to go sightseeing, but I also wanted to wait for my family. I decided to go sightseeing without my family and meet them later. The first thing I did before I went sightseeing was that I wrote a note that I would go sightseeing and I would meet them in Times Square. Once I finished writing the note, I wanted to see the Brooklyn Bridge. I walked on the Brooklyn Bridge and gazed at all of the cars passing by. I was amazed at how many cars passed by the bridge without paying any attention to the wonderful sights.

When I finished walking through the Brooklyn Bridge I noticed a subway station and I wanted to ride a subway. I went inside the subway station and I felt the rumbling of the subways. I bought a ticket for the subway and I got on the first subway that arrived. After I got on the subway, I realized that I didn't know where the subway was going. I looked at a map and noticed that this subway was going farther away from Times Square. At the next stop, I got off the subway and waited for a subway that went toward Times Square. After fifteen minutes, I started wondering why there was no subway. I looked around and I saw a sign that said that all of the subways going toward Times Square were closed.

Once I got out of the subway station I looked for a taxi, but I couldn't find a taxi because I was in a quiet neighborhood. I found a telephone booth and looked for money, and realized that I spent all of my money riding the subway. A policeman walked by and I told him what had happened, but the policeman told me that he couldn't help me. After walking a few miles, I found a taxi and told him to bring me to Times Square. When the taxi driver said that he could take me to Times Square, I was relieved. The taxi arrived at Times Square and I got out and searched for my family, but the taxi driver told me that I needed to pay him. Suddenly, I felt petrified because I didn't have any money.

I told the taxi driver that I didn't have any money, but my family did. Frantically I looked for my parents. After a few minutes, I thought that it had been an hour and I started begging the taxi driver to give me a free ride. When the taxi driver said that I had to have the money, I saw my family looking at the buildings, and when I tried to get their attention, they turned around and noticed me. My family went to the taxi driver and gave him the money. I was relieved that I found my family and we went sightseeing together. I told my family what had happened and they didn't mind. Then I went to see the sights with my family.

After a few days in New York, it was time to go home. It was an exciting trip, but it was also a frightening trip. I was glad the trip was over and I was ready to go home. When my family and I arrived home, we were relived that we were all safe. I was glad I was home and I couldn't wait for school to start. I wanted to tell everyone about my trip. My trip to New York was very scary, but I saw a lot of sights and I learned a great lesson.

Michael Yu
Age: 12

DIRT BIKES

Once upon a time there was a boy named Barrny. He wanted a dirt bike. He bugged his parents for one. One day he got one. But one day it wouldn't start. So they went to the mechanics. When they got there, "Junk," he said. "Hold on for a minute. It's just a piece of cardboard blocking the carburetor. I can get it out."

One hour laterrrrr!

"Yea," Barrny said. And Barrny loved his dirt bike. And Barrny's dad and him had fun. They had fun going on trails together.

Jordan Gilson
Age: 7

"Ouch!" Liana grumbled. A large, brown-haired man peered through his spectacles at her while chiseling away at her head. Liana's head throbbed with pain and her vision was blurry and dull.

"Done!" the man finally announced to Liana's relief. She became dimly aware of herself being transferred to another table.

"Oh great," she whispered. To her surprise, the young woman at the table grasped a large pallet of colorful goo and a long stick with some clumps of hair on the end.

Liana sighed happily.

"Okay, let's get to work!" the woman smiled.

She dabbed the hair on the stick in a chestnut brown. She leaned forward; small, wispy, black curls falling into her face and her tongue peeking out of the side of her mouth.

The goo was creamy and cool on Liana's hurting head.

"Ahhhh," she sighed contentedly. "That feels gooooood!"

The woman chatted with Liana as she smeared the colored goo all over her body. Liana listened, relaxed and comforted.

After about an hour, the woman halted.

"Ohh," she gasped, "you look magnificent!"

It was true. Liana's soft ringlets carved out of wood were a soft, gentle brown. Her long, flowing dress was a pale yellow and was covered with the same mauve roses that nestled in her beautiful locks. Her peachy-colored feet poked out from under her dress. Her face glowed and her eyes sparkled a subtle violet.

The most wonderful of all, a pair of crimson and cream-colored wings arched behind her back.

Slowly and cautiously, the woman picked Liana up and set her on a wooden shelf.

"Well, I've got to go," she whispered. The woman removed her smock, draped it on a hook, and left.

That night, the air whistled outside the workshop windows. Liana sat dreaming of herself in a beautiful home.

"Ahh!" she screamed as thunder boomed and lightning skipped across the sky.

"Calm down!" Liana scolded herself. "It's just rain!" The floorboards creaked.

Suddenly, a large shadow loomed in the door. Liana's breath froze in her throat. A robber!

The man stole swiftly and silently towards the shelves. He grabbed Liana and a few others and stuffed them in a sack.

The rough fabric bristled against Liana.

"Is everyone okay?" Liana inquired. The other figures murmured back, their voices thin and scared.

All of a sudden, the thunder became deafeningly loud and water soaked through the bag.

With a sudden lurch, the bag slipped open and Liana tumbled out, landing on a patch of wet grass.

The night was dark and cold. Liana waited and waited for dawn to break. Finally the rain stopped and the sky grew lighter.

Hours later, a little old man was walking when he saw something glittering in the grass.

"Why, what a beautiful fairy," he marveled as he inspected Liana. "I think I'll bring it home and give it to my wife!" With that, he picked up Liana and set off.

"Oh, she's beautiful!" cried the little old lady, as her husband handed her Liana. "I think I'll hang my jewelry on her!" She clapped her hands.

"Jewelry?" her husband asked.

"Jewelry?" Liana repeated in disbelief.

Moments later, Liana sat on a shiny wooden vanity. A collection of bracelets and necklaces adorned her body.

"We have to hang on this?!?" a pretty diamond necklace groused.

"It's probably filthy!" groaned an amethyst bracelet.

"This is soooo disgusting!" whined a topaz brooch.

"I do have a name, you know!" Liana snapped.

"Whatever," the diamond necklace replied. Liana grunted in frustration.

"Eeeek!" A shrill scream vibrated through the air.

All the jewelry groaned.

"What—" Liana started to ask, but suddenly, a small, chubby face peered over the edge of the vanity.

"Ohhh, faiwee!" the little girl crowed, her brown hair bouncing up and down.

She reached up and grabbed Liana, sending all the jewelry clattering. They all snickered.

"Shh, faiwee, be quiet," the little girl whispered, with a finger on her lips as she stuffed Liana into her backpack.

The textured fabric scratched at Liana. She shivered, reminded of the previous night.

Sometime later, Liana blinked in the bright light. The little girl was moving Liana around in the air, pretending she was flying. They were sitting in front of a big, white house.

"Faiwee doll! Faiwee doll!" the little girl cried over and over again.

"Jenny," a voice called.

"Stay here," the little girl, Jenny, commanded Liana as she ran inside.

"Phew," Liana sighed, happy of the little girl's departure.

"Why what do we have here?" a voice boomed. Liana groaned. Would she ever find a home? A young man with sleek, black hair picked Liana up. All of a sudden, the man's face lit up.

"I'll put her in my garden!" The man smiled happily as he tucked Liana under his arm.

Liana looked around dizzily as the man walked up to a big, gray and crimson house.

Gently, the man set Liana down in a clump of yellow roses. He rubbed his chin looking very pleased with himself.

Slowly he walked into the house.

"Will this journey ever end?" Liana asked herself. With a sigh, she fell asleep.

That night, Liana awoke to a bark.

"Wha'?" she mumbled bleakly.

Suddenly, her vision cleared. Now she knew what had barked!

A huge, heavily muscled dog lumbered toward her, his jaws hanging open to reveal a large and sharp set of teeth. The spiked collar around his neck pulsed with every growl.

"Ahhh!" Liana screamed.

"Grrrr!" the dog growled, just as he slammed into Liana, sending her hurtling into the air.

Liana emitted a final screech before crashing into the ground with a dull thud. Everything went black.

When Liana opened her eyes, she was immediately surprised. Someone must have taken her again!

She was in a warm, pleasant room filled with puffy chairs, chubby pillows, and velvety-looking couches. Fuzzy blankets were draped everywhere and a cozy, yellow glow illuminated the room.

Liana herself was perched on a polished mahogany shelf above a crackling fireplace.

She stared at all the furniture and paintings, her eyes shining.

"Ohh," she breathed softly.

All of a sudden, someone strolled into the room. It was none other than the lady who had spread that glop all over her!

"I hope you feel at home," the woman whispered as she reached up and stroked Liana.

Then, as quiet as a mouse, she aroused and crept out of the room. The lights flickered off. Liana sat in the warm dark, her mind racing.

Before she drifted off to sleep, Liana whispered to herself, "I'm finally home!"

Kasey Huntress
Age: 11

Have you ever driven a truck or car without seeing? One day this teenager was about to get his license to drive on the road not the sidewalk. Do you think he will be able to drive an automobile? It all started with a rich, sixteen-year-old teenager that had tons of friends and wanted a new car for his birthday. But first he had to get his license.

When Billy the rich sixteen-year-old went to go get his license he thought of happy thoughts while walking down the sidewalk. When he got to driver's ed, he had to fill out a form, when he remembered something. He remembered that he used a blindfold when he drove. So he asked the desk for a blindfold and got it. Billy got in the driver's ed car with the driver Ed and put his blindfold on and drove. When the driver Ed looked at Billy, he said, "Sir, please take off the blindfold."

Billy stopped the car in the middle of the track and took off the blindfold. Billy went on and was getting worse than when he had the blindfold on. Billy started to go over the cones and hit the wooden people.

The driver Ed yelled, "Stop." Billy slammed the brakes to a huge halt. The driver Ed said firmly to Billy, "You have one more chance."

Billy asked the driver Ed if he could wear his blindfold. Billy promised the driver Ed that he would do very good and would not blow up the car. The driver Ed said, "Very well then." Billy put on the purple, striped, blue blindfold and started to drive. The driver Ed said, "Very good, Billy, but you know that you are going to have to drive with your eyes open."

Billy got his license and had a huge party and got a new car. He now drives without a blindfold and he's happy. Billy had to keep on practicing without the blindfold. Billy is now twenty-one, has a job, a wife, and two kids.

Grant Gadbois
Age: 9

I'm C.J. I like to go for a ride with my friend. I'm a frog. I live in a classroom. I like to eat my crickets for lunch.

Zachary Kennedy
Age: 7

SQUAB'S ADVENTURES

Chapter One: Squab

Squab, the crab, was happily eating plankton drifting in the sand. Squab bent down and grabbed one with his small pincher. Making sure it was green plankton, he popped it in his mouth. There was a small crunch, then silence.

Suddenly, a sweeping noise came to his ear. Squab began inspecting his area. He searched for where it was coming from. Usually intruders hid behind small boulders.

Then, Squab knew what it was. He burrowed under a few rocks and popped out next to the intruder. There, lying in front of him, lay the source.

Squab sighed. "Get off my rock," moaned Squab.

"No, I refuse," argued Stark, a four-armed starfish with antenna-like eyes.

"I really dislike you, Stark." Squab gently pinched Stark with his small claw.

"Ooh!" complained Stark as he slid off Squab's favorite rock.

"Thank you," muttered Squab as he hopped on his rock.

"Darn you." Stark circled the rock and slid into Squab's den.

"You've got a nice den." Stark complimented.

"Get out!" Squab charged Stark.

"Aaaahhh!" Stark pulled himself out of Squab's den just as Squab leaped in. Squab spun around and pinched Stark with both claws.

"You're mean . . ." Stark fled to Squab's rock.

Squab searched his den for green plankton. When he found them he would devour them.

Squab lazily waddled out into his territory, snooping for larger food. He didn't notice that he had stepped into the cod's territory. The cod was looming above him. The cod lunged at the unsuspecting crab.

"What?" Squab pulled his limbs into his shell. The giant fish smacked Squab back into his territory.

"Out," the cod commanded in a deep voice.

"Out," mocked Squab as he turned around.

He turned to see a huge lobster, sweeping its antenna across Squab's face.

The beast was at least fifty times bigger than Squab.

"Wow," Squab said as he began to flee. The lobster was right on his tail!

The lobster had Squab cornered when a giant reef shark swooped down and swallowed the lobster whole.

"Oh, yeah!" Squab called to the reef shark. It turned and swam toward Squab. "Oops."

Squab hopped in his den.

Chapter Two: A Jewel

The next day Squab took a walk. He saw green plankton and popped it in his mouth. Crunch.

He scurried to his favorite rock. There was Stark, lazily being himself. Squab crawled on the rock and gave Stark a small pinch.

Stark glared at Squab.

SWAT! Squab was swatted off his favorite rock.

"Ow." Squab knew he couldn't win so he gave up. "I hate you."

Squab continued his walk when something caught his eye. It was a blue, shining jewel, but it was in the reef shark's territory.

Squab wanted that jewel. He trotted into the reef shark's territory then grabbed the jewel. Wow, that was easy, thought Squab.

He turned to see the reef shark glaring at him.

"My, my! Look at the time. I really must be going," Squab said in a quick voice. Squab shot out of sight.

The reef shark shot after him.

"Oh, no!" Squab tossed the jewel into his den as he ran by.

When the reef shark got bored, it swam away, looking for something to eat.

Chapter Three: A Starfish On The Roof

Mrs. Puff, a relative of Squab, was coming in three hours. Squab needed to prepare. He scurried around his den, getting ready for Mrs. Puff's arrival.

Mrs. Puff isn't the nicest aunt in the world, a snot-nosed, pig-faced brat of a puffer fish.

Though she was a brat, she was an aunt, and an aunt is an aunt.

Squab tidied his bed and hopped on it. That was some hard work. Squab rolled onto the floor just as the doorbell rang. She's here! Squab ran to his closet and slipped into his best suit. Squab opened the door.

"Squab, why are you wearing that hideous shirt?"

"Stark? SSSTAAARRRK! Get out! My aunt will be here any minute! Out, out, out!" Squab peeked behind Stark. "Oh, no. GET OUT! My aunt's behind you!"

Stark pulled himself onto the ceiling.

"Hello . . . um . . . Squab. Is that your name?" She didn't wait for an answer. "Squab, that is an extraordinary ceiling, it looks expensive."

Suddenly, an unexpected starfish fell from the ceiling.

CRASH!

Mrs. Puff puffed up like a balloon. Squab's den filled with spikes.

"Stark!"

"Squab?" asked Mrs. Puff.

"Me?"

"No! Stark!"

"I am Stark!"

"Who's Stark?"

"Him!"

"Me?"

"Yes!"

"Where?"

"On you."

"Who's on who?"

"Stark is on you."

"Who?"

"Stark!"

"Stark?"

"Stark."

"Me."

"QUIET!"

"Why?"

"Because I said so." Squab stood up, carefully dodging spikes. "Stark, get out."

Stark pulled himself out of Squab's den. "See ya later."

Stark left, not knowing what he did.

Squab turned and left before you could say "fish paste."

"Oh, darn." Squab started cleaning his house.

Chapter Four: Shopper

Squab dodged shells, left and right. Weaving through rocks he leapt behind a bunker.

The enemy fish were pinning him in!

"Time for lunch," Squab thought aloud.

Squab turned off his GameCrab and scavenged for plankton on the sea floor. A small group of plankton floated by.

"Delicious!" Squab began his feeding frenzy. "Mmm." Squab twisted and turned to catch every last one.

While Squab was happily chewing, a hammerhead shark trotted up to him.

"Hello, Mate," he said in an Australian voice.

"Aaaaaaaaah!" Squab leapt three feet in the water.

"I'm Deater. I'm from the Great Barrier Reef. Where are you from, Mate?"

"Who are you?" Squab asked.

"Me responses are limited. Ask again."

"What are you?" Squab asked again.

"A robot. I'm programmed to get you to buy our products."

"Go away, you barnacle brain."

Squab threw a rock at it and walked away.

"Fine, I'll go buy off something else." The robot swam away. Squab guessed it was swimming towards Stark.

A few minutes later Squab wandered over to Stark. Stark was holding a bike, a computer, and a jack-in-the-box.

"Where'd all that stuff come from?" Squab asked Stark.

"A shark sold it to me," answered Stark.

"What? But it was a robot!"

"And I should care why?"

"I hate my life," mumbled Squab as he walked away.

Chapter Five: And Then . . .

After everything was back to normal, something strange happened. Weird metal hooks with dead fish started to drop from the surface.

"Mmm, fish." Squab popped a hook in his mouth. "Delicious."

As Squab grabbed the last, it yanked him up to the surface. "Aaaaaahhhhhh!" Squab screamed as he was yanked up. His voice got quieter and quieter as he went.

When he broke the surface he gasped for water. The human threw Squab in a tank full of water and took it to a house.

The man dumped the tank in another tank with fish.

"What is this?" screamed Squab in horror.

"A . . . human house," answered a puffer fish.

"Well I don't like this . . . human house. I want out!" Squab attacked the wall. "Take that, and that!" To everyone's surprise, a crack formed in the glass.

He turned and looked at them.

Squab threw himself at the glass and it shattered. Squab knew the fish couldn't walk like him so he pushed them two by two out the door and into the water. When the last fish was in the water, Squab had no moisture in him. He started to shrivel up! He couldn't move! He couldn't breathe!

Then something strange happened. A young boy picked up a shriveled Squab. "Poor little crabby," said the human. It brought Squab back over to the shore. "There you go," said the happy human and watched as Squab perked back up. He walked away smiling.

"Wow." Squab shot like a rocket towards home, not knowing what life had in store for him.

Jesse Ricardi
Age: 9

TROUBLE IN CIRCLE LAND

Once upon a time, there was a circle and his name was Bingo the Bouncy Ball. He had a best friend and his name was Bob. Bob was different than all the other people in Circle Land because he was a pentagon. But nobody really cared because Bob was funny and nice and all the Ping Pongs, the town folk of Circle Land, liked him just fine.

One day Bob and Bingo were walking along and they tripped over Tom the Triangle. He was so small and gray you would think he was a rock. Tom the Triangle was so angry, he started screaming jibberish to Bob and Bingo. Bob and Bingo just looked surprised that something so little could be so loud. After a couple minutes, the triangle stopped screaming and Bob and Bingo apologized.

You would think Tom would say, "It's all right," but he just lectured them. "Why did you trip over me? Why didn't you see me? It's not fair." So Bob and Bingo just walked away.

Tom was so determined to get everyone back in Circle Land for always tripping over him and ignoring him because he was too pointy, and small, and gray. He hatched a plan, not meaning he hatched an egg, but he thought up a plan, to change Circle Lane into Triangle Terror! "Moo, haa, haa, haa, haa," he sniggered to himself. His plan was to go to the Rectangular Witch of Mount Shape-a-topus, to make him a special, green, bubbly, gubbly potion that would change all the Ping Pong folk into triangles with triangular hats. This was phase one of his sneaky plan. Then he got Bob the pentagon to meet him for a secret meeting in his not-so-secret hideout, which was in a strange-looking tree house that you couldn't miss because it was right on the main path. Bob agreed to meet with Tom because he felt bad about tripping over him earlier in the day. Tom told Bob that he had a new energy drink that he made that will make all the Ping Pongs and Bingo the Bouncy Ball bounce higher and faster—but it doesn't work on pentagons or triangles. He called the new drink The Bubble Ubble Energy Drink. The next phase of Tom's plan was to get Bob to convince Bouncy Ball to try the new drink.

On Bob's way to Bingo's with the drink, he was tempted to try it, even though Tom the Triangle said it would not work for pentagons. As Bob walked further and got thirstier, he thought he would try just a sip. It tasted delectable for two seconds but then he shrank and turned into the shape of a triangle with a little, triangular hat that was blue!

Bingo came bouncing along and landed right on the top of Bob's new, triangular head. Bob explained everything about the new energy drink and how amazed he was at how he had underestimated this very mean, tiny, gray triangle, Tom.

Bob, now a triangle, and Bingo went to see Tom and find out why he would want to change everyone in Circle Land into little triangles with little, triangular hats. Tom looked at Bob, very surprised to see him a triangle and very small, and said, "I told you not to drink the Bubble Ubble Energy Drink!"

Bingo asked, "Why would you want to make a drink that turns everyone into triangles?"

And Bob adds, "With little, blue, triangular hats?"

Tom said, "I am sick of you all being colorful, and happy, and bouncy, and round, and always stepping on me! I wanted people to be more like me and know how it feels to be smooshed like me."

In the end, Bingo, Bob, and Tom decided on a different path, which was to have a Triangle Holiday once a year, where everyone in Circle Land would wear little, blue, triangular hats. Everyone decided that every shape should be a part of the Circle Land Community.

Mason Robertson
Age: 10

THE VOLCANO ACCIDENT

One day, Stewy was walking on a volcano in Hawaii. All of a sudden the volcano began to erupt! Just then, his safety cord broke and what will Stewy do now??

Luckily, Stewy had an idea. "I can't go to the side because the lava is coming down. I can't go up because the lava is coming down. I can't go down because it is too steep." But the lava was flowing down and it was about to crush him. Stewy threw out his shoes and socks and hopped onto his shoes to walk on and he jumped onto his socks to try and get the top of the volcano. Next, he hopped onto the top and saw a plane! Stewy jumped up and down and cried, "Help me!" Suddenly, Stewy fell into the volcano. Stewy yelled as he fell, "Maybe someday someone will get me out of here!" No one ever found Stewy, but legend has it that if you go really close to the top of the volcano and yell "Hello!" someone will answer: "Get me out of here!"

Nicholas J. Bush
Age: 9

"... Twenty-seven ... twenty-eight ... twenty-nine ... thirty, ready or not here I come." I opened my eyes and started to search behind all the hay bales. After about ten minutes of searching, I started to think they were up to something. "Guys, where are you? I give up," but there was no answer. "Alex? Grant? Travis? This isn't funny, oh, and if you're trying to scare me ... it's ... it's not working ... not at all."

But oh boy was I lying, I thought to myself. Here I was playing hide-and-go-seek with three guys (who love to torture me) in an old, abandoned barn, at night! I was more scared than a mouse being chased by a cat with sharp claws. I was just about to go down the ladder to leave and go tell on the boys, when all of a sudden, I felt a haunted, cool breeze on my back. I quickly turned around to see hundreds of bats fly over my head and out a broken window. "Ahhhhh," I shrieked. With my hands over my head, I slowly got up and turned to where the bats had flew out of. "You have got to be kidding me," I said aloud.

It was the only area that I hadn't checked, a hole in the wall that leads to another hay room. Except this one is worse. It is darker, it's where the floor creaks the most, it's a lot colder, and there are holes in the ground that are covered in hay (like a trap). It's absolutely terrible, and now I had to go in there and find those stupid boys. With much hesitation, I took my first step into the hole, then eventually lowered my whole body into what I called "the haunted hay room." With each step I took, a creak in floorboards would follow. There were only a few stacks of hay bales in the room, so, thank the dear Lord, this meant less time I had to spend in this treacherous place. I checked behind all of them, except for one that was in the back corner.

I slowly made my way over there and the very second I looked behind it, I heard a "Boo!"

"Ahhhhhh," I screamed at the top of my lungs.

"Gosh, Girl, it's only us," Alex said laughing.

"Yeah, Big Boy," my brother said in his "manly" voice.

"OK, do you really know what just happened there?" I asked them.

"Yeah, we really scared you," Alex replied while giving my brother a high five.

"Wow, are you guys that clueless? About two minutes ago something really odd and scary happened."

"What, did a cat meow?"

"Oh, be quiet, Grant. Anyway ... guys, what's with Travis?"

"Uhh ... I ... dunno," said Alex with much hesitation.

I stared at Alex oddly, "Why are you hesitating ... Oh, you knew what I was talking about, but you just didn't want to admit it."

"What? I felt a breeze and a few bats flew out of ..."

"Exactly, you don't know," I said, "you know why? Because they came out of nowhere."

"What are you saying, that it's haunted or something?" I looked down.

"Yeah," Grant replied for me, "she's always said that this is a haunted hay room."

"What, are you scared?" asked Alex.

"That doesn't matter," I said trying to switch the subject. "You know that I'm not making this up, I mean look at Travis." He was staring with his eyes wide open, at nothing. Suddenly he broke out of the trance and into tears.

"Alex," the seven-year-old boy sobbed, "that was scary," and he ran to give him a hug. I looked at Alex.

"See," I said. "Travis, you probably just had a dream, a very bad dream, that's all."

"Okay," he said with trembling lips, "but can we go inside now?"

"Definitely, yeah, sure," we all replied.

When we got in the house, Travis immediately fell asleep, so we were safe to talk about what just happened.

"Okay, I'll talk about this with you guys if you guys swear never to say a word about it again. I don't want to be known as a freak at school, being cool is a lot better, okay?" asked Alex.

"Whatever," we replied.

"Okay," Alex went on now that that was settled, "there is something weird going on in that barn and we have to figure it out. I have no idea how we will do that though, any ideas?"

"Well, we could just start off my writing down a list of things that happened," I suggested.

"Okay, but I have no idea how that would help us though, cool breeze, bats flying out of nowhere, white ghost-like figure in hay room . . ."

"What, I did not see any ghost."

"Oh, I didn't tell you? My bad."

"Well, that's kind of a big deal. There is a ghost haunting my barn!!!" I screamed.

"Well, actually, it's not your barn, it's your grandfather's," said Alex.

"That's it. I'll call him. He might know more about it."

"At two o'clock in the morning?"

"Hey, he said to call if there was an emergency, and I would call this an emergency." So I picked up the phone and dialed in the number. Ring, Ring, Ring . . . Ring, Ring, Ring . . .

"Hello?"

"Hey, Grampa, I was wondering if I could ask you a few questions."

"At two o'clock in the morning?" he asked, in a very tired voice.

"Well, it's kind of an emergency," I replied.

"Well, then I guess I could help you out. What is it?"

"Do you know if we have a ghost in our barn?" He was silent. "Grampa?"

"Oh, yes," he was very serious now, "a long time ago when I was a youngster like you, me and my cousin decided to play in the barn. There was a rope hanging from the ceiling that we liked to swing on. Problem was it wasn't that secure. Anyway, it was his turn and he swung on that rope like there was no tomorrow."

"So he died??" I asked.

"Yes, the rope came loose when he was swinging and he fell hard to the ground, and that was the end of Freddy. He's been haunting that darn place ever since."

"Wow, thanks Grampa, that really helps," I replied, then I hung up the phone.

"What did he say?" asked Alex. So I told him the whole story.

"Well, I'm never going in there again," said Alex.

"Me too," I agreed, "how about you, Grant?"

"ZZZZZZ"

"I guess we will tell him in the morning," I laughed.

"Yeah," Alex replied. The mystery of the haunted hay room was finally solved.

Danielle E. Thibault
Age: 13

MEAN BULLS

My mom has a bull and he is mean! The bull's name is Talladega. He is very, very big. He has a black and white body. He also has a large, white head. He looks scary, fat, mean, and he watches us. He stares at us and follows us with his frightening, black eyes!

I was at school one afternoon and my mom was out back at the barn. She was checking the water so that the cows don't get mud on themselves. That is when my mom saw Talladega. He put his head down and the next thing she knew, he had her pinned against the wall of the barn! She started yelling to her dad to open the door because she couldn't get to it. He opened the door and she jumped inside. She was all right but he did hurt her leg a little bit. Thank God my gramps was there to open the door or my mom might have had to go to the hospital.

Brittany Ornberg
Age: 10

THE HAUNTED VIOLIN

There was once a girl named Jacky. The only thing Jacky loved to do was play the violin. She would play all day, all the time, and anywhere. Jacky performed almost everywhere.

But one day, Jacky's violin got worn out. Jacky and her mom had to get a new one. Jacky got in the store, and on a shelf she saw a shiny, beautiful violin. Jacky just loved it. Her mom bought it. Jacky was overjoyed to try the new violin. She ran to her bedroom excited to try the violin. She played and the violin sounded great. It sounded almost like a voice.

The next day, Jacky went to a recital to perform. She played a note, but it didn't sound as great as she had played before. In fact it was a horrible sound. Everyone wondered what was wrong with the instrument. Jacky became very worried. She went home feeling very sad.

The next day Jacky picked up her violin. She looked at it and something was different about it. It didn't look as beautiful as it used to. It looked dirty, scratched, and almost burnt. Jacky said to herself, "What is wrong with this violin? First it didn't sound good, now it doesn't look very pretty anymore."

Jacky the next day went to school worried. She was so nervous about her violin. She wondered what it would look like when she got home. Would it look black? Will the strings be broken? Was it her fault all of this was happening? Jacky was worried all day that day.

After school Jacky actually didn't want to play the violin. She was too scared to even look at her new violin. Would it look hideous? Was the violin haunted? It couldn't be. Jacky was very scared at this point in time.

Jacky got home and ran upstairs to her room to see the violin. She was so nervous, that she started to sweat, her blood pressure rose, and her teeth chattered. She opened the case and she saw a black, filthy, moldy violin. What was wrong with this violin? Should she tell her mom? No, she couldn't tell her parents. She would just make them just as nervous as she was. She would probably make them even more nervous than she was.

Suddenly, Jacky heard a voice out of nowhere speak to her. It wasn't just a noise, it almost sounded like words, words in a very hushed tone. Was the voice from her mom? Was there someone else in the house? Jacky didn't know what was going on.

She didn't know much about her violin. The violin she had was haunted. A lady once owned that very same violin Jacky was currently owning. The woman who owned the violin used to love playing the violin, too. She was very good at it. She would play the violin every day no matter what. She'd play in recitals, bands, orchestras, and even in church. But one day the woman mysteriously disappeared. No one was exactly sure what happened. Some said she just got killed. But the real reason was that the violin was haunted. It actually sucked her soul in the instrument.

Jacky then heard a voice out of her violin. The voice said, "You have used the Haunted Violin. Whoever uses this violin will be trapped in here forever! Since you have used the violin, your soul will be stuck in here forever." Jacky was never seen again.

Addie-Eileen Paige
Age: 11

THE MYSTERY OF THE MISSING FISH

Antarctica, December 13, 2006

Where is my fish? thought penguin.

Penguin's fish had been outside last night, as he had seen on his way to bed. But when he woke up this morning, it wasn't there. Then penguin wondered if his friends had taken his fish. So he went to his friend's house.

KNOCK KNOCK "Hello? Anyone home?" Penguin's friend, Polar Bear, opened the door.

"Hi! Come on in!"

Penguin walked into the igloo. It was filled with fish.

"So . . . why are you here?"

"My fish is gone. It was there when I went to bed, but when I woke up, it wasn't there."

"Oh . . . well if you're wondering about this fish, it's mine. I caught it yesterday by the iceberg where Snowman lives."

"Snowman! I'll go ask him!"

"Good idea! How about we both go?"

"OK! Should we take my sled?"

"Sure."

"OK."

Penguin and Polar Bear walked outside and got Penguin's sled. Then they went down the hill to the iceberg where Snowman lived.

KNOCK KNOCK "Anyone home?"

Then Snowman opened the door. "Hi, Penguin! Hi, Polar Bear!"

"Hi!"

"Hi!"

"So . . . why are you here?"

"I lost my fish. It was there last night, but when I woke up, it wasn't there."

"Oh. That's too bad . . ."

"Wait a minute! The Snow Monster! He loves fish! We can use Polar Bear's fish to distract him and get my fish back . . . if he stole it . . ."

"He probably did! Let's go check and if he does have your fish, we'll do the plan."

"OK."

So Penguin, Polar Bear, and Snowman walked outside and went to see if the Snow Monster had Penguin's fish.

"There he is! He has fish! MY fish!"

"They'll never figure out I took the fish . . . heh heh heh."

The Snow Monster was talking about how he had stolen the fish, and Penguin, Polar Bear, and Snowman then knew that it was Penguin's fish and they got ready to do the plan.

"OK. So . . . we go and get Polar Bear's fish, and you guys use it to distract the Snow Monster. Then I go and get my fish back and we escape. Got it?"

"Got it."

"Got it."

So Penguin, Polar Bear, and Snowman went up the hill to get Polar Bear's fish.

"Go get the fish! I'll get the sled ready!"

"I'm going!"

Penguin then got the sled and Polar Bear came out with the fish.

"Down we go!"

"Down!"

"Down!"

Penguin pushed the sled, and soon they were all going down the hill.

"Snowbank! Twelve o'clock!"

"Turn!"

"Turn!"

"Aaaah!"

The sled turned so quickly that Penguin went flying off and flew over the snowbank and then landed on the front of the sled again.

"OK. I'm going to jump off!"

"OK!"

"OK!"

"Get ready to stop and show him the fish while I go around him!"

"Got it!"

"Got it!"

And so, Penguin jumped off the sled and Polar Bear took over.

"And now, the plan starts."

Polar Bear and Snowman stopped the sled in front of the Snow Monster saying: "Fish delivery!"

Penguin then went around to get his fish while the Snow Monster wasn't looking.

"My fish delivery!"

While Polar Bear and Snowman were distracting the Snow Monster, Penguin got his fish and signaled for them to come on the sled.

"Gotta go!"

"Huh? But I didn't even get my fish!"

"Too bad Big Boy!"

Polar Bear pushed on the sled, and they went to get Penguin.

"Hop on!"

Penguin jumped on the sled and they turned the sled around just before they went off the iceberg into the water.

"You'll never get away!"

The Snow Monster had turned around towards them and was coming for them.

"Oh yes we will . . ."

The sled went between Snow Monster's legs, and he tripped on himself and rolled into the freezing cold Antarctic Ocean.

"That shows him!"

And so, Penguin, Polar Bear, and Snowman went up the hill to Penguin's house to have fish for dinner. HIS fish.

Ian W. Graham
Age: 10

A CIVIL-WAR ANCESTOR

My ancestor was a general in the Civil War and the leading general in the war was Ulysses Simpson Grant. The North and the South entered into the Civil War due to slavery. They were a nation divided.

The slaves tried to escape and start a new life. It was very dangerous for them and for others to help escaping because their owners would hunt them down and if they were caught, it could mean their death.

Abraham Lincoln was the leader of the Union and the President during the Civil War. The President did not stop slavery, but intended to stop Southerners from getting new slaves. He planned where they would attack the confederates. He went to General U. S. Grant's camp to talk about their strategies they would use during the war.

The soldiers were trained at West Point. They taught them how to shoot and how to sword fight. During the battles, a soldier would hold the American flag and if he fell down, another would continue to hold the flag.

My ancestor was in the all the Civil War battles. He was also the United States President before the Civil War started. My ancestor's name was General James Knox Polk.

Jonathan A. Knox

MY TRIP TO PENNSYLVANIA

Last summer I went to visit my grandparents in Pennsylvania with my mom, my dad, and my brother named Zack. My grandparents live on the best fishing spot on my favorite lake called Lake Hauto.

They have a huge pier with a really tall ladder leading into a part of the lake that is fifty feet deep. But the other side only goes up to my knees. They also have two motorboats that go really fast!

On the first day, I ran at about 50 mph down to the pier and grabbed a fishing rod before casting out to a one-hundred-foot section of the lake. Five minutes later, I felt a huge tug on my line. I whipped back the rod and began to frantically reel in the line. This was a true whopper! I could just feel it!

At halfway reeled in, I was exhausted! I ran to get the net. I called for my dad to get two more nets and a saw. I sawed off some metal, grabbed some glue from my backpack and made the world's largest net. I swung it through the water and caught a muskie. It was eight feet high and thirty-seven feet long. It was a keeper.

I was still hyper with energy after catching a few more giant fish. So I went swimming at noon. I told my dad that I'd be underwater for a few hours. He said that I couldn't do it. So I said that I'd try anyway and would come up if I needed a breath. "Fine, but you won't last more than a minute," he said, and with that I jumped in.

I saw lots of things. Suddenly, a great white shark swam up to me. I had an eight-hour, underwater battle with it and I won! Just then I needed a breath. I swam to the surface. "Holy moly!" I cried. It was already dark. I then went to bed.

The next day, after eating breakfast, I went down to the pier. After casting out and reeling in a few times, I got a bite. I whipped back my rod as fast as lightning and began to reel in. Eight feet, seven feet, six feet, five feet, four feet, three feet, two feet, one foot . . . in! This was officially the largest bass in the world! I ran up the hill to show my dad. I was so excited!

My dad was very happy for me. He was so happy about my accomplishments that he took the time to filet and cook the fish for us and the rest of the family. It lasted a year! I had a great vacation fishing at my grandparent's lake house.

Douglas Dubosky
Age: 8

FRIENDSHIP LASTS FOREVER

It was a bitterly cold afternoon at Logan International Airport. While thousands of people tried to push their way through to catch their flight, Jack, a fourteen-year-old boy, was also trying to push his way through the bustle to catch his flight to Kenya to see his grandma.

He was prepared for what would be an extremely long ride. Jack could not wait to see his grandma. He had not seen her in over a year, but he always e-mailed her or talked to her on the phone. While Jack was on the plane he wondered what adventure would happen at Grandma's this time.

The plane finally landed at the airport late the next morning. He had to find his luggage which took him what felt like forever. When he was all ready, he went outside the front door and there was Grandma waiting for him in her old, beat-up Land Rover. He jumped in and they drove off.

You could tell they were happy to see each other, just by the expressions on their faces. Jack asked Grandma what she had done while he was gone. She said she had fixed up the house a bit and planted some more flowers around the house and spent a lot of time talking to him on the phone and by e-mail. Jack just laughed and told her that the family really missed her a lot and that she should come live with them. Grandma said no every time anybody asked her. She said there were things in Kenya that were not in America like the jungles and the animals, and she did not have to worry about the hustle and bustle.

When they got to Grandma's house, Jack remembered it just as it was the last time he was here; an old white house with red shutters and flowers that ran all along the house. He couldn't forget the African jungle right in Grandma's front yard that spread as far as the eye could see.

As Jack went into the house to take all of his luggage in, Grandma went into the kitchen and fixed Jack's favorite sandwich, peanut butter and jelly. After lunch Jack went out into the jungle to explore, remembering to stay within eye distance of the house. While he was exploring the jungle, he heard what sounded like an animal cry. He ran where he thought he heard it, but he did not find anything. Then he heard it again and ran in another direction, and sure enough there was a baby lion crying next to his dead mother lion.

Jack cautiously went over to the baby lion, picked him up, and took him to his grandma's. Grandma, shocked to see what Jack had, was nervous and thought that it might bite him. She took the lion, put him in the bathtub and washed him all up. When she was done she could not believe how much water one little lion could splash around.

After the lion's bath, Jack took a water bottle, filled it with milk and fed it to the hungry little lion. After the lion was done eating, Jack and the lion went out back of the house and played catch. Jack started to play catch with his tennis ball, but the lion ruined it with his sharp teeth. So hoping that a baseball would be a little bit harder to ruin they tried playing with that. Still the lion tore it to pieces too. Finally Jack gave up, he just didn't have anything for the little lion to play with.

When Jack and the lion came in, Grandma went up to the attic to get the old, baby pen that Jack's mother used when she was little. When Grandma brought it down, she looked all over the house finally she found Jack and the baby lion in the living room all cuddled up asleep on the sofa, so she just left them alone.

When Jack woke up the next morning, he saw that the lion was not sleeping beside him. He got up nervously, wondering if Grandma had taken the lion back to the edge of the jungle. All of a sudden, he heard a big crash from the kitchen. He ran to the kitchen and found that the lion was in the fridge eating breakfast. The lion was too busy wrestling with a pickle jar lid to even notice that Jack was there. Jack picked him up and put him in the baby pen, but it was no use, the lion bit right through the netting. Jack took a piece of rope and tied him to a post on the porch.

After Jack had cleaned up all of the mess that the lion had made, they went out into the jungle to explore some more. While Jack was exploring, the lion ran off into a great big field. Jack, watching the lion, had no idea what he was doing. After a while, the lion came back with a dead rabbit in his mouth. The lion started purring. Jack thought it was time to let him go even though he had had him for only two days. Jack didn't want to worry about that just yet. He wanted to play with the lion and that's what they did all day without lunch and until supper.

A week passed and it was time for Jack to say what might be good-bye forever to the little lion. While Jack was packing everything to go back to America, the little lion just stayed by his side. When it was time to go, Jack couldn't do anything but hope that he would se the little lion next time he came to Grandma's.

While Jack and his grandma drove off the lion tried to keep up. Jack just started to cry. Jack said silently, "You were the bet pet anyone could want."

Every time Jack went to his grandma's and yelled out "Little Lion," he never came. But Jack knew that the little lion was still out there somewhere, and he knew that their friendship would last forever.

Zachary A. Parker
Age: 13

A LONG WALK HOME

Sabrina was thirteen years old and she was already in the ninth grade. It was only because of her massive intelligence that she had skipped a grade. She had taken advanced math lessons for at least two years now. She was the only one to participate in the class. Some people thought she was smart sometimes, but other times, they hated her for it. They mocked her saying, "Oh! Look! I'm Sabrina the smartest girl in the school! Wow, I should just leave the rest of the ninth grade alone and just go off to college!" But those weren't the meanest things that they could say. Some things they weren't even allowed to say in school. But they said it anyway.

It was the first day of ninth grade for Sabrina and she couldn't be any happier! She had skipped eighth grade because her teachers believed that the eighth grade would just slow her down. So they just bumped her up a grade.

The day was half over and Sabrina had not made one single friend. She figured she wouldn't because she did not know anyone. So she sat at an isolated table in the corner of the lunchroom. Not a very comfortable way to start the first day. But it was the only thing she could do since she had no idea who anybody was. So she just sat there, quietly, alone, until the lunch bell rang and it was time to go back to class.

"I can't believe it turned out like this," she mumbled. "This day was suppose to be fun . . . but it is a nightmare." She was so disappointed of what her day was like. But then, a lifesaver happened. The final school bell rang and it was time to go home.

Little did Sabrina know that a group of her classmates were planning something horrible, something inhumane. They were going to make sure that Sabrina wasn't going to come back to school the next day. Oh no! They weren't going to kill her! That would just be so mean and shocking. They were just going to scare her, in the worst possible way. They had a pen and paper and they were jotting down ideas of the way they were going to do it. They came up with things like chase her with hockey masks and baseball bats. Also, follow her in our car and make her go the other way, then hunt her down! These things were horrible to do to a very smart girl who could make history someday. But they were going to do it anyway.

It wasn't long before Sabrina was not even halfway home and she heard a rumble. It wasn't like an earthquake, but it wasn't like a metal trashcan, either. It was a car, with four people with hockey masks on . . . with baseball bats. They chased her down and made her run the other way. They heard her scream and saw her shed tears, but they didn't stop. It was like their hearts were made out of barbed wire and coal, or they didn't have hearts at all. Sabrina soon found an alleyway where the car couldn't get through. So the teenagers got out of the wide car and chased her on foot, not knowing that there was a police officer on the other side. Sabrina swung around the corner and crashed into the police officer.

"What is wrong, Miss?" the police officer asked.

"I am being chased by teenagers with baseball bats and hockey masks! You have to help me! Please, I am so scared!" responded Sabrina.

"I will do what I can." The police officer ran into the alleyway looking for the hockey-masked strangers. But there was no trace of them. They were actually on the balconies above him! So the kids jumped off the balconies and started up the chase, again.

After a long run, the hockey-masked maniacs ditched Sabrina, and she had no idea where she was. It was dark now, which made it even harder to find her way home. Then she heard the same rumble of the car that started the chase in the first place! She soon went even further than she was. She probably traveled all over New York by now.

The next day when the start of school bell rang, Sabrina never showed up. It turns out that the teenagers were there, but she was not. Then more days came, and she was nowhere in sight. Then more days, then more days, then more days. Pretty soon, it had been a month and no one, not even her mother, had seen Sabrina. Sabrina was never found.

Jason Taylor
Age: 11

THE HAUNTED HOUSE

Once there was a haunted house that everybody avoided. One night I walked past the house and I realized that there was a creature moving behind the door. My heart pounded, but I went onto the path that led to the house. Very slowly I reached for the doorknob. Then I heard a familiar sound coming from the other side of the door. I grabbed the handle. Suddenly, a trap door opened right under my feet! I fell through the hole and into a cage! I was trapped! I had an idea. I quickly rolled the cage onto the floor and the cage split open! I was free!

Quickly, I ran back to the front door and grabbed the handle, but I jumped away when the trap door opened. When it closed, I slowly opened the door. I found a trail of slime leading upstairs. So I followed the trail and it led to a door. I tried to open the door but I was really hoping that it was locked. Bad news, it wasn't. When I opened the door, I saw a slimy green monster that could change into anything! I ran up and down the stairs screaming with the monster right behind me! Suddenly I came up with a brainstorm. I ran home as fast as I could and got my vacuum cleaner and ran back into the house. I sneaked up on the monster and sucked him up!

Nobody was ever afraid of that house again. But sometimes I still would think I'd hear it; a strange music coming from inside the house. Once I swore I saw the monster in the window. Did the monster have babies and hide them before I sucked him up? If so, was his child planning to attack the city? Well, I thought I could save that investigation for another day.

Danielle Dottor
Age: 8

RABBITS ARE INNOCENT

Do you own a garden? Have you ever blamed a rabbit for stealing YOUR carrots or hopping through the lettuce? I know all of you humans do. NEWS FLASH! Technically, we rabbits are the whole reason why there are such things as gardens! Don't believe me? Listen to this legend I have about my rabbit ancestors that will prove once and for all rabbits have a right to all gardens!

Randy The Rabbit Legend

Randy Rabbit was doodling through the village on a breezy day in 1001, way before humans ever lived. He was famished from the long moose hunt. Of course he didn't catch anything. To be quite honest he really didn't care, he was sick of meat. For some strange, reason cold, raw, fly-infested carcass did not appeal to him.

"But what's a rabbit to do? If I don't eat, I'll starve, but if I even whiff the putrid smell of meat I will most definitely gag! Aha, decisions, decisions, moaned Randy. Sadly, Randy, against his gut feeling went home and had the leftovers from the previous lunch.

"Someday I'll invent a scrumptious recipe that nobody can resist. I am giving my solid word that until that happens I will not, repeat, I will not, eat anymore unsanitary food that only makes me sick!"

Well, two weeks later Randy was singing a different tune.

He was in such dire need of food, anything would be a treat. Unfortunately, all the fellow rabbits thought he was crazy and refused to help him. Randy began scavenging around. He searched high and low only to find a clump of leaves, a wee bit of cheese, and cold, hard ham.

"Well, I am not against trying new things, but if I mix all these unusual ingredients, the product might be very nasty," Randy said to himself, "but then again, I'm in no position to be picky. Besides, maybe I'll make millions off this new recipe!"

So now Randy was on a mission to make a five-star recipe that rabbits would love and possibly gain some friends at the same time.

As he walked back to his house with his strange new goodies, Randy pondered over what he could make with these elements—cheese, meat, and leaves.

"I got it!" screamed Randy. "I will shred the cheese over the torn-up leaves and put lemon juice on top. It is brilliant, I will call it s-a-l-a-d."

So that night Randy ate this salad and found it to taste quite delicious. In the following weeks Randy discovered that there are many other foods you could put in a salad, like carrots, cucumbers, and peppers. He began to plant and harvest food; it became all he ate. Randy noticed that the new foods he discovered didn't make him gain weight or feel tired. Amazing!

Randy told everyone he passed on the street about this new diet. Rabbits didn't know what to think at first, they decided that it wouldn't hurt to try this new diet. The first taste was so intriguing that they soon devoured it all. They too began planting these new elements of food.

The rabbits would have loved to live on leaves, and fresh, crisp vegetables, but one horrible day changed life as they knew it.

It was a rainy night and all the crops they needed blew away and all the seeds got washed out. The village was taking on water from the nearby river and everything was being destroyed. They had no food and had no idea where they would go for shelter. One thing was for sure, however. They had to move to high ground or they would drown. Leaving everything behind was hard, but everyone had high hopes for finding new crops or possibly the old ones.

Over time in the new village, rabbits forgot about the food they once adored. They accepted the new unappetizing diet of nuts, and life became very dull, until a little rabbit wandered off and should have starved to death, but found a place where leaves were plentiful and nobody went hungry. You could get food whenever you wanted, as long as it was after dark. If you even thought of sneaking out into the open during the day, the creatures with two legs would trap you and keep you as a pet!

With this new information the rabbits devised a plan to sneak into the garden, dig up the plants and transfer them back to their garden. The plan was a sure way to get the plants back, but one rabbit thought it would be wrong to take another's source of food.

This rabbit was Randy.

"Do you remember that terrible night when we lost all that was dear to us in a flood? We had no food, no shelter, and no secure place. But we got through it and we're fine now. Please, don't be greedy. Don't take another's prized possession for your own happiness. Think how they will feel when they have no food for their kids!"

That speech really hit home to the rabbits and they all agreed to NOT go through with the plan because they have a heart. Every now and then a rabbit will get sick of nuts and go to a garden and swipe a carrot or two, but never a significant amount. All they need is a taste of what was once theirs and it keeps them going. So, now, seeing how we rabbits invented a new type of food and don't want to ruin the gardens, couldn't you cut us some slack? Do you want to know what I think? I think the humans need to relax and let us come and go. Besides, it's not like we're asking for . . . nevermind that's another story!

Abbie Eastman
Age: 12

TROUBLE AT SCHOOL

Jason had just woken up when he heard the school bus coming, so he slipped into his clothes and ran outside just as the bus was leaving. So once again he had to ride his electric scooter to school. Jason was eleven, and his best friend was named Jeffry. Jason's favorite sports are soccer and golf, and he has a pet piranha.

While riding his electric scooter to school, Robert, a bully from his neighborhood ran in front of Jason. Before Robert could punch Jason, he took a sharp turn and was safe for now.

By the time Jason got to school, Robert was already there. He got there so fast because Robert has a dirt bike. When Jason got to class, they were studying adding and subtracting fractions. Unfortunately, Robert was in the same class as Jason, and he was staring at Jason in the meanest way you could think of. Robert asked if he could go to the bathroom and Ms. Rose said, "Yes."

While the teacher was reading, and when we were writing, Jason looked out the window and saw Robert ripping out the wires in his electric scooter. When he raised his hand Robert came in, so he put his hand down before Ms. Rose saw it. So Jason had to walk home with his electric scooter. When he showed his dad, his dad frowned. Luckily Jason's dad was a mechanic, so his dad found the wires and fixed the electric scooter.

When he was in bed that night, he realized that if he stood up for himself, then maybe Robert would back off and pick on someone else for once.

When Jason got up the next morning, he looked at the soccer schedule and the championship soccer game was today. Jason's team is the Rockets and they haven't lost a game yet.

Jason was getting ready in the locker room when Robert barged in and said, "Are you ready to get your beating before the big game?"

"Actually, Robert, if you hurt me before the big game, you'll let the team down and I'll tell. I guess if you want to hurt me, do it after the game, but I'll still tell."

When Jason was playing the game, he felt great about standing up for himself. He was rushing down the field when he yelled, "Pass it!" Jeffry passed it with five seconds left in the game. The game was tied one to one when Jason shot the ball and scored. The Rockets won the championship game and everyone picked up Jason and cheered.

Robert apologized to Jason, for now at least. For the next week Robert decided to try to find a hobby. However, that didn't work for long and he went back to his bullying self.

What can I do just to stop Robert? Jason thought. Then suddenly he had an idea. If he got Robert to bully someone else, then he might stop bullying him. When Jason tried to talk to Robert, he didn't listen and just laughed and walked away. By the time he tried to think of another plan, it was the end of the school year.

Now it was time for the vacation in Florida that was supposed to be the congratulations for winning the game from Mom and Dad. He was happy that he would actually get the whole summer off with no Robert. That's what he wanted. When his family got packed, they started to leave for the Sport Resort for Kids. When they got there, he saw a kid learning how to play tennis but he wasn't very good at it. When they got into their hotel room, it was puny. It was made for two people. So they decided to leave and just have a fun vacation at home. Jason doubted that he'd have as much fun at home, though.

When the family got home, the house was destroyed and the only thing left was Jason's piranha.

In the fish bowl was a piece of paper. It said:

How do you like me now, Jason. P.S. From a bully at school.

It sort of looked like Robert's handwriting, so Jason called the police and when the police got there, they agreed that it was Robert's handwriting. Now Robert's family has to pay a fine of three million dollars because of private property destruction. He had to sell everything to pay Jason for what he did.

After that a new kid came to school. His name was Carter, and he was mean. However, he didn't hurt other students, but he found things that scared them. He hurt Jeffry's feelings first. Jason said that he would help Jeffry to try to stop Carter. Jeffry and Jason had a plan to find a weakness in Carter.

The next day they found out that Carter was afraid of frogs because Carter screamed when he saw one. So they filled Carter's locker with frogs and when Carter opened his locker he yelled, "Helllllp meeeeee." Then Jason and Jeffry said that if Carter didn't hurt them, they wouldn't hurt him.

After lunch Jason and Jeffry went out to recess. They couldn't play kickball because Carter was bullying the captain of kickball team. The next day, the captain told on Carter, and Carter got expelled for five months. The school was better than before. Since Carter had been gone, though, it had been kind of boring and not as much fun as everyone thought. Even though Carter bullied people, he was fun to play with. However, Jason and Jeffry thought that maybe Carter bullied others because he didn't have very many friends.

Then Jason got to thinking. If he became Carter's friend, Carter would be nice to him. When Carter came back to school, Jason and Jeffry made friends with Carter. Then soon enough, they became best friends.

One school day, Carter saw Robert's best friend, Josh, taking someone's lunch money. Then Carter told Jason and they decided that maybe little by little Josh was becoming just like Robert. "Jeffry, we have to do something before Josh starts punching or kicking people." Now the only thing they could do was to tell a teacher and the teacher could keep an eye on Josh.

At that same time, Jeffry's mom and dad were planning to take the family plus Jason to Utah and stay and play at the Big Mountain Fun Park to get Josh off their mind.

When they got there, Jason started to write a note to his mom and dad.

Dear Mom and Dad,

     I'm having so much fun. Jeffry and I went down a one-hundred-foot water slide. I hope you are having as much fun as I am.
Love,
Jason

Jason and Jeffry spent a week there and slept all the way back on the airplane.

Back At Home

"That was a great vacation, huh Jeffry."

"Yeah, it was awesome! The best part was when we came back and found out that Josh was expelled for the rest of the year."

Jason and Jeffry hoped that they would have a great school year. They had saved the day and prevented the school from chaos.

Cody Brann
Age: 10

THE SPACE WAR OF SISCO

As the earth spins around and darkness comes, the brightness of the stars and moon reveal Sisco, a huge space station. Sisco is a five-thousand-person space station close to the planet Earth that appeared thirty-five years ago. Its inhabitants are super intelligent life forms, who survive by drinking oil from large blue oil rocks found in space. These aliens are all males, five feet tall, with four arms, three short legs, with white faces, and wrinkly skin. Their faces have one small eye with a pointy nose underneath. Their mouths are in the shape of an upside down "U". They can hear with large antennae, which stick out both sides of their head.

The men are getting their ships ready for a scout run in space to explore the area for food. Coca, one of the captains of the fleet, was the only one to find an oil rock on the last voyage. He brought it back to the station. It was huge and had bright little light blue crystals that kept growing each day. One of these crystals got so large that one night it reflected on a new planet in space that was never seen before. Like Earth, it was a brown and blue planet. The planet had life forms, meaning there were people on the planet. "They must have had a cloaking device so we could never see the planet. Also the oil rock had enough energy to reveal the new planet," said Jumba, the king of Sisco.

"Yes you're right," said Coca.

"Coca we need your scout fleet to explore the surroundings of the planet," said Jumba. "Then I will send a scout group for the surface of the planet," said Jumba.

After Coca's space scouting he came back to the space station and he said, "They have a space port, but no ships. The ground scout says our elite ground force was captured. That means they have ground soldiers," said the scout.

"We must get all of the troops and invade the planet."

After the troops landed they tried to find the creature called the nursa. Then they saw a small, green, big-eyed creature and screamed nursa. The men secretly followed the nursa into a huge mysterious underground "city". They went over and attacked the base. Momba, the head guard for the nursa, saw the men first and sealed the entrance. Musa, the king of the nursa, put all the defenses up so the men would not get in.

Jumba came out and said, "Free the prisoners and we won't attack you."

Musa replied, "OK, if you come in peace."

Jumba offered to pay the nursa a treaty of peace and to forge an alliance. Sisco now owned half of the new planet and the nursa owned the other half of the planet. Sisco constructed many cities and soon became one of the most powerful forces in the universe.

Reid F. Jerue
Age: 10

ANIMALS MISSING

Chapter One

One day Mrs. Call and Lexie went to school. Mrs. Call has brown curly hair and is twenty-six years old. She has blue eyes and is very tall. Then there is Lexie. Lexie is three years old and has black and white fur. She has green eyes, a pink nose, and big ears. She is a bunny.

When Mrs. Call and Lexie got to school, Lexie fell through a hole in the school parking lot and disappeared. Mrs. Call never knew that Lexie was gone. So the class asked, "Where is Lexie today, Mrs. Call?"

"She is in her car. See. Look over . . . OH! Where is my wonderful Lexie? She is gone!"

"Don't worry, Mrs. Call, we will find her! Yes we will!" replied Jimmy.

"Oh thank you, class! You are the best in the world."

"It will be like a field trip. If you put it that way, it does sound pretty interesting. Okay, like a field trip." So after all the classes were done, the kids all met up after school and stared at each other, but none of them came up with a suggestion. So they had to go to Mrs. Call for a plan. Mrs. Call told the class to split up first and she helped them with that.

Chapter Two

Maddie is one of Lexie's friends. Maddie is Mrs. Tabby's kitty. Maddie has brown and black fur and is three years old. She loves to go to school and have fun. Mrs. Tabby was screaming her head off.

There is one more character I would like you to meet and his name is Ben. He is a pug. That is a dog, and his owner is Mrs. Kelly. It is really sad for all three teachers because their little animals are missing.

On the animal side they are having a blast because they met up in the hole and stayed with each other. They were so tired looking for a way out, Ben just dropped to the ground and Lexie and Maddie were in front of Ben so they did not see that he had dropped.

"Lexie, I'm getting tired. What about you , Ben . . . Ben, are you still here?

Lexie hopped around. "You aren't going to believe this . . . Ben is gone."

"Okay, we can't flip out. Okay, yes we can. Now let's think. We thought he was behind us the whole time. We don't know where he went. He might have fell or tripped over something and gotten hurt really bad. Oh my, we need to go find Ben before anybody else finds him."

On the way back to find Ben, they got in trouble because they ran into a mole. It was a very aggressive mole and the animals had to run for their lives.

Ben was still lying on the ground and he was sound asleep. The animals were running from the mole so fast that they flew by Ben. They didn't even notice that he was lying there.

They were so far ahead of the mole that the mole had started to walk and he had seen Ben and ran away. So they turned around and started to run back. They got Ben up off the ground and brought him to a different hole. They went up that hole and found themselves in someone's house. Maddie said, "I don't think we went up the right hole. We need to go back down this hole and find that right one." That night the three animals went up and down every hole, until they finally fell asleep at the bottom of one.

At 6 a.m. all three animals had woken up. They were already looking for the right hole again. It took them most of the day until finally at 3 p.m. they found the right hole and they saw their owners again. Except for Lexie, she had turned around for a split second, and Maddie and Ben were already gone by the time she turned back around. Lexie went the wrong way, but she had found the other side of the hole and arrived fifteen minutes after Maddie and Ben got there.

On the kid's side, it did not turn out as good. With Jimmy in charge, they didn't even get out of the school. So that's the story.

Samantha Libby
Age: 10

THE SECRET OF THE ATTIC

I have always wondered why I was never allowed in the attic. The door is right next to my room and Mom had a key. It was always so hard to resist opening the door. One day I thought I would give it a shot. So . . . I walked up to the door, put my hand on and . . .

I was interrupted by, "Allison . . . Allison . . ." That was my name. I closed the door tight and ran into my room. It was morning and Mom did not know I was up yet, so I flipped myself under my covers and pretended to be fast asleep.

Bethany walked into the room. Bethany was my best friend. She had beautiful blonde hair and blue eyes with a hint of green. "Phew," I said as she walked into the room. "Why are you here?" I asked. She reminded me that I had asked her to help figure out the mystery of the attic.

I told her about my mother. Whenever she speaks of the attic, she always acts weird and awkward. I need to figure out what is so important about that attic. We walked out of my room and went past the attic door.

I tried opening the door again, and it opened, just with a twist of the door and a pull, it opened. I looked and saw old creaky stairs all the way to the top and spider webs everywhere on every wall. It seemed like nobody had been up there in thousands of years.

Bethany and I walked up the stairs frightened that there was something up there that would do something bad to us or hurt us. We tried not to touch the spider webs but they were everywhere. The floorboards creaked and sounded like they were going to crack on us. However, I tried to be brave enough to even open that door. I tried to be as quiet as I could. I looked around and I was very disappointed when I saw nothing in that room except for a small box in the corner.

I walked over to the box. I started to open it until something startled me. It was my mother. She had called me down for soccer practice. I heard her coming up the stairs. I ran downstairs before she came up to get me and saw me in the attic. I shut the door. She looked at me the way she looks at me when she thinks I am guilty. I was scared that I was going to be in big trouble but she did not do anything.

We walked into my room to get our soccer equipment on and then went on our way. I was thinking maybe Mom did not say anything because Bethany was there. She probably didn't want Bethany to tell her mom she was crazy, but I know she would never do that. When I got home my mom was going upstairs to change her clothes to work in the garden. I walked upstairs and saw that my mom was looking at the door suspiciously. She looked and saw that the door was cracked. I thought I closed it tight. How could I have done that? She closed the door and I ran downstairs, ran out the door, and came in again pretending like I just got home.

"Hello?" I called. "Mom?" I called again.

"Upstairs," she called. I went upstairs.

"Hi," I said.

"Hi. How was soccer practice?" Mom asked.

"Good," I replied.

I went to my room and took my things off. I knew I had to go up in the attic sometime to figure out what was in that box. I knew it was not going to be tonight because my mom was already suspicious. Maybe I could do it tomorrow if Mother wasn't there.

The next morning, I was called downstairs for breakfast. I ate pancakes with maple syrup. Yum! Mom said she was going to the store to buy some groceries.

"Yes!" I screamed in excitement.

"What did you say?" Mother replied.

"Nothing," I said.

"Maybe I should stay home," Mom announced.

"No, that's okay," I said as she walked out the door.

My father, Brian, is never home because he is always on business trips. I never see him because he always goes around the world selling a bunch of fantastic items. He is a salesman. So far, he has gone to Hawaii, Mexico, China, Canada, and Costa Rica. He lives in a big house in California right now. I always wondered how he could afford it. But, oh well.

Then I remembered that I did not have much time to look in the attic, so I ran up to the door leading to the attic.

I went through the spider webs, walked up the creaky stairs, and got to the top. I walked to the very corner of the room and went to the box. The box was sitting there as still as could be. I opened it and a poof of smoke slithered out like a snake. I jumped as a figure that looked like a fairy started to form. It was a fairy. I stood there with my mouth open and my eyes stunned and very confused. It spoke.

"Whatever I may do will be my pleasure." This fairy was beautiful. She had shining blue slippers and a beautiful white gown. Her hair was back in a bun. She was very pale. She came out and flew around almost as if she was a butterfly. Her wings were very white. She came over and landed on my shoulder. I was frightened. Her hands looked very soft and she had a beautiful, twinkling star in her hand. I thought to myself of what it could be. Maybe it was for decoration. But no! It couldn't be. She was a magical fairy. It would not be for decoration. I hopped up and started to run down the stairs. I was scared that it might be something bad and that's why they had kept it up in the attic where it cannot be touched. I thought that for a while but then I stopped. She said whatever I may do will be my pleasure, so you would think that she is a nice fairy. She caught up to me and landed in my hand. She said again, "Whatever I may do will be my pleasure." I wanted to see if she really granted wishes, so I tried.

"Um . . . Um," I said as I was trying to think of a good wish. "I wish . . . I . . . I . . . could be what I always wanted to be—a fantastic drawer that can draw anything."

The fairy waved her twinkling star and granted my wish that very second. Glittery dust flew around and around me. It spun so fast you could barely see it. It scared me for a second but then I calmed down.

I went into the workroom and got a piece of paper and a pencil. I started to draw and I could not stop. I just drew the best I could. I was so surprised. My drawing was fantastic. I drew a monkey in a tree with lots of leaves. Maybe I should go in competition I thought, but I knew that would be cheating, so I decided not to.

The fairy really did grant wishes. Then I realized that that was how my mother and father met. Mother asked the fairy to grant her wish to marry my dad and . . . and . . . I went on and on until I heard my mother walk in the door.

I ran in my room still with the fairy in my hand as she started to walk up the stairs. I shoved the fairy in one of the jars that I had kept for a butterfly collection. I never caught anything. The jar was just sitting in my room waiting to be used. She walked into my room and with my back to the jar, I said hi. The fairy was making a racket in there trying to get out and be free.

"What was that?" Mother asked.

"Nothing," I said.

She walked over and looked over my shoulder. "You! You! You went in the attic. How did you get in? It was locked, and I even have the key. How did you get in?"

"It . . . it . . . it was open!"

"What?" Mom said.

"Yes I . . . I . . . I turned the knob and it opened." Mother walked over and opened the attic. The smoke was still there from the fairy. Mother shut the door and came back into my room. She said very firmly, "You can keep the fairy only if you use her wisely," and then she left.

From then on, the fairy and I never left each other's sides. I told Bethany about the fairy. She was shocked.

My father came home and decided to find a job near home to be closer to his family. Secretly I wished that from the fairy.

Julia Ritter
Age: 11

92

SEAL DAY

One day I was walking to the beach with my mom, sister, and three friends Nick, Emma, and Jessica. When we got to the beach we saw a seal that had hurt its side. We called the animal shelter to ask what to do. They asked, "How big does it look?"

I answered, "It looks about six months to me, maybe one and a half feet long."

"Do you have a wagon? If you do, go get it and bring the seal to your house. Once you're home, call us again." Then they hung up, not waiting for an answer to their question. I turned off Mom's cell and told everyone what the shelter had told me to do. So we all ran back to my house got my wagon, some blankets, and some fish, then ran back to the beach to get the seal. To get the seal in the wagon and come with us we used some of the fish I had brought. She ate it all up and we gently put her in the wagon and took turns wheeling her home. When we got there, I called the animal shelter and asked what to do. They said, "You need to feed it cut-up, raw fish four to five times a day and make it so she can't move her side. Then they added, "If she moves her side she'll reinjure herself."

"Well thank you for your time," I said not so sure of myself. Then I hung up.

"OK let's set up a plan. Mom every day you send me a note saying I can come home from school to feed the seal."

Mom said, "Fine, I'll go write the note."

The next day at lunch I biked back home as fast as I could. When I got there I ran inside to my closet and opened the door where I had set up a small space with a bed so she couldn't roll around much. She seemed OK so I ran to the kitchen, got some chopped-up fish, and ran back to my closet to feed the seal. Then I started the music box that helps put the seal to sleep, then closed the closet door, ran back to get my bike, and sped back to school.

After I got home from school, I ran to get another bunch of chopped-up fish, and went back to my closet to feed the seal again. I started making it a ritual to do my homework in the closet with the seal. Once in a while she'd nose the ball that I had gotten her over to me and I'd bump it back. This routine kept going on for half a month. By this time her side had healed and she was ready to go back home to the ocean, except for her age.

One day my mom and I went to the beach to collect seaweed when we saw and heard a larger seal barking. Then I said excitedly, "Mom! Maybe that's our seal's mom. Let's go get our seal and bring it back to the beach and see if that's what she's looking for!"

Mom speed-answered, "Let's go!" We ran back home got the seal in the car and quickly drove back to the beach. As soon as we let the seal out of the car it waddled over to its mom and they were reunited. Then they swam away and everyone was happy.

Amanda Sancomb
Age: 9

THE DISCOVERY OF THE HEFLUMPS

Chapter One

"Hey, Tommy, did you see that thing in the tree?"

"No."

"I wonder what it was," said Sam.

"Let's go see. Quick! Quick! Let's go before it runs away!"

Tommy and Sam were breathing hard.

"Where did it go?" said Sam.

"I don't know."

"Come on! Let's keep going. We might see it. Oh, it's too late now. Let's go back exploring now and check tomorrow."

The next morning at 4 a.m., Tommy woke up and met Sam in his backyard. Tommy and Sam went down to the exact same spot in the woods. They kept hearing sounds and seeing leaves thrash, but they never saw anything for two weeks. Then one day they saw something blue sticking out of the trees! Tommy and Sam exploded like an atomic bomb, but very quietly so it wouldn't run away. Sam knew it was an animal that kept making sounds. The animal moved a little so they could see its whole body. It looked like a bright blue animal with two legs, a round head, and a very long tail.

The next day Sam and Tommy met each other at 4 a.m. in Sam's backyard, and they went to the same spot in the woods. That day they decided to make a tree house. It took them just one day to build it, but the tree house wasn't really a tree house. It was just a big board stuck in a tree with a rope ladder going up to it. The tree that had the awkward animal in it was the tree they chose to build their tree house in.

For a couple of days it seemed that the animal was starting to become a friend to Sam and Tommy, so it was easier for them to get a good look.

(The next morning they went to look out for the evil sakakas and the wufer. They are very ferocious animals that can easily kill you.)

Chapter Two

Thummmp! Crakkk! Crashhh! "What was that?!"

Tommy and Sam were horrified as the crashing got louder and louder. The little blue creature ran away like it was a lightning bolt. The two boys could see a huge, orange head coming towards them. A few seconds later a tree fell in front of the tree house. Then the head turned into a huge, bright orange lizard. A gigantic monkey came out of the trees right after the tree fell. The two monsters were fighting each other very intensely while Sam and Tommy were running home. They told Sam's mother about the sakakas and the wufer. The next day Sam looked at what the giant animals did. When Sam got there he gasped. The tree house was smashed to bits. Lots of trees were broken down, and there were lots of holes in the ground from the sakakas' claws drilling down into the earth. Sam ran back to the house and called Tommy on the phone.

"Tommy, Tommy, did you hear what the wufer and the sakakas did!"

"No," said Tommy.

"They destroyed everything, the tree house and the ground, but not the tree that the little animal sat in."

"Can you show me?" asked Tommy.

"Uh-huh," said Sam. Tommy came over to Sam's house. Sam showed Tommy the damage in the woods.

"How did those animals do that?"

"I don't know," said Sam.

Sam and Tommy built the tree house, but the animal didn't come back.

Chapter Three

"Where is it?" asked Sam.

"Is what?"

"The little blue creature."

"Maybe it will come back sometime soon." And so it did. The little blue animal finally came back. Sam and Tommy named the creature a heflump. It seemed that he liked that name.

The next day Sam and Tommy went into the woods. "Holy cheese!" said Sam. "Look at them all. There are hundreds of them! Heflumps, heflumps, heflumps!" There were tons of heflumps. There were heflumps on the tree house. There were heflumps on the rope ladder. There were heflumps on the ground, and there were heflumps in the trees. The two boys couldn't believe how many heflumps there were in the forest.

Sam and Tommy finally got their parents to look at what they had discovered. Their parents had never seen this type of animal, so they called the Ching-Wow-Pow.444. It is a group of high-tech Chinese animal scientists. They know every little bit about animals. The group came over and checked it out. They thought that it was a new species of animal, so they checked on the animal map. It was a new animal.

The news spread around the world in a day. Every TV that was on had a heflump on it. Sam and Tommy were the first kids ever to have discovered a new animal.

Chapter Four

Sam and Tommy were sure that the heflumps were reptiles, but they didn't know why they didn't go away in the winter. The heflumps stayed all year.

That day . . . Thuddd!!! A giant bird came flying down from the sky and started chowing on the heflumps like a hungry pig eating grain.

The next day . . . Thuddd!!! It happened again, but there were no heflumps to eat.

Sam's mother didn't know about this creature. The next day and the next day and the next day . . . Thuddd!!! Thuddd!!! Thuddd!!! Still there were no more heflumps.

But one day . . . Booommm!!! The giant heflump-eating bird blew up. Sam and Tommy set a mine right where the bird landed and it exploded. Sam was glad that the evil bird was gone, but they were sad that there were no more heflumps.

Chapter Five

Tommy and Sam checked if there were anymore heflumps. There were tons of them, but they were floating around in spacesuits and eating CHEEZ-ITs. When Sam was running back to his house, the heflumps followed him, so Sam asked his mom if he could have all the heflumps as pets. His mom agreed, so for the rest of Sam and Tommy's lives, they had a bunch of heflumps flying around the room in spacesuits eating CHEEZ-ITs.

Eric Wilcox
Age: 10

VACATION TO THE OTHER PLANETS

My name is Jack. I am in the third grade. This summer my family went on a vacation. This was not an ordinary vacation. We went to the other planets in our solar system.

My dad drove the rocket, but, as usual, he got lost. So, there we were, flying around in space with no idea where we were going. My idea was to head for the sun.

The first planet was Mercury. I liked Mercury, but it was way too hot. So, we went to the next planet. The next planet was Venus. Venus was also too hot. So, we went to the next planet. The next planet was Mars. I liked Mars and wanted to stay, but Dad said we had to keep going. After Mars, we went to Jupiter. It was colorful, but too windy. So, we left. After Jupiter was Saturn. I liked Saturn's rings, but it was too cold. So, we went to Uranus. Uranus was also too cold. When we left, we went to Uranus. Uranus was also too cold. When we left, we went to Neptune. Neptune was way too cold, so we left.

After our Neptune vacation was over, we went back to Earth. During this vacation, I learned that the other planets were cool, but Earth is the best of all. I was not too happy when I had to go back to school.

Jack Charbonneau
Age: 8

THE LITTLE SPARROW

Once there was a little sparrow who lost his mother. He would eat blueberries because if he caught a worm he would say, "Oh, you cute little thing, why would a sparrow like me eat you?"

He also went to Sparrow Elementary School. There, he would learn how to catch worms. One day in Sparrow Elementary School, they learned how to fly. He fell and hurt his wing. It healed and he was able to fly. Now this is weird, but this little sparrow had a cat friend. This was a cat that was vegetarian. All she ate was sushi.

Every day the sparrow would say, "Want to play?" and the cat would say, "I am very old, as you know, and my muscles are too old to play." So they would tell stories.

One dark, foggy day, the sparrow went in the woods to get food. When he saw a cat, he thought it was his friend and he went to it. That's when it jumped out. Frightened to death, the sparrow stood still and fell over. The cat who lost sight of it said, "It must be a leaf blowing in the wind." Then the cat walked away. The sparrow jumped to his feet and then thought, that was close!

Now let's talk about the cat. This was an old cat. Her owner took good care of her and gave her the best milk in town. The cat had silky fur that swayed in the morning breeze.

Now let's go back to the sparrow. While we talked about the cat, the sparrow had grown and now he lives with his wife and five kids who go to the Sparrow Elementary School.

One day Mrs. and Mr. went with their kids to find a new home because their last home fell apart in a recent, fall storm. On their journey to find a new home, they met a rat that got chased by a hunter who wanted to make rat filet. So Mr. Sparrow swooped down and grabbed it, then flew away. On the other side of the lake, he gently placed it on the ground and said, "Are you okay?"

The rat thankfully said with a big smile, "I surely am." When the rat left, Mr. and Mrs. Sparrow left with their kids to find a new home. They found one right next to Mr. Sparrow's friend's house. Every day the owner would feed the birds food or pieces of bread. Now the sparrow family lived happy lives and the cat at home is as happy as ever to get visits from the sparrow family.

Hannah Schiffner
Age: 10

DARK STORM

During the storm, the family took shelter in the root cellar. This is a classified story about a demi-god. His name is Electric. Age twelve. His father is Zeus, god of thunder. Remember this. It started five weeks ago.

Week One

"Mom. MOM! Hey, Mom. I got the best grade in the class," Electric yelled. No one answered.

"Roar!!!" Wave yelled. Wave and Shadow are Electric's brothers. Wave is Poseidon's son and Shadow is Hades' son.

"Don't do that Dude," Electric told him.

"So what's this about having the best grade in class."

"Just a 115—highest possible grade in class. Shadow, refresh his memory please."

"OK. The deal was that Wave gives you a dollar for each ten points and ten cents for each point that isn't ten."

"Thanks, Shadow. That will be $11.50."

"Fine. Here."

Week Two

The boys are watching TV when a news section interrupts. "A three-headed dog, a giant squid, and a giant bird made of thunder are attacking the quad city area . . ."

All of a sudden the power went out and Electric said, "I know what they are. The three-headed dog is Cerberus. The giant squid is the Kracken. And the giant bird made of thunder is the Roc. Ahhhh!"

BIZZZZZZT

"Man! Was that spicy! And why are my clothes all covered with gold thunderbolts?"

"What's a Kracken? Duuuuuddddeee!"

SHPUSH GUGLG

"Whoa! Hang ten! Dude. Why am I wet?"

"I don't know. But I've heard of Cerberus. Whoa!"

GRRRR ROARRRRR

"Cool. A black tunic."

All of a sudden they all fainted. Then they all woke up. "Where are we?" Electric wondered aloud.

"Why are our clothes different?" Shadow asked.

SNIFF SNIFF

"Dude. Why do I smell like wet dog?"

Do I have to say who said that? All of a sudden four old men stepped out of the dark. When I said old, I mean VERY old. So old that their wrinkles had wrinkles. OK, back to the story. Each man took a turn talking.

"In our tree house in the outskirts of town, Electric."

"They changed when you said your fathers' pets' names, Shadow."

"Wave, we're not answering that."

"How do you guys know our names?" Electric said.

"We know all," they all said in unison.

"Who are you guys?" Shadow asked.

"Our names are Ferien, Alexander, Trek, Even. Take the first letters of our names and that's who we are," they said.

"F-A-T. Fat? Why fat? None of you are fat!" Wave said, confused.

"It's not fat, it's fate. They're The Fates," Electric said.

"But aren't you guys girls? And there are supposed to be only three of you guys?" Shadow said.

"In myths as time went by, people thought we were shes and Even was asleep and sharing one eye is wrong. We share two eyes. Ferien and Even has them today," they said.

"Why are we here?" the boys asked.

"To train."

Week Three

All that week they trained day and night. On the first day they got their weapons. For Shadow: the Midnight Helm which turns him into a shadow at his will and allows him to walk through walls, and if he walks into someone he's in control of them for as long as he's in their body. Wave got the Tsunami Trident. He can make tidal waves with it. With it he can change into any sea creature possible or any child of Poseidon. And Electric got the best weapon there is. It is known as the Thunder Blade. This sword allows its user to strike the opponent with thunder, also giving you the ability to run at the speed of sound and super-human strength. Plus you could become a bolt of lightning. Now back to the story.

"You must go down to the labyrinth and fight the Minotaur and Hydra to begin your training," The Fates told them.

"But aren't they dead!?!" Electric said.

"Nope. Just go down and fight," The Fates said.

As the boys climbed down the staircase, CREAK CREAK PLOP PLOP, that was all they heard. They climbed down the lonely path to the labyrinth. When they reached the bottom step everything went dark.

"OK I'm out Dudes! I bet it smells better in the Kracken."

SPUSHGURGEL!

"Ah man! I smell like wet dog again, Dude," Wave said.

"Yeah. It's not you who stinks. It's that Hydra that stinks," Shadow said.

"HYDRA! RUN!" they all yelled. But Shadow stayed behind pulling out his Midnight Helm. Then he ran to catch up to them and said, "Grab my hands."

When they did, he put on the helm and soared into the Hydra, leaving his passengers behind.

Inside the Hydra, he told them to "Strike him in the head with the crimson crescent on its forehead. Don't worry about me. Attack when I say now!" He lowered the head and said, "NOW!"

When Electric struck, Shadow jumped out and landed right next to them. "One beast down. One to go! Dudes!" Wave apparently said.

"Let's find the last one!" Electric told his brothers.

As they searched the labyrinth, they heard the clip clop of hooves. CLIP CLOP CLIP CLOP. Then they saw three things: the Minotaur, and two very big metal bulls that were on fire.

"I got the beach bull—e's," Wave said going headfirst into the flames, he pulled out his Tsunami Trident and yelled, "Cyclops!"

All of a sudden his eyes fused to one, moved to the middle of his forehead and he started to grow. He went from four feet, eight inches to nine feet, eight inches.

When he got to the bulls, he bashed their heads together and yelled, "Bad bulls. No setting my bros on fire!!!" Then, like they were stuffed animals, he threw them against the walls of the labyrinth and said, "Wave!" and with that, his one eye turned back into two eyes and he shrunk back to four feet, eight inches.

All of a sudden Electric said, "I got an idea! Just follow my lead!" Then he jumped up taking his lightning blade out and said, "Use your weapons like mine!" and he turned into a lightning bolt.

"Got it!!!" Wave and Shadow said in unison. Shadow put his Midnight Helm on and turned into a shadow.

Meanwhile, Wave turned into a PIRANHA!!!

"Whoops I didn't know what a piranha was. Well then let's go with this. KRACKEN!!!"

Just then he started growing ninety feet tall and the labyrinth was only fifty feet tall. So you can guess that Wave changed.

So he chose great white shark!!!

After all of that they started going right toward the Minotaur and launched the final blow! The Minotaur faded into dust.

Week Four

As the days passed our young heroes battled many monsters, and learned special attacks. They also got armor: for Electric a thick celestial bronze plate armor with the symbols of Zeus: an eagle and a thunderbolt, for Wave a celestial Hydromith (a blue metal that is found at the bottom of the ocean) chainmail which has a fin on the top of his back, for Shadow a celestial, black Cion plate armor which has a skull arm cannon, which can fire a skull over 90 mph, its range is over 100 miles, and can shoot 9 skulls a minute, talk about deadly! But it won't phase a mortal like every celestial weapon or armor and other abnormal stuff like monsters or a place made by immortals.

Week Five

"Ferien, we're ready to fight them," Electric said

"OK. You guys are ready," The Fates said. "Go!" yelled the Fates.

The boys ran all the way to the city. And when they made it there, the city they remembered it being was being destroyed but the monsters could be seen by the mortals.

"Let's hit them hard!!" Wave yelled and so they used all their weapons the same way they did in the labyrinth.

In the end they won the battle and saved the city.

Dallion Labonte

I am Weberly the elephant. I like to swing like a monkey. I like to play hide-and-go-seek. I can spout water from my trunk. I am big!

Kaitlin Tourgee
Age: 7

"I'm running away!" Adam said. He was talking to his stuffed animal, Jake. Adam has always had bad days at school. Kids punching him, swearing at him, making fun of his glasses. He hated it. In order to run away he had to sneak past his mother. That was going to be hard, he thought. Adam quickly packed his bag.

"Let's see. Jake? Check. Sleeping bag? Check. Glasses? Wait. No, I'm not bringing my glasses. I'll never be seen in public again with these things." With a disgusted face, he chucked his glasses into the garbage can and snuck out of his room. Slowly he went down the stairs and into the kitchen.

"Hi, hon', where are you off to in a hurry?"

"Just getting some . . . uh . . . fresh air. Yeah, fresh air."

"Oh, all right, but have some breakfast first."

"Uh . . . that's okay. I'm going over to a friend's house first and I'm sure he'll let me have a Pop Tart or something."

"All right, I guess, but be back for lunch okay?"

"Okay." Finally Adam was outside. He hated lying to his mom, but if you really thought about it he wasn't really lying. He was going outside to get fresh air right? Well, partly, but anyway, Adam was walking along on a dirt path deep in the woods when all of a sudden he heard a voice.

"Who goes there?"

As startled as could be Adam squeezed out a little, "Uh, Adam, sir. My name is Adam."

"Adam? What kind of name is that? My name is Mozaily."

"Mozaily? Show yourself." Adam was all of a sudden showing some bravery. All of a sudden Mozaily came out from behind a tree. Ew, Adam thought. Mozaily was the ugliest creature Adam had ever seen.

"Um . . . don't worry. I'm not gonna hurt you," Mozaily said, coming towards Adam. Adam didn't know what to do. Run? Scream? So he decided to do both.

"AAAAHHHHH!"

"Wait!" Mozaily was a giant so every one hundred steps Adam took it only took Mozaily one or two. Mozaily sat down and started crying!

"WWWAAA!"

Adam was starting to come forward.

"What's wrong?"

"When I was a little squirt—that's what my brothers called me—my parents got killed by these BIG hunters. My brothers and I were so sad that we decided to go our own ways because everyone was scared of us so it's not like anyone was going to hurt us. So that's why I was wondering if you could be my friend. Will you?"

"Why, of course!"

"Now, what brings you out here?" asked Mozaily.

"Well I decided to run away because I've been having a hard life. Everyone makes fun of me and everyone makes fun of my glasses."

"Why, how about if we take care of each other in the woods? We could watch out for each other and I'm sure no one will harm you or me because as I said before, everyone is scared of me."

"Okay," Adam said. "It's a deal!" After a few hours of trying to find shelter they saw a little hole in a tree. "It'll be perfect!" Adam said, already hopping into the tree.

After a few days of hunger Adam had a very sick look on his face.

"I'm SO hungry!"

Mozaily is a giant which means he has a bigger stomach than Adam. So Mozaily could go without food for one whole week without even complaining about food. Adam was starving and was getting homesick and wanted to go home. In fact, he would have but he didn't want to break Mozaily's heart. He was thinking of just running away instead but that would be too cruel so he finally decided to tell Mozaily. Mozaily actually didn't take it as bad as Adam thought. So Adam gave Mozaily a big hug and headed for home!

When he got home his mother was sitting in a rocking chair and crying like a little baby. Wow! Mom was actually crying over HIM! Now that was something to cry about!

"Mom?! I'm home! I'm home!"

"Honey? I was so worried!"

I'm so happy I'm home and I'm REALLY sad and mad that I ran away and I have a WHOLE LOT to tell you! So after every hug and after every kiss Adam told his mom about EVERYTHING just as he said he would, but his mom didn't believe him about Mozaily and neither did his friends OR his teacher at school, but now everything would be all right! Finally! Maybe at school people would finally appreciate his glasses. He'd have to wait and see. And I'm the only one who knows. But that's a totally different story!

THE END . . . I think . . .

Courtney Brown
Age: 11

SAND RACES

Sand. That's pretty much all Jason saw out the hotel window. Ever since coming to Arizona for the Sand Dune Racing Championship, there was a lot of it. His team, Team Avalanche, had managed to win a regional sand dune racing championship and come here. It had been hard, as spinning out of control wasn't uncommon, but it was fun. The competition looked tough, with Team Burnout, Team Light Speed, Team Iceberg, and the overall favorite, Team X.

Jason looked at the clock. It was 11:10. Then he remembered there was a team meeting at 11:00! Great. Why do I always have to be late? thought Jason, as he hurried down the stairs to the room where Team Avalanche would be meeting. He came bursting through the door.

"Fast on the race track, slow off of it." That was Steve, one of the members of the team and Jason's best friend.

"Yeah, yeah, hold your applause," Jason said. He looked around the room. All the members of the team were there; Steve, Scottie, James, Matt, and the captain, Josh. They were his friends, the people he had to fly with on the red-eye flight to Arizona.

They sat there discussing the competition, and what they were likely to do. Team Burnout was very aggressive. They would crash, bash, and burn their way to victory. Team Light Speed would stay out of the way and try to cruise on forward. Team Iceberg was all about stunts. They would jump, take turns full throttle, and even drive backwards in their quest for the finish line. Team X would head straight for the finish line and destroy anyone in their way.

By the time the meeting was over, it was 12:30. It was time for lunch. Jason called room service for a sandwich and while he sat munching away, he looked at the schedule.

SDR Championship Schedule

Saturday:
11:00 a.m.—Team meetings
3:00 p.m.—Work on dune buggies
5:30 p.m.—Practice race
6:00 p.m.—Refuel and fix dune buggies from practice race
Sunday:
11:30 a.m.—Championship race

It was one o'clock, two hours 'til they had to work on the dune buggies. As he was reading a book that he had brought with him, someone knocked hard on the door.

"I'm coming, I'm coming," Jason said, as he made his way to the door. He opened it, and there was Steve.

"Guess what!" Steve said excitedly.

"They're going to let you drive for once?"

"Ha, ha. No. The Sand Dune Racing Association has a few junky but still running dune buggies. They were going to throw them out, but I said I'd keep them and they gave them to me!"

"How many?"

"Two. And I thought we could try them out before we have to work on the dune buggies!"

"Well . . . Okay. Let's go."

Steve led him to the Avalanche's small garage and showed him the two dune buggies. They weren't high quality, but they were OK. They climbed into the dune buggies and drove over to the starting line.

"3 . . . 2 . . . GO!"

"Hey!" Jason said, as Steve drove off with a head start. They drove as fast as they could go, bumping into each other to try and get ahead. They were rounding a tight curve when . . . Bang! Jason's dune buggy hit a rock, making the car flip sideways many times until it smashed against another rock.

"Jason! You okay?"

"Yeah. A bit shaken up, but okay. The dune buggy's destroyed, though."

"I see that."

They hauled both dune buggies back to the garage, where Jason's would sit until it went to the junkyard. As they were walking back, Jason glanced at the clock.

"Oh no."

"What?"

"It's 3:10. We're late!"

They rushed to the garage where the teams had gathered to work on the dune buggies. They got a few stern looks from Josh, and then they started to work on the dune buggies. They sand-proofed the tires so they wouldn't slide, made sure there was enough gas, checked to see they didn't have to change the oil, and put in necessary racing advantages. The advantages include: oil slick, metal bumpers, and a fire hydrant. It was legal in the SDRA to add things to your dune buggy that could mess up the other teams. It made sand dune racing more exciting.

At last it was time for the practice race. They drove the buggy to the starting line and Jason got in, while Josh got in the passenger seat to instruct him and help him in the practice race. Steve, Scottie, James, and Matt would be the pit crew if there was a blowout or something.

Jason got ready. "3 . . . 2 . . . 1 . . . GO!" And they were off. Team Burnout got the lead, with Team X, Team Light Speed, Team Avalanche, and Team Iceberg in that order behind them. Team X got the lead in the second lap, with Team Burnout smashing anyone who got close to them. As Team Iceberg was slammed by Team Burnout, Team Light Speed snuck by them. Josh used the fire hydrant to temporarily blind Team Iceberg, and then took out Team Burnout and Team Light Speed with some oil slick. As the fifth lap approached, Team X was in first, followed by Team Avalanche, Team Light Speed, Team Burnout, and Team Iceberg.

Team Light Speed used nails to blowout Team Avalanche, who had to stop by the pit crew to get a new tire. Then something very unexpected happened. Team Burnout spun out of control, and Team Light Speed and Team Iceberg smashed into them, creating a barricade of buggies. The safe thing would be to drive around the buggies, but Jason had a different idea. He headed straight for the buggies, planning to jump them. "Are you crazy, Jason?!"

"Well . . ."

Jason slammed his foot on the pedal and they sped towards the barricade. Surprisingly, they managed to jump them, and it was a battle the last four laps between Team X and Team Avalanche for first place. At first, Team Avalanche took the lead, but going into the ninth lap, Team X took the lead. At first, things looked hopeless, but then, right before the finish line, Jason saw another opportunity.

"What if we rammed them in the post that holds up the finish line?"

"Well . . . fine. That's our only chance,"

So they came up neck and neck with Team X, and they pushed the buggy towards the finish-line post. The plan work perfectly. Team X was stuck against the pole, inches away from the finish line, and Team Avalanche cruised past the finish line, winning the practice race.

"Nice—if not crazy—driving there, Jason," said Josh.

"Well, I do my best."

"Yeah. Let's hope you do just as well in the real race."

They fixed the dune buggies, and they really did need fixing. Then they went to bed, Jason too excited to get any sleep. At last, morning came. It went by pretty fast, so did most of the afternoon, until the race came about. They got the dune buggy to the starting line, and soon it was the same situation as yesterday.

"3 . . . 2 . . . 1 . . . GO!" They were off again. This time though, Team Iceberg took an unexpected lead, followed by Team X, Team Light Speed, Team Avalanche, and Team Burnout. Josh took Team Burnout out with some oil slick, and they soon passed Team Light Speed. Team X soon ran Team Iceberg off the road, and the order was Team X, Team Avalanche, Team Iceberg, Team Light Speed, and Team Burnout.

As they were coming to the seventh lap though, Team Burnout smashed and crashed their way to first. Team Avalanche managed to stall Team X with some oil slick. Then they were coming to the ninth lap, and Team Burnout was followed closely by Team Avalanche. Soon though, with the finish line in sight, it became clear to Jason and Josh that Team Burnout was going to run Team Avalanche off the road at the last second. As they were making their move though, Team Avalanche deployed the oil slick and Team Burnout spun out of control! Team Avalanche glided triumphantly past the finish line and was greeted by the cheers of their teammates.

"Awesome!"

"Cool!"

"That was great!"

And so on and so forth and all that congratulations stuff. Everybody was congratulating him and he went to bed stunned. He just couldn't get his mind off of it. He didn't know how to get his mind off of it, but what he did know was that he couldn't wait to drive that dune buggy again.

David W. Hartman
Age: 11

106

TREASURE

One day five dogs were bored so they threw a ball around in the doghouse. The five dogs' names were: a Bichon Frise named Bones; a golden retriever named Daisy; Jessie, a German shepherd; and two Bernese mountain dogs named Otis and Annie.

Then, they hit an old picture! "Oh no! Mom is going to kill us if we don't fix that picture!" cried Bones.

"We are so busted!" whined Jessie.

But then they noticed a door that used to be behind the picture. Daisy said, "Should we open it?"

Bones answered, "Yes." They opened the door and found a treasure map.

"This will pay for the picture," exclaimed Otis.

"And we can buy some dog treats!" said Annie in a strange but happy voice.

Bones said, "Let's get ready."

They packed for their adventure: dry dog food, water, and dog biscuits. The five dogs went on a speedboat to an uncharted island.

"The treasure is north," said a faraway voice.

"Okay . . ." said Annie.

Just then, a bird flew out of a tree and Otis yelled, "Are you the voice we heard?"

"What? I can't hear you!"

"Never mind," said Otis. "Let's go."

They went north and dug. "Wait on the map the treasure is south," Bones remarked.

"That bird lied," said a nearby cat. "The treasure is south."

They went south and dug some more and a while later the five dogs found the treasure. Jessie asked, "Can we have a break?" They munched on dog biscuits and when they turned around, the treasure was gone! They searched the island until they found the cat and the parrot with the treasure! The five dogs reclaimed the treasure.

"Let's go home, this place is too risky," cried Annie. The dogs ran to the speedboat and went home as fast as the boat could go.

When they got home they paid for the picture and got some dog biscuits. Bones woke up and had breakfast.

"All the stuff we bought is still here and the map is gone," said Daisy.

"Did you have the same dream too?"

"Yes, I'm afraid so."

Jessie, Otis, and Annie had the same dreams, too, and they told each other endlessly about their dreams and they lived happily ever after eating dog biscuits.

Jack Felag
Age: 9

A WOLF'S LIFE

Chapter One: A Dangerous Decision

"Can we play outside?" whispered Copper.

Carla woke up annoyed and very tired. "Not now," she said sleepily standing up and shaking the dirt off her fur coat. "I must go out and hunt," she said as she left the den out the long tunnel. As she did so, Copper, Charlie, and Flower all started play fighting. When Carla came back she looked disappointed.

Meanwhile, the pack was trying to find food. There was a big problem. Steve, their leader, was leading the pack out of their territory. This could mean fights—big fights.

"I must go out one more time," Carla said hopelessly. "If we can't find food, we'll starve." She left, leaving three pups alone in the dark.

As Steve began to cross the line, he heard a howl. It didn't sound familiar. He started to slow down, knowing what would happen next.

Chapter Two: Badger

While Steve and the rest of the pack were out hunting, the three pups were bored to death. "Come on there has to be something to do!" yelled Charlie waving his paws in the air.

Flower was not listening to a word he was saying. She had her paws over her ears.

Copper was listening, but uninterested.

Then they heard a noise coming from one of the tunnels. Then they saw it. It was a badger. Flower screamed and ran for the other tunnel, her two brothers right behind her.

The badger was getting closer and closer. After all, the pups aren't that fast. As they ran they saw a tunnel that said EXIT.

Chapter Three: Down In

"Help!" they all yelled together as they ducked into the small exit tunnel. The tunnel was so small that the badger couldn't fit.

"Whew," said Copper thankfully.

"I wouldn't be so sure about that!" said Flower. "Badgers can dig!"

They all ran as fast as they could. The badger was catching up quickly.

Just then they found out that it was a dead end. "Flower!" Charlie howled as his sister fell through a trap door. Flower howled as loud as she could. The howl was so high-pitched that the walls caved in and Copper fell with her.

Charlie knew he had to do something. Just then he realized that the ceiling was a tunnel. Charlie jumped up and grabbed on with his claws. There was a giant rock ahead. I might be able to jump on that, he thought to himself.

Chapter Four: Run!

Steve stopped in his tracks seeing the other pack. "I'm not so sure about this," said Pusca wearily.

"She's right. There's ten of them and only three of us," said her twin brother Pusco, taking a step backwards. The other pack leader started to growl.

Before Steve, Pusca, and Pusco knew it, they were being chased by the enemy.

Chapter Five: Up, Up, And Out!

Charlie climbed and climbed until he reached the rock. Charlie realized that it was easier than he thought. He realized this when he noticed that there were two other rocks next to it. One rock was next to him on the opposite side. The other rock was above the one he is on now. That pattern kept on going until it reached the top.

Slowly he climbed up rock by rock. Once he slipped and almost fell fifteen feet in the air.

Charlie was worried and a bit clumsy. He was worried because he didn't know how or where the others were; he was clumsy because he was worried.

Finally after all of that work, he made it.

Chapter Six: The Fight

After hours of being chased, Steve had no choice but to fight.

It was one hour until the other pack, called the Aces, finally left.

Pusco couldn't walk. Pusca could walk but barely breathe. Steve was the worst. He was lying on the ground not moving, barely breathing. To Pusca and Pusco's surprise, he got up and sat.

Chapter Seven: Howl To Home

"Steve, Steve, wake up," Pusca said repeating it one million times. Finally after thirty minutes, he woke up.

He lay there for a minute, forgetting where he was.

"Okay, everyone," Steve said in a shaky, worried voice. "We have to howl so that Carla knows where we are."

They all howled as loud as they could. Carla could hear them but couldn't leave the pups behind. She started home, oblivious to the danger her pups were in.

Chapter Eight: Oh, No!

As Carla got closer to the den she started to get worried. She didn't hear any noise coming from the den. Normally the pups would hear her five minutes before she even arrived.

Carla started to run towards the door. She ran down the tunnels searching for them.

Finally she came to the exit tunnel. She heard whining coming from the back of it. Carla ran through it, only to find that her pups had fallen through the hole.

Chapter Nine: Clues

Carla looked up and saw the scratch marks from Charlie's claws. She howled, hoping that Charlie could hear her.

"Mom?" Charlie said above ground. "Where are you?" he said trying to be quiet.

Carla couldn't hear him and went back to the beginning of the tunnel to search for clues to the fact that her pups fell into the hole that she had dug the day before. She looked and smelled every rock. She could see the marks from the badger and smell what had caused the fall of her children.

Chapter Ten: Copper And Flower

Copper and Flower were ten feet underground in a dark tunnel. It was so dark that they could barely see. Copper walked around for a while. Copper was going towards a straight tunnel. Flower, however, was going nowhere. She was using her memory. Since she is trained by her mom she gets trained by the best of the best.

But Copper and Charlie are trained too. Flower is the only one that listens to their mother.

Chapter Eleven: Wrong Way!

"Flower, where are you?" howled Copper.

"I'm over here," exclaimed Flower.

"Where's over here?"

"Turn around and walk straight," she said in an "of course" attitude.

But there was one problem. Copper couldn't walk in a straight line. "Okay," Copper said in a hopeful voice. At first he was in a straight line, but he stumbled and walked into one of the other diagonal tunnels right next to where Flower was.

"Can you hear me?" asked Flower, which to Copper sounded far away.

"Are you sure I'm going the right way?" asked Copper.

"Of course I'm sure. Aren't I always?" Flower said in response.

Chapter Twelve: A Wonder To Wander

By now Copper should have figured out that he was going the wrong way. Suddenly he realized what he was doing wrong. He started to go back.

He heard Flower and howled. She came down his tunnel and barked out with joy. They were so happy to see each other that they played together. Soon they were back where they fell.

"I'm hungry," said Flower unhappily.

"Me too," said Copper.

Flower let out a big sigh and said in a low voice, "When is Mom going to find us?"

Chapter Thirteen: A Short Nap

Copper and Flower decided to take a walk around the tunnel.

"I'm tired," said Copper.

"Me too," said Flower. "And I want Mom."

"Let's go back to the place where we fell," said Copper, actually making sense this time.

"Good idea," said Flower. "And this time walk in a straight line!" she said laughing.

So they walked and walked until they reached the spot where they fell. There they went to sleep hoping they would be rescued in time.

Chapter Fourteen: Together Again

"Let's go home," Pusco said.

"You don't have to tell me twice," Steve replied. He found enough strength to walk.

Pusco stood as best as he could, and he and Pusca walked behind Steve.

When they got home they found the two pups fast asleep. Soon they were back to safety.

An owl scared Charlie. He ran, found the entrance, and barged in as a terrified puppy. Carla thought there was no hope until she got home.

"It's good to be together again," Flower said. And they all agreed to that.

Makala MacLean
Age: 10

THE BEAR VILLAGE

Once there was a cute village, and in that village there lived many bears. So, one day, a little bear wandered off in the woods to get wood for the fireplace. But when the little bear got home, no one was home. So he looked, but he didn't see anyone there. Then he looked around and he found out he was in his friend's house.

The next day the little bear named Teddy went to his cousin, Freddy's house. Teddy and Freddy went to the park. They played on the swings, seesaw, and the jungle gym. When they got home, they played The Game of Life. Then they played checkers. Then Freddy slept over at Teddy's house that night.

The next day Teddy and Freddy played soccer, baseball, chess, and air hockey. Then Freddy went home and went to bed. Both bears had a great time together.

Ryleigh Alfonse
Age: 8

A TALE TO TELL

Prologue

"Grampa!" exclaimed Jamie. "Tell us another story!"

"Yeah, please?" asked Max.

Jamie and Max were brothers. Jamie was eight, and Max was five. Their grandfather, John, has come for a visit. Jamie and Max love it when Grampa and Johnny would tell stories he had heard about the sea.

"All right," said Grampa Johnny. "This time, I'll tell you a story about myself, but I hope you kids learn something."

"We will, Grampa," said Jamie.

"Promise," said Max.

"All right. It happened when I was sixteen. I was on the merchant ship, The Old Mary . . ."

The Story

"It started below deck. Some men were gambling. Songs were being sung like 'A Pirate's Life For Me!' or '15 Men On The Dead Man's Chest,' or 'Yo, Ho, Ho, And A Bottle Of Rum.'

Our mysterious crewman, Jones, was leaning against the wall drinking rum. I looked at Jones. He was staring at me. He's enough to scare the heck out of ya! With his emerald and fish skull necklace—well, you get the idea. I walked over to him.

'I sense something bad is going to happen,' said Jones.

'How can you tell?' I asked.

'See that mist?'

'Yeah?'

'That's the start of Davvy Jones' locker. Many ships have sunk there.'

'I don't believe in ghost stories, Mr. Jones.'

'You should, Johnathan, you should.'

He walked away and Percy walked to me. 'That Jones is a weird man, isn't he?' said Percy.

'Yeah, real strange.'

Jones walked on deck, alone.

A couple days later, everyone was below deck except Jones. I walked up the stairs to the deck. Jones was staring at the ocean intently. There was a ship on the horizon. It had not yet spotted us.

Then Jones raised the emerald in the crossbones locket. It glowed quickly, then another ship appeared. This ship looked strange, but the only strange thing I could make out was torn sails. I knew there was more."

Max broke in at this point.

"What was the ship?" he asked.

"Oh, you'll see," said Grampa Johnny. "Right after that ship appeared, the old one sank. I remembered what Jones had said:

That's the start of Davvy Jones' locker. Many ships have sunk there.

I don't believe in ghost stories, Mr. Jones.

You should, Johnathan, you should.

A chill went down my spine. I managed to spit out a few words.

'Jones, what's going on here?' I asked.

'What?' he said in an awkward voice.

He wouldn't show his face.

'Jones?'

'Run along now, Boy. This is none of your business.'

I ran down below deck.

'Percy,' I yelled.

Everyone looked at me.

'Percy, come here!'

Percy came to me.

'What's going on?' said our captain.

'Nothing,' I said. 'Percy, come on! Let's go!'

We ran above deck.

'What's wrong?' he said as we raced up the stairs.

'It's Jones. He's acting really strange.'

I got to the top of the stairs just to find Jones holding a sword at my throat. I was too young to carry a weapon so I stood there, helplessly."

"Did he kill you?" asked Max.

"Max!" yelled Jamie, "If he was dead, he wouldn't be here telling the story!"

"Oh yeah," said Max. They all laughed.

"Well, there you go!" said Grampa.

"You don't have to answer my question," said Max.

"Yes, I know," said Grampa. They all laughed some more.

"So then he plunged the sword at me and I ducked. Then, I heard a yell and a sword flew through the air to me. I turned around. It was the captain who had thrown the sword! He was giving me a weapon. He lightly saluted me. That meant, 'you're in charge now'. I couldn't believe it! The captain put me in charge because he was afraid! He was trying to back out of the fight!

I made a disgusted look and turned around. I had to fight him. I didn't know why he was turning on us, but I had to fight him. I might not be old enough to carry a weapon, but I did know how to use them."

"You know how to sword fight?!" exclaimed Jamie. "Can you show us?"

"Maybe some other time," said Grampa. "But now, I'm telling you the story. Jones yelled and sliced at me, aiming to cut the length of my neck, but I countered it. It repeated more and more but I blocked them all. I was too stunned and scared to offend, just defend. Then, Jones made a bloodcurdling scream and made a hard swipe for my sword. It flew out of my hands and out of my reach. I backed up, but I hit a wall. I was trapped. Jones made the swipe that would kill me. I closed my eyes."

"Did you die that time?" asked Max.

Grampa chuckled. "No, Max," he said. "I didn't die. Percy had grabbed my sword and jumped in front of me. Apparently Percy knew swordsmanship, plus wasn't afraid of Jones like I was. He was right in the battle, and he always had the sword right in Jones' face. Then, their swords clashed hard. Sparks flew through the air. They backed up.

'Now it's my turn to be an attacker,' said Jones. He charged and attacked. Percy was almost too late to protect himself. Jones' sword was fast and all over the place. Up, down, left, right. Percy was just barely blocking them all. Then, their swords clashed for a long time.

While this happened, Percy asked, 'What do you want?' in a stern voice. 'What do you want of me?'

'It's not you I want,' Jones pointed at me. 'It's him.'

Jones spun away from Percy and came at me. Percy threw his sword and knocked away Jones' before he could hit me. They both went into the ocean.

'Jones,' called a ghastly voice. 'Have you got me those men?'

'Gah!' cried Percy.

'Whoever you are, get down here! Show yourself!' called the captain.

'No,' Jones replied to the voice.

'Jones!' the voice yelled. 'I'll have to show them who you are!'

'No!' yelled Jones. 'Please don't!'

'I have no choice,' said the voice.

Jones's teeth fell out. His skin and tongue began to rot. His nose went crooked. A scar ran down his forehead and through his eye. His hair grew long like a girl's and became a sparkling blue-green. It swayed like the ocean. That was the only thing on him that looked good. His fingers were like tentacles. His right hand was missing a middle finger. His clothes were brown rags with torn shorts. I knew right away who this man was. This man was a legend. This man had to be Jones. Davvy Jones."

"You met Davvy Jones?!" exclaimed Jamie.

"Yes I did!" said Grampa. "Only he's not the kind of Davvy Jones in stories. He was much worse.

'Davvy Jones!' I said.

'Yes,' said Jones. 'And the voice was the Flying Dutchman. He acts as a ship for me, and my boss.'

'Now kill them,' said the Dutchman.

'I'm powerless,' said Jones. 'My sword is gone.'

'Jones!' said the Dutchman. He turned to a human. 'I'm going to have to kill you!'

Jones was choking. I quickly stole the gun from the captain's belt and shot the Dutchman. I half expected it to go right through him, but he fell to the ground, dead. I ran to Jones.

'Are you all right?' I asked.

'I'm fine.'

The Dutchman's body disintegrated.

'Who did you want to kill?' I asked.

'You and the captain,' said Jones.

'Why?'

'I don't know why he tells me to. I just do what the Dutchman—'

A voice spoke. 'You're dead, Jones!'

The Dutchman.

The mysterious boat sank and a huge wave struck The Old Mary. I was almost flung off-board, but Jones pulled me back. He lost his balance with his tremendous pull and fell into the water. He splashed and went under immediately.

Then, the storm calmed. It must have been Jones. The Dutchman wanted payback. But all in all, we had won. Davvy Jones and the Flying Dutchman were both dead. The sea was safe."

"What goes around, comes around!" said Jamie.

"Yes," said Grampa. "And I want you kids to know that if you help someone, they'll help you back and be rewarded. Now, can you kids go help someone and see if the same thing happens to you?"

"We will, Grampa!" said Max.

"C'mon!" said Jamie. "Let's help mom do the dishes!" The kids ran into the kitchen.

"Ah, kids these days," said Grampa. "They'll believe anything."

Casey Myhaver
Age: 10

115

SARA

There had always been something odd about Sara. Even at age twelve, she had clung to that childhood fantasy of talking dolls. She insisted that they be brought to dinner, to bed, even school with her. She had coveted and spoiled these dolls as if they were her children. Then, one day, Sara just . . . disappeared.

I put down my notebook. I couldn't write anymore. That horrible day was coming back to me . . .

Mother had woken Father and I at the crack of dawn, saying that someone had called and said that they knew where Sara was. Mom and Dad had been worried sick all week. Sara was the baby of the family, even though we were the same age. She was twelve, and very quiet and shy. She never said anything at school. It was only when I was around did she show her true nature. Once, when we were playing Truth or Dare, I had dared her to steal a cookie from the cookie jar. When she was caught with the cookie in her mouth, Mom and Dad blamed me. They couldn't get it through their heads that Sara, of all people, could do something wrong. So we went where the mysterious caller said, and there she was. Beautiful as ever. Blonde hair spread out across the rocks where she had evidently hit her head. Blood spilled from the wound and into the water that was running by. But her eyes weren't their usual blue, they were green! And her hair was a full shade darker than it had been before. Nobody else noticed.

THUMP! Startled, I whirled around to see Sara and somebody else with eyes as green as the forest, and hair as black as midnight. "Sara? Is that really you? And who's that other person? Why aren't you dead? You know, I never really believed that you were dead. That wasn't you by the river in the woods, was it? Why are you here?" I paused for a breath, and Sara cut in.

"Jacki, this is really me. That other person is Jane, and she helped me escape. No, I was never really dead, and that wasn't really me by the stream in the woods. Now, let me tell my story, okay?" I nodded obediently. "Now, where was I? Oh yes. All my life, dolls have been able to talk to me. That's why they came everywhere with me. They were eager for a taste of the human world. Some threatened me, others pleaded. Then Jane came along. You remember her? I got her for my birthday last year. She offered to take me to Drossignol, where dolls live. Of course, I jumped at the chance. I was bored with this life, and had only stayed there a week before the Darkest Queen caught me. She immediately ordered one of her slaves to make a copy of me, but the slave got nervous and made it wrong. Luckily for her, most humans see what they want to see. Only a very special few see what is right in front of them." At this point, she looked directly at me. "Then Jane rescued me, and we hightailed it straight here. Now give me a long stick and we can be on our way."

I wordlessly handed her a magic wand that I had gotten for my sixth birthday. Then I blurted out, "Where are we going?"

Sara looked at me oddly. "Drossignol, of course. What were we talking about?"

I wanted to leave a note, not for Mom and Dad, but my friends at school, Marissa Jones and Victoria Avella. I wouldn't miss school that much. Seamus Tiernan was always making fun of me, and so was Torren Talon, Brandon Dexter, and Corey Anderson. But I thought that my friends had the right to know not to worry.

"Can I leave a note first? For Marissa and Victoria?" Sara said of course, and don't worry about giving it to them, she would take care of it.

My note said,

Dear Marissa and Victoria,

I will be out for a few days. Please do not worry. I cannot tell you where I will be, but I am pretty sure that I will be safe. Burn this note as soon as you are finished reading it.

Jacki.

With a wave of her hand, Sara sent the note to Marissa's desk so she could read it in the morning. "Now, are you ready?" Sara inquired politely. Without a word, she took the magic wand and drew a door in the air, mumbling to herself as she did so. I gasped. Following the tip of the magic wand, a shaft of sparkling, rainbow-colored light drew a real door in the air. Sara added, almost as an afterthought, a doorknob and window. I looked through the window, not knowing what to expect. Below the floor, a road stretched on and on, and there were skyscrapers and museums, just like in New York City. And there were even people, little tiny ones because we were so high up. Sara opened the door and jumped! "It's okay!" she called back, her voice almost drowned out in the noise that had poured out when the door was opened. Then Jane jumped, and finally, I did, too. As I tumbled down through the air, I wondered if I was going to die. Suddenly, I landed hard on a small stone shelf, about three feet wide. I can't tell you how afraid I am of heights.

Then a voice said, "Don't worry, it will be all right," and a hand grabbed me. Then I was climbing down a flight of fire stairs. You know how they never put endings on those things? We had to jump.

"On the count of three, everybody jump!" That was Jane's command. "One . . . two . . . THREE!" We jumped . . . and landed right on top of a car! We sped through the city, not talking because even if you shouted, nobody would hear you. Sara locked eyes with me and took my hand. When the car we were on got out of the city and into a meadow, we jumped again. I landed in the meadow and blacked out. When I woke up again, I was staring at a huge black castle straight ahead. This must be the Darkest Queen's castle, I thought to myself. As it turns out, it was. The plan was this: go into the Darkest Queen's castle disguised as slaves, gain access to her bed chambers, and kill her while she is sleeping. Jane and Sara had already put on the appropriate clothes, so I went into the bushes to change. When we were done, we really did look just like slaves of a dark queen. Now to get in the castle. We limped our way to the front door, looking for all the world like we had been mining jewels for Her Majesty all day.

The guard didn't even give us the slightest glance. We were in! The main hall was black as Jane's hair, maybe even darker, if that was possible. Shadows flitted around like gruesome, black, evil ghosts. My knees went weak. Another guard came up and asked us, "Now what are your numbers, slaves?" Numbers? What numbers?

"Ummm . . . 12076987627," I gabbed furiously, making up as I went along. Jane said hers was 12074902234, and Sara's was 12076461820. The guard eyed us suspiciously, and for a moment I thought that he wasn't going to let us in. Then he smiled, a cruel smile, and told us to get along to our cell. I'm not kidding! He said cell! We didn't "get along to our cell" as the guard so eloquently put it. We tried to get to the queen's chamber, but we kept getting lost. Whenever we tried to get to a door right in front of us, it ended up in the back. Finally, Sara had the idea to try going in the opposite direction of the door, and it worked! Now we knew the trick of this place. But where was the bedroom? We asked around and one jovial, fat chef told us that it was the right wing. She had a whole wing as her bedroom!

We waited until midnight, then crept silently to the right wing. We got there, and stared in disbelief. The whole thing was a collage of Barbie posters! The Darkest Queen was a Barbie! And she was . . . awake! She turned to us, and I saw the evil glint behind her blank blue eyes. "Now, what are three little slaves like you doing here at midnight?" Her voice sounded like honey over a steel blade.

"Nothing, Your Majesty. We only wanted to get a glimpse of your beautiful face," Sara and Jane chorused. They were good actors. I remained silent.

"Now get along to your cell, and maybe you'll get extra gruel in the morning." The Darkest Queen's voice had even more honey in it.

"Yes, Your Majesty." Their voices were blank, too unintelligent. As we turned to go, I caught a look into their eyes. The sight made me gasp in horror. They had no irises! Their eyes were completely white. She had hypnotized them! I realized that it was up to me to save the day. When they walked down the corridor, I stole Jane's knife from her hand. She didn't even notice. When the queen had her back turned again, I walked silently over and stabbed her in the back! Well, I'd like to think it was this way, but she turned again and walked right into one of her own booby traps, stepping on a tile that sent a knife down from the ceiling. She screamed, but it was cut short when she suddenly dissolved into black dust. Sara and Jane came back, rubbing their eyes, which had the irises back again. After that, we hugged and cried and everybody was happy again. But when it was time to go, Sara hung back at the door.

"What's wrong?" I asked her.

"Oh Jacki, I don't belong out there! Don't you see that I belong here?" I didn't want to admit it, but it was true. She did belong here, and there was nothing I could do. I cried, but in the end I went through the door. Sara was right. I hated it, but she was right.

Moira Wright
Age: 12

Fun is coming my way again! I'm a big sister and I will have so much fun! But there will be some parts I don't enjoy along the way. The noise will bug me too. Her name is Emma. She was born on February 21, 2007.

I'll have lots of fun! I'm so excited! I'm glad I'll get to drive her around. I'll also have something to do other than sports. I'll get to do her nails when she gets bigger. It will be fun to teach her different things. But, the first thing I'll teach her is how to say Kandyce, then Tayler (my other sister), then Daddy and Mommy.

Most parts I won't enjoy, like babysitting. I'll have to clean up after her, settle her down, and clean up her slobber. I will have to change her stinky diapers when she cries. I will have to help her a lot. Emma will cry so much. She'll cry and I'll have to figure out what she needs; a bottle or maybe her diaper needs to be changed.

I will hate the noise very much. She'll cry a lot when she is hungry. Emma will take toys away from other kids. She will want everything. Whining will be a problem too. When she gets hurt or doesn't get her way with something.

I'm glad to be a big sister again. I'll learn to live with the noise, some good and some not so good, but it will all be worth it later, knowing she learned a lot from me.

Kandyce Langlois
Age: 9

THE TINY TIBET TOWN'S KEY

It was a nice day in Tibet Town, but the mayor was screaming for help! It was up to Tiny Tib Tim to save the day . . . again!

"Help! Help!" said the mayor.

"I'll have to call Tiny Tib Tim at 444-4444," said the mayor's husband.

"Hello," said Tiny Tib Tim.

"I need help," said Mr. Tib Tyler, the mayor's husband.

"OK, I'm coming," said Tiny Tib Tim.

Knock, knock! That was the sound Tiny Tib Tim made knocking on their door. "Come in quick," said the mayor's husband.

"What is the matter?" said Tiny Tib Tim.

"The key, the key is stolen!" Tib Tyler said to Tim.

"Good, the police are here," the mayor said.

"The key is in China!" said the police.

"How do you know?" asked the mayor.

"There is a chip in the key," said the police.

"Oooh. I love chocolate!"

"Not that kind of chip, a microchip!" said the police.

"Tiny Tib Tim, we will get you on the next plane as soon as we can to find the key."

1 a.m. Ring, Ring, Ring, Ring!

"Hhhheellloo," said Tim.

"We found a plane to China. Be here in one hour," said the police.

"OOOKKK," said Tiny Tib Tim.

Tiny Tib Tim got up , got dressed, got in the car, drove to the airport, and got on the plane.

On the plane Tiny Tib Tim asked for food.

"Can I have . . . apple juice, a chocolate doughnut, oranges, pancakes with syrup, an omelet, and a cinnamon bun?"

"Is that it?" asked the stewardess.

"For now," said Tiny Tib Tim.

The next day he woke up and the pilot said, "We have landed in China."

Leaving the airport, Tiny Tib Tim was hungry. He asked many different people where the diner was, but he heard the same thing over and over.

"Toshina."

Finally, he found a building. He saw a sign and wondered if it said diner. Tim walked inside the building. He ordered macaroni and cheese. He saw a bunch of people eating. As soon as he took the first bite of his macaroni—BOOM! A huge monster appeared and ran out of the building. Tiny Tib Tim went to the largest building he could find and climbed it to find the monster. He saw the monster.

What should he do? He found a brick. "Hhhmmm!" Tiny Tib Tim had only one chance at this. He threw the brick. CRACK! It hit the monster right in the head. The police were amazed at the throw.

"Whatever you want, you can have. That monster has been wrecking our city forever. Thank you," said the Chinese police.

"I would like a plane to Austin, Texas, in North America," said Tiny Tib Tim.

"Yes, of course," said the police.

When Tiny Tib Tim got back, he went to his friends', Tiny Tib Tasha's and Tiny Tib Tommy's.

"Let's play hide-and-go-seek," said Tiny Tib Tommy and Tasha at the same time.

Tiny Tib Tommy was it. "One, two, three . . ." Tasha hid in the bathtub. Tim hid in the closet. "Four, five, six . . ."

"Ow," said Tiny Tib Tim.

He got out of the closet. It was the key! He had stepped on it. Both of the kids came in the closet door.

"I like the key," said Tiny Tib Tasha.

"I just helped her take it, because I was bored," said Tiny Tib Tommy.

The police came and got the two robbers the next day. They both were found guilty in court. Then something bad happened the next day. They broke out of jail. The police could not find them, so they gave up.

Megan Cunningham
Age: 11

Nadia Jones was a normal girl living a not-so-normal life. When Nadia was three months old, her mother and father were killed in a tragic fire at a local restaurant. Nadia became an orphan. After spending only one month in the orphanage, she was adopted by a man named Tim Laine. Tim nurtured and spoiled her as a baby, but once she turned five, he couldn't care less about her.

When Nadia turned eight, Tim lost his job, made some bad investments, and lost most of his money. He and Nadia moved to a run-down apartment on the east side of San Francisco. Tim struggled to find a job for two years. He eventually found one, but the job paid minimum wage. To make a sensible amount of money, Tim worked fourteen hours a day.

The year was 1989, and Nadia was fourteen years old. She cooked, cleaned, did her own laundry, rarely saw Tim, and was basically her own parent. Aside from being her own parent, she did what a fourteen-year-old girl did. She loved music, arts and crafts, and volleyball. If she ever had any frustration built up inside her, she called her friend Sarah over to play volleyball to relax her.

One day at Nadia's school, there were announcements that volleyball tryouts would take place every day next week from 3 to 5 p.m. Nadia was excited because she had never played on an actual team before; all she did for volleyball was play at the YMCA for fun. She ran up to Sarah and asked, "Did you hear that announcement?"

"That tomorrow's lunch is macaroni and cheese? Yes. Why?" Sarah replied, wondering why Nadia cared.

"No. About volleyball tryouts. Are you going to try out? I am," exclaimed Nadia, excited.

"Yes, of course I am," said Sarah, getting excited along with Nadia.

"Cool. I have to tell Tim about them, and when I say tell him I mean leave him a note. Bye!"

When Nadia reached home, she was surprised because Tim was there. Yet, she thought this was a good thing because now she could tell him about the tryouts in person.

"What are you doing home?" Nadia asked flatly.

"I decided to come home early and see how your day was," Tim lied.

"What are you really home for? Tim, you always have the hardest time lying," Nadia said.

"Sit down," Tim told Nadia sadly. "It's hard for me to tell you this, but I lost my job. It's going to be extremely hard for me to find another one since I have lost all of my other jobs. I'm going to need your help, and I was hoping you could find a job to support us."

Nadia sat there in silence taking in everything Tim had just said. At first, she thought she could probably find a job and would love to help Tim. Then she thought aloud, "Who is going to want a fourteen-year-old as an employee?"

"A lot of people! If you can't find one, we're not going to be getting anything new anytime soon, and I would be really disappointed," Tim said, putting a lot of pressure on Nadia.

"When am I going to do it, though? Between school, three hours of homework, and volleyball, how is it going to work out?" Nadia asked Tim.

"Since when do you play volleyball?"

"There are volleyball tryouts all next week from three to five, and I think I have a really good chance of making the team. Can't I go? I mean, I think I deserve a little fun in my life."

"Nadia, I'm sorry, but you can't do it. That time should be spent finding a job. What do you mean you don't have any fun?"

"Tim, I cook, clean, do my own my own laundry, on top of school and homework. You're never home. By the time I finish all of my work it's too late to do anything with my friends. Now you want me to find a job? What are you going to do? It sounds like you're not going to even try to find one. It's not fair. Honestly, I feel abnormal doing everything I do around here. Half the girls at school make fun of me because you're not around. I would like to do something that makes me feel good about myself, and that's volleyball. I'm going to play and there is nothing you can do that's going to stop me!"

Nadia left the apartment, steamed and crying. She ran to Sarah's house twenty blocks away and told Sarah everything that happened.

"How inconsiderate can Tim be?" Sarah asked, astonished at Tim's behavior.

"I don't know. I can't go back there, Sarah. I can't face Tim. He expects me to find a job and help him. It's his fault he lost his jobs, not mine," Nadia broke down.

"You can sleep over for as long as you need to, Nadia," Sarah sympathized.

"Thanks."

When the Monday of volleyball tryouts arrived, Nadia's stomach churned from nerves and thoughts of Tim. She had slept over at Sarah's the whole weekend being unable to face Tim. As the tryouts started, Nadia couldn't think of anything but Tim. This distracted her from her play and she didn't do too well. The coach had seen Nadia play before and knew that Nadia was quite good. So at the end of tryouts, the coach called Nadia aside.

"What's wrong, Nadia? I've seen you play and you always seemed to play well," the coach said.

Nadia told the coach everything, even the part about how abnormal she felt. She also told the coach that she can't concentrate or play well when something is bothering her.

"Tell Tim that you just can't find a job on top of everything else you do. Nadia, you're a good girl and I know you'll make the right decision. Just go with your heart," the coach told her.

"Thanks I needed to hear that," Nadia said.

After her conversation with the coach, Nadia ran home to see Tim. She was surprised to see that the apartment was spotless, dinner was made, and Tim was sitting there waiting for Nadia.

"Tim, I'm sorry for the way I acted the other day. It's just . . . how do you expect me to find a job on top of everything else I do? But I've decided that if we really need the money, I'll get a job and put off volleyball for a while," Nadia apologized.

"Nadia, that's unnecessary. I talked to my parents, and they said that we could live with them until we get back on our feet. I have a few jobs in mind and I have a couple of interviews scheduled for later on this week. Since we're going to be living with my parents, this means that you don't have to cook or clean and you can spend more time with your friends. Nadia, one thing got to me, though, when you said you felt abnormal. Everyone has some flaws in their life, but no one is ever abnormal. Finally, Nadia, I'm sorry for not asking you about getting a job and just assuming you would get one," Tim apologized.

"Tim, it's okay, and I can do volleyball now, right?"

"Of course!"

Nadia gave him a big hug and they sat down to eat dinner together for the first time in a long time.

The next day at volleyball tryouts, Nadia dominated. In the end, Nadia made the team and was voted captain. Tim got a good-paying job and managed to keep it. Nadia had more time to spend with her friends and Tim. They ended up getting a small house across the street from Sarah's and they lived together happily until Nadia moved out on her own.

Courtney Mansfield
Age: 13

A CHRISTMAS WONDER

It was five days before Christmas in 1990. The Cantigo family was sitting together quietly in their San Diego home. They were sadly remembering when their grandfather died on this day only two years ago. There were three children in the family; two girls and one baby boy. The oldest girl's name was Lillie and she was age ten. Next came Molly who was five years old. The baby's name was Charlie. He was almost two years old. The children had a mother who had to work part time and their father worked full time. The parents' names were Anna and Tom. The next day would be Charlie's second birthday and that would be a very happy day. When tomorrow came, the family didn't have enough money to have a big celebration; they even had to get the smallest Christmas tree they could find for Christmas Day.

The mother and father tried not to let the kids notice this, but the only child that did know was Lillie. Lillie was worried that the family would become poor. Poverty is the main conflict in this family's life. Lillie tried to get some extra money, but her mother would not let her go out in the big city of San Diego. Lillie and Molly each got six presents before Charlie was born, but now they all get four and sometimes five. But this year was different. Anna was working more so all the kids got five good-sized presents and four more smaller ones to play with all together.

The children receiving more presents wasn't the only difference between this Christmas and last. A very nice man had stopped by their small house the other day. This man gave Tom $10,000 because he had bought one lottery ticket to see if maybe the family had luck and they did. With the money, Tom and Anna bought all the kids new clothes and two pairs of shoes each. Anna was very happy that Tom had bought the lottery ticket because now they put $5,000 in the bank account and $500 toward the medical bills from when Charlie was born. The Cantigo family invited all of their family over for a Christmas Eve and Christmas Day celebration. The family had never felt so blessed before in their lives. Two years later, the Cantigo family was living in a two-floor house in San Diego, California.

The family now has more than enough money to send all the kids to school. Tom got a better-paying job and now Anna has to work three days a week and the family is enjoying their life. The Cantigos will never forget the Christmas miracle that happened at their front door in 1990 in San Diego. The Cantigo family feels like God is watching over them every second of their lives and I am sure He is with all of His power. In three more years, the Cantigos hope to have two cars so the family doesn't have to walk everywhere, but they aren't greedy like some people in the world who have much more than them. They are just thankful that they have each other.

This Christmas of 1995, a new member of the Cantigo family was born. His name is Timothy, named after the grandfather who was also watching after them on Christmas. Now the Cantigo family gives to the poor hoping that someday the families that live in poverty can be saved with a big miracle like the miracle of the Cantigo family.

All things can happen as long as you never give up and always pray to God for help.

Madeline Lewis
Age: 12

125

SWEET SIXTEEN

It was 5 p.m. on a Tuesday when my phone rang and it was my friend Julie. My best friend Julie Barry is calling right now so I have to pick up the phone. We made plans to go car shopping and have a sleepover. I then said, "OK, we can also go to the mall while were are out." Oh by the way, my name is Ariel Sandler and I am fifteen years old. I live in Orlando, Florida. My birthday is in three days on July 2. I am having a sweet sixteen party and Usher and Nick Lachey are performing at it. They are my two favorite singers and they both are singing three songs. My dad is a millionaire and he spoils me!

Julie arrived fifteen minutes later. I grabbed my purse and walked out to her car. I had on a white polo, a pink skirt, and light blue shoes that were one inch high with a pink star on the toe. Julie turned sixteen on June 5. Our plans for the summer were to have my party and then go on a road trip, but I still need to get my license.

As I stepped into the car, Julie said to me, "Hey, I love your shoes!"

We buckled up and we drove to the car dealership. She has a hot red Porsche, I want a light blue Lamborghini with a hot pink leather interior, but I knew that it would have to be custom made, and already knew where to go. We were car shopping for fun. I'm hoping to get my dream car on my birthday.

After we went car shopping, we headed over to the mall. Somehow, when we came out of the mall, we had twenty-five shopping bags altogether. I have no clue how we spent only three hours in the mall and came out with twenty-five bags of clothes, shoes, and accessories! Well, I do know how we did that. I mean, we were just having fun and half the stuff we will probably only use one time. When we got back to my house, we went to my room and watched TV. While watching TV, we both fell asleep.

We woke up at 2:30 in the afternoon when my phone rang again. It was my dad and he was calling to tell me that I could drive to my party in a Hummer limo with one other person. Of course I would choose to have that one person be Julie. I said, "Thank you so much, Daddy, and I will see you there." The theme of my party is Hollywood and gold stars. I am also having a red carpet which is one of my favorite parts. There were two hundred fifty kids and twenty-five adults coming to my party.

The rest of the day, I made sure that I called The Crown Plaza, which is where the party is. I also called the place that I ordered all my deserts, Fredrick's Pastries. Julie called the caterer and made sure that there were no peanuts in any of the food. That is because my other best friend, Charles, is allergic to them. Just if you are wondering—my cake is as big as a wedding cake that is vanilla cake with a light layer of vanilla frosting. Once we were done with all that, it was dinnertime and we were too lazy to cook, so we called a pizza joint and got a small pizza and in ten minutes the pizza had come. We ate it and went right to bed since we had to get up in the morning so I could take my driving test and get ready for my party, which starts at 6 p.m.

When we woke up, all I knew was that this day was going to be awesome. We got out of bed, got dressed, and left. On the way, we stopped at Dunkin' Donuts to get coffee. When we finally got to the place that I was taking my test, it was 10:35 a.m. I sat down at a desk and pressed start. After I answered all the questions, I pressed end and I then started to cry. I was crying because I got seven right and eight wrong, which, in simpler terms, means that I failed and could not get my drivers license. I was so mad because I really thought that I would pass. I then got over it and Julie and I drove back to my house.

When we got there, it was 4:30 and time to get ready. So we first did our hair then makeup and finally we put on our dresses. When we were done we realized that something was missing—our shoes! Then by the time we were done it was 6:05. People were arriving at the hotel now and we would have to leave in ten minutes. When we got there people went crazy. Then Usher and Nick Lachey performed and it was such a surprise to the guests because he sang "Happy Birthday" directly to me. When they were done my dad gave a huge speech and at the end told everyone to go outside. Everyone did and this is when he gave me keys to my car that backed out of a garage. This was my favorite part of my party, even though I couldn't drive it yet, it was just perfect. After that the party went on and people went home.

The next day when I got home I had a message on my phone from the place where I took my drivers test. It said that the computer that I took my test at had a failure and I actually got seven questions wrong and eight right and that I can go down there and get my driver's license. So I called Julie and told her the news. She came over and we went to that place, got my license, and went back to my place. So after all this occurred, Julie and I really did get to go on our road trip. I think that this summer is going to be the best summer yet.

Naomi Noiseux
Age: 12

GROAN

Hi, I'm Dave.

Have you ever had one of those days when absolutely nothing goes right? Most of us do at some point in our miserable, little lives. But hey, that's life.

Well the worse day of my life, so far, occurred a few days ago. Chapter one starts when I woke up on a (not-so-wonderful) Friday.

Part One

Yaaaaaawwwwwwwnnnnnnn . . . Ugh, I really hate early mornings. Especially when I have to wake up early (8:30) or go to bed late. As I walked downstairs from the loft where I slept to go to the bathroom to wash my face, I tripped on my own feet and fell half of a flight of stairs. It hurt like a hundred rusty, plastic spoons being thrown at you. (My boss wants me to try to think up weird figures of speech to use.)

I got up and reached the bathroom. There I washed my face. My brown eyes were still half asleep. I washed my face with cold water and I woke up instantly. I walked into the kitchen and made myself some pancakes. I heard the phone ring in the other room and ran to answer it and when I got back the pan was starting to smoke.

The pancakes were burning. I ran, turned off the stove, took the seared pancakes and dumped them in the trash. And to top it all off, I just made enough batter for one pan's worth of pancakes. I had to have boring, old toast.

After I got dressed, I headed to Wal-Mart to get some junk for around the house. And what to my eyes did appear? The entire store had a sewage backup, so everything but the registers and the women's clothing aisles was covered in a greenish powder! The walls had an interesting color that reminded me of my friends chunky guacamole. Let's just say the color isn't the prettiest flower in the field.

And guess what? Today was the 60% off sale! Of all days for this for to happen, why during the second-largest sale of the year?

I spent the rest of my morning doing the most mind-numbing errands in the world. I had procrastinated on my bills so I had an avalanche's worth of mail to send and groceries to buy. And I need to go to another superstore to get the items that I needed at the Wal-Mart that was flooded. Ugh!

Part Two

I had lunch at the nearest McDonald's, which happened to be the most disgusting place on the face of this planet (third most disgusting in our universe), so I just got a burger. To my surprise, when I bit into my burger, the patty was completely raw! I looked at the burger more carefully and found that they just warmed the meat. I ran to the bathroom and got sick.

As I drove home, I saw a squirrel run across the road so I swerved and grazed a tree which knocked off a mirror and my antenna. Now that's going to really cost a lot. As I was pulling into my driveway, I hit my mailbox, which dented my car and now I need a new mailbox. I went inside and tried to feed my dog, Foofie. Foofie then tried to gnaw me! I made a snack and tried to look up the meaning of life on my laptop. Sadly, I couldn't even do that! My laptop had crashed! And guess what? The warranty expired yesterday!

I called Pizza Hut and ordered a large pizza with the works. I turned on the TV and waited. Ten minutes. Twenty minutes. Thirty minutes. One hour. After one hour and ten minutes, you get a bit mad at the pizza guy. When it came, I paid for it and just felt how warm it was. And of course it's cold. I put it into the fridge then I went to bed. That was the worse day of my life. Then, to add to it, my bed collapsed!

Chris Figueroa
Age: 13

HUBERT THE HOBO

Hubert is a hobo that came from a large family of eight. Ma, Pa, Sis, Bro, Nana, Gramps, Aunt, and Uncle. He was the ninth, until he got sick of all of the commotion in the small house. "There just isn't enough room for me," he said, taking a small handkerchief and tying it to a long stick. He took a suitcase and stepped out the door.

Hubert walked to the most far away woods and found a nice soft patch of grass, put down his bags, and sat to relax from all of the walking he had done. "Gee," said Hubert, "I didn't think I was stupid enough not to bring any water."

Before he knew it, he was walking his way to a stream. He picked up a leaf and shaped it as a cup to put in the stream for water. "Ahh. This sure is cold," Hubert said. "This is the best water I've ever had." He was on his way.

On his way back to the grass he found earlier, he saw something green and paper-like. This was money! He went running to the money and picked it up. "Wow," he said. This wasn't a one. It wasn't a five. It wasn't a ten either! It was a whole twenty-dollar bill! A hiker must have dropped it while walking. Hubert knew what this was for. He was going to go the market and buy his dinner.

Hubert could buy a lot with this. So he went to the meat section and picked up a fine-looking steak. He thought it looked good so he put it in the basket. Then he went to the canned goods. He bought some canned baked beans. Last, he bought a small pot. Just a cheap one so he was sure he had enough money.

He stood in line at the checkout. The cashier rang everything up with the scanner. "Okay, your total is twenty dollars and one cent," the cashier said.

"Oh my gosh!" said Hubert. "I only have twenty dollars on me. I don't have anymore money!" But then he looked on the ground next to him. And then he saw it. One penny. "Here you go," he said sighing with a huge sigh of relief.

"Well, you sure are a very lucky man," said the cashier.

Hubert walked back to the woods. He put down his bags. Then he collected sticks and rocks. He formed the rocks into a circle. He took two of the pieces of wood and rubbed them together until he made a spark. He uncanned the beans and put them in the pot and let them cook. He took out the steak and cooked that. He ate his meal.

It became dark at about six o'clock. Hubert lay down. He was looking at all of the beautiful stars. "Hey! That sure looks like a spoon or an upside-down baseball cap," said Hubert. Hubert had spotted the little dipper. He soon started to doze off when he heard a noise in the woods.

When he heard the noise, he was startled. He slowly, quietly followed the noise. The noise was coming from a bush. He pulled apart the leaves to see what the noise was coming from. Then he saw it. It was a baby wolf.

"Well, hi there. Where did you come from? Did you lose your mama?" Hubert asked. The wolf's eyes were barely open. "Li'l baby."

Hubert picked up the animal and put it in his lap. They watched the stars, then soon they both fell asleep. When they woke, Hubert had the wolf at his side. "Good morning," Hubert said. He was hungry and thought the wolf (Wolfie) was too. So he went walking back to the stream, holding the pup. He picked up a long stick with a nice hook-like end. He was hungry, so he had his best hopes up for catching a lot of fish.

He stuck the stick in the water with his eyes on some trout, cod, and tuna fish. He sat there for about an hour with no bites. He was just about to give up hope and take his stick out of the water when he felt a hard tug.

Hubert pulled on the stick and the huge fish came flying out of the water onto the grass. "This looks like a tuna. It's my favorite, Wolfie. I hope you like it too." Well, I think everyone knows fish isn't my favorite breakfast (or anyone's), but they enjoyed it.

After they finished, they took a long walk through the tall pine trees, taller pine trees, and the ground of moss, dirt, and grass. They even saw some toads following each other as if they were playing follow the leader. There were squirrels running past them and a doe and buck with a fawn prancing all through the trees. Hubert and Wolfie enjoyed seeing the animals.

On their way home, they saw so much more wildlife, including butterflies whizzing by and landing on dandelions and daisies along with bluebirds and robins in nests in tall trees and a lot more wildlife. "So, Wolfie, now that we're back to our spot, let's do something else!"

Julia Melidossian
Age: 11

"Cough! Cough!" Timothy said. "This place is getting smoky around here."

A few years ago, this place was a normal village. It was a perfect place to live. But then, these unusual, clothed men came, and started to build tall buildings. It was a terror for the animals that lived in the village. Cars started to come out more, smoke everywhere. Everyone planned to escape. But small animals, such as mice, found it hard to escape.

One morning, I gathered every suffering animal in the village (because I am the animal mayor of the town), to the animal hall. One of them was the Cheese family. Mr. Cheese, Mrs. Cheese, and Timothy, their son.

I started to talk. "Since I am a bird, I can fly. And since I can fly, I can see what is over the forest . . ."

"JUST GET ON WITH IT!!!" everyone shouted.

"I saw a wonderful village, just like what this place used to be." Everyone in the meeting cheered. They clapped, and hugged each other. "But . . . there is one problem. While I was flying, I saw an owl. Then another owl flew out, and the next, and so on. There are tons of owls there. It's very dangerous for small rodents. So it's either you risk your life, or you stay here in this smoky place."

Everyone whispered to each other. In the end, everyone except the Cheese family decided to stay. On the day when they were leaving, everyone gathered to say good-bye. Though the Cheese family decided to leave, they were still very nervous, mostly scared. Timothy even tried to stay. Just when they were leaving, Timothy started to cry, screaming, "Mooommy!!! I don't want to get eatennnnn!!!" His mother calmed him down. She said to him that she didn't want to go either, but she didn't want to stay either. She told him they had to take the risk.

They went in the forest, hearing cheers, cries, and laughs behind them.

"Mom, this place is scary. Only about an hour has passed, and I can already hear owls hooting," Timothy said, shivering.

On the other hand, the owls were smirking with excitement.

The first owl that spotted them reported to its king immediately. "King Bucher! I saw three mice walking in the forest!"

The owls had not been eating mice for about five years. But now, there were three actual, live mice! It was a rare, delicious treat for them. "I, myself, will go get the three mice," said the king.

Everyone gasped. The king had never gone hunting himself before. He trained, was an expert at it, but he never went to hunt for a real, live animal. He went swooping down, completely silent. He saw three mice, warily walking.

"Huh? Honey, did you hear anything? I think I heard something. Maybe it was just the wind," said Mr. Cheese, the best hearer of all.

"Good ear," said a deep voice behind them. They looked up, and saw the enormous king. They ran as fast as they could. Timothy, the fastest, escaped. But Mr. Cheese and Mrs. Cheese got caught. They bit the king on his toes as hard as they could. The king, however, had always been treated carefully, and had never felt the "pain." He released them because of his pain, and flew back to his place.

"Mom! Dad! Are you OK?" yelled Timothy.

"We're fine. Don't worry," comforted Mrs. Cheese.

The king went back to his place, screaming. "King Bucher! Are you OK, Sire?" one of his servants asked. The king's pain healed in a few minutes, and the king was OK.

The Cheese family walked and walked, and they started to wonder something.

"Why aren't the owls attacking us anymore?" asked Timothy.

The truth was, the owls were scared of them because they had defeated the king.

One day, two hunters came to the forest with some traps to get owls. The owls never knew about this.

"Heeeeelp!! Heeeelp!!" an owl shouted. He was trapped.

"Honey? Do you hear someone shouting?" Mr. Cheese asked.

Everyone stopped and listened for a while. They heard it. Far off, somebody was shouting for help. They ran towards the sound. When they arrived, some owls were already there, trying to help. But since owls have no teeth, it was no use.

The Cheese family was scared. They did want to help, but they were scared the owls might attack them afterwards. The owls were struggling very much. The Cheese family knew it was impossible for them, but they still couldn't step up from the thick, dark bush. Mrs. Cheese's feet were itching to go up. And her head was fighting the force. Mr. Cheese and Timothy were the same too, fighting themselves. Finally, when it seemed like such a long time, Mrs. Cheese stepped up. Then Timothy, then Mr. Cheese.

"Excuse me, Sir. We think we can help your friend," Mrs. Cheese said, nervously.

The owls gasped. They flew away at once, hiding.

"What's wrong with them? We are supposed to run away from them."

Though the Cheese family was confused, they started to free the trapped owl. They bit, bit, and bit.

"Ah, thank you, Mr. and Mrs. . . . ?"

"Cheese. And this is our son, Timothy," Mrs. Cheese finished.

The owls reported to the king immediately. "King Bucher! The three mice just spotted the trapped owl, and we think they are going to kill him!!"

The king somehow knew they weren't. They were just trying to help. The king stood up, saying nothing at all, and flew away. The king was thinking. He wondered why, why these three unbelievable mice helped their biggest predator. Were they sure they could beat us all? No. He didn't think so. It was their great courage, and their open heart. He finally decided to reward them for their kindness. He went down, very quietly. The Cheese family backed up, but didn't run away.

"Sire, please, I swear. They were just helping me . . ."

"I know," interrupted the king. "And for that great courage and the great kindness, I will reward you three. I will give you a safe place to live, where nobody will attack." He paused. "But if you go out of the limited space, we will attack. That is the deal."

The Cheese family discussed it together, and finally decided. "Yes, we will take the deal."

He gave them enough space for three mice to live, and forbade the owls to hunt there. The king kept his promise for as long as they lived.

Kaede Yoshioka
Age: 11

THE LONELY YORKIE

Most dogs in the world have a home and the owners care for them. But there is something different about my owners. Is it me? What am I doing? Well anyway, my name is Krista I am a female Yorkshire terrier dog. I live with Mr. and Mrs. Anderson in Providence, RI. I can't complain. I love my life. But . . . OK, I do get a little lonely. Now that I think about it, I think I'll be lonely for the rest of my life because Mr. and Mrs. Anderson have a baby. I do everything to make them notice me. It takes them about an hour to finally get the picture that I have to go to the bathroom! That's why one night, I left. I didn't even think twice about this. But I did miss the delicious food Mrs. Anderson gave me, and how much fun we used to have, but that was all before baby Steven came into the picture. All he does is scream at night, which makes my ears tingle, and he poops in his pants! Come on! I'm better than him! I wait at the door very patiently. But . . . then I realized, maybe they do care about me. Take last night, for example. They were watching TV and Mrs. Anderson was petting me. Steven was actually sleeping. Maybe when Steven is not in the way—wait . . . maybe it's me who is in the way . . . not Steven. Maybe Mr. and Mrs. Anderson just need a little time with Steven and then they can spend time with me. I thought about this for a long time and then I ran home as fast as my little legs could carry me. When I reached my house, Mr. and Mrs. Anderson and even little baby Steven were waiting for me. I was attacked with kisses. Even Steven gave me a big hug. And right then and there I knew I was loved.

Krista Tramonti
Age: 11

STUCK ON THE MOON

Vrrrrrooommmm! We zoomed down the hall to find Maria in a space shuttle. We ran inside. "What are you doing here?" we asked.

"Aaahhh!" Maria pressed another button.

"Please stop pressing buttons!" I moaned.

"Spacesuits everyone!" screeched Bianca.

"Owww!" I said melodramatically, turning my fingers in my ears. Now we were off to the moon.

"Look, I see stars and it's only 11:30 a.m.!" said Nick.

"I know. That reminds me. I forgot to eat breakfast," I bellowed.

Then, Boooomm! Then silence—pure silence. The space shuttle had stopped. We all ran out.

But just as we stopped, "Hhheeelllppp." Maria was trapped! Craters are formed when meteors hit an object in space. I crouched down, took out my hand, and pulled her out.

"Guys, we found you. We thought we'd never find you! Hey, Nick . . . Bianca? Where are they, Maria?"

"Are they lost?" Maria gasped.

"Are they lost? You mean they are lost!" I yelled so loud it's a wonder I didn't lose my voice!

"I've got today's forecast: meteor shower!" We screamed. We ran like a monster racecar!

"Ooff!" I slammed into Nick, and Maria slammed into Bianca.

"Come on, guys. I know exactly where I—or Maria—parked the space shuttle," I said. "Well, she parked it right here," I said. "Oh, great," I mumbled. We looked up, down, right, left, front, and back. Then we found it! We went in.

This time I controlled the space shuttle. We looked out more for Maria and she watched what kind of button she pressed. When we got back, I had double the lunch. Maria, Nick, Bianca, and I had a sleepover. We told spooky stories about a space ape destroying the Earth.

"And the space ape . . ." said Nick.

"Ah, here it is!" we yelled.

"Drinks anyone?" It was my father.

"Sure," we said.

"Now when you're done, time for bed." Gulp.

"Done," we said.

"Okay. Now sleep time."

In my dreams I think of what I said in different words.

"This time I'll drive the space shuttle, so Maria doesn't drive us to another planet," I had insisted. We had traveled back home. It was nice to see the grass and trees again. I like the bees in my garden a lot more now, but I wish I had brought back some moon rocks because they would have gone great with my flowers.

Michael McCann
Age: 8

PUP NUMBER FIVE

It was a cold, dark, and dreary night. Rain trickled down through the brisk air and moistened the ground below. All alone in the depths of the meadow, lying under a pile of brush, poor Mamma Dog shivered in fear. It was time for her litter of pups to be born into the world and she had no one to comfort her. Brave and courageous, after four long, tiring hours, Mamma gave birth to five precious golden retriever pups. Instantly, she snuggled them to warm their tiny, little bodies from the cold. She could feel the small pups wiggling beneath her body. Mamma counted one, two, three, four . . . but where was pup number five? She stood tall and looked down. To her surprise, pup number five was less than half the size of his siblings, much too small to be felt under his mother's fur. At that moment, she feared the worst. Her instincts told her to abandon the little guy. Being the runt, she knew he wouldn't survive. Mamma picked up pups one through four in her mouth, and carried them away to a safe spot where she could feed them and care for them. Pup number five lay all alone in silence, frightened and confused.

The morning sun arose and woke the little pup from his sleep. The grass was becoming dry and the sky clearing from the night before. The warm sun felt good on his tiny, damp body. Being so small, the pup could not walk well or get to the other side of the street safely in a short time period. The small but strong-willed puppy set out to try to go across the street where houses were lined up for at least a mile.

Barely escaping an eighteen-wheeler Doritos truck, he made it to the other side in five minutes. Hungry and exhausted, the little pup wandered around looking for a meal to eat. He gazed with sad puppy dog eyes at every person he saw, but no one paid attention to him. People passed by him and never even noticed the small, sad baby. Then something happened. It was something wondrous.

A girl, no more than six years old, noticed him! This is when little pup's life changed forever! The young girl, Sarah, called out to the pup. When she saw the look in his big brown eyes, she understood completely. Sarah picked him up gently in her warm hands, snuggling him against her wool coat, and carried him up the stairs into her apartment. She felt his tiny belly rumble in her hands. The first thing Sarah did was offer the pup a cup of tapioca pudding. He ate it all up! He needs a name, thought Sarah! Tap E. Oca! That was it! So the little pup got his name!

Tap E. Oca grew to be strong and healthy with Sarah's help. She fed him well and cared for him. They spent winter nights together under their favorite blanket on the sofa watching movies. In the spring, Sarah and Tap enjoyed running in the park and playing fetch! During the summer months, Tap learned to swim in the local lake and even taught Sarah how to doggy paddle. Autumn was their favorite time of year when they rolled in the crisp leaves together. Sarah and Tap were inseparable. The two best friends grew to be adults, enjoying the years as they passed.

One sunny day when Sarah was at college she received a rather sad phone call. Poor Tap was hit by a car while chasing the neighbor's cat into the middle of a busy street. Although Tap was gone, he was never forgotten. Tap always lived on in the heart of his loving owner, Sarah.

Sabrina Mollicone
Age: 11

NIGHT OF THE MONSTERS

Once on a dark and stormy night, three kids were watching TV. But they did not know that a monster was watching them. Then one night it happened! When the girls were sleeping one of the monsters took one of the girls. A girl heard a scream in the night. Kay woke up in the night and realized that Daisy was missing. Then Kay was up. She screamed! It woke up Rose. Then there was silence—complete silence. Then their mom came in. She said, "What is going on in here?"

"Nothing," said Rose curiously.

"I thought that I heard you scream," said Mom.

"No we did not scream," said the girls.

"Are you sure?" said Mom.

"Yup," said the girls.

"Okay," said the mom.

The girls said, "Good night."

The mom said, "I love you, girls."

It was silent, then Rose was first to speak. This is what she said, "I hope that Daisy is OK"

"I think she is OK"

"YOU THINK! You never think!"

Then suddenly Boom! went the lights. Then in the blink of an eye, Kay was gone, long gone. Then all there was left was Rose. She was all alone in the dreary, dark night. Then she heard a scream. It came from the basement. As she opened the door, the scream got louder and louder and louder until suddenly it stopped. She could hear a noise that went Crunch! Crunch! Crunch! Then there was a sound! It went, "I'm going to get you! I'm going to get you!"

Then she saw her sisters. They were strapped to a table. Rose unstrapped her sisters and defeated the monsters and they all lived happily ever after.

Chasity Rian Pike
Age: 7

UFO

Part One

One day, I was in my room playing video games. The game I was playing was Alien Smash. My mom wanted me to go outside, so I stopped playing. I got on my jacket and went outside. When I got outside, I made a little snowball. Then I decided to make it into a big snowman. It took a lot of work, but I finally got the head on.

I went back into the house and got a carrot nose for my snowman. I couldn't find the carrot, so I asked my mom. When I got the carrot, I ran back outside. When I got out, I looked up into the sky. I saw a big, flashing light coming closer and closer. To my astonishment, it turned into a twenty-foot-long UFO.

The UFO got closer and closer until it was above the treetops. It zoomed past me and chopped off the head of my snowman. I was so stunned that I dropped the carrot and backed off. When the UFO landed, part of the outer wall of the ship folded down and became a ramp. When the ramp was completely down, a ton of smoke came pouring out. I heard a hissing sound from the spaceship.

I heard big, loud footsteps approaching me. To my surprise it was a robot alien. It stood ten feet, seven inches tall. It was very shiny and silver. It stopped and stared at me. Then it suddenly said, "Would you like to come for a ride?"

I asked, "Where?"

The alien just pointed to the sky and said, "Up there!"

I replied, "Okay," and I stepped into the spaceship.

There were thousands of colorful, flashing lights. I saw hundreds of joy sticks, switches, and levers. I asked the alien what his name was and he replied, "Tonamore." Then I told him my name. He pointed out to me the Milky Way. It was so beautiful up close.

He asked me where I wanted to go. I told Tonamore, "I want to go to Pluto." Once I finished speaking, off we went. The trip would have taken over seventy years, but though we went in hyper speed, it only took us a couple of hours. When we got there, I saw miles and miles of rock. I was getting bored, so I got back into the spaceship.

He asked me if I wanted to go to his home planet. I asked him, "What is the name of the planet?"

He said, "Wegea." The planet was in another dimension. It only took us a few minutes because we went in hyper speed. When I looked out the window, I saw swirling black holes. Then the alien said, "We are here."

When we exited the spaceship, I was astonished. I saw thousands of aliens just like him. They all talked weird. The planet was a deep blue. There were little stone houses with aliens in them. I was getting hungry so I asked for a snack. And alien approached me and gave me something. Once I saw it, I was not hungry anymore. It looked like a big, slimy caterpillar with hundreds of legs.

I was starting to get tired so I got back on the ship with Tonamore. When we got back home, he dropped me off in my backyard. Once I got off, the ship vanished. In a matter of seconds, my mom called me to go to bed. I got ready for bed and thought. I figured I should not tell my mom because she would think I was crazy.

The next day I went to school. I told all my friends, but they didn't believe me. At lunch I went to the bathroom. When I was walking to the bathroom, I heard something knocking on the window, so I went to investigate. To my surprise, it was Tonamore. He told me that he had to go back to his home planet and will never come back to Earth. I ran to the next door and went outside to talk to him.

I asked him why he was here. He said, "I wanted to say good-bye."

"Why?" I asked.

He said, "I am not allowed to come to Earth anymore because I can only stay on Earth for a certain amount of time and I have exceeded my limit."

I said my good-byes and went back to lunch. At the end of school, I went home and did my homework. I went to go look at the stars and I swore that I saw the same lights that I saw the night before and I knew that it was Tonamore.

Part Two

A few weeks after Tonamore left, I was looking at the stars. I saw the big dipper and saw a bright light inside of it. It came closer and closer. I knew that it must be Tonamore coming back. When the spaceship landed, Tonamore exited. "I thought that you were not allowed back," I said.

"I know. I left without telling them," Tonamore said. "I want to take you for a ride," he said. I hopped into his ship and we blasted off into space. We circled around space for a while.

When we landed on Earth, I put a disguise on him so other people would not recognize him. The first thing we did was go to Denny's Diner. I had chicken tenders and fries. Tonamore had steak and potatoes. After the meal, we went to get ice cream. We both had coffee ice cream in a waffle cone. A little bit later we went to a movie. Halfway through the movie, I went to the bathroom. While I was washing my hands, I heard a loud thump. I ran to the movie screen and saw a big hole in the roof. Tonamore had fainted in his chair. When I woke him up, he said he did not know what had happened.

When we looked outside, we saw hundreds of spaceships destroying the town. Everybody was running for his or her lives. There was nothing that Tonamore or I could do. The attack lasted all day. When the aliens left, Tonamore was relieved. A few hours later, he collapsed on the ground. He said that the other aliens must have poisoned him because he came back to Earth. His voice became weaker and weaker. His last words were, "I will miss you." While he said that, he closed his eyes.

"Don't die!" I cried. But there was nothing I could do. I watched him slowly dissolve into the ground.

When he disappeared, I picked up a piece of the dirt and brought it home. I ran into the house and got a jar. I put the dirt with his ashes into the jar. Now whenever I miss Tonamore, I just need to look at the jar. Sometimes on a sunny day, when the light reflects off the jar, I can see his face smiling at me.

On a wintry cold day, I heard something outside and I went to investigate. To my astonishment, there was a spaceship that looked just like Tonamore's. A small alien that looked just like Tonamore looked at me. "I am the son of Tonamore," he said.

"Will you be my friend?" I asked.

"Yes," he replied. Now I will never be alone.

George Melidossian
Age: 11

MY HERO

"Pass me that screwdriver and give me that bolt. They need these planes in Korea." These are the words my grandpa spoke when he made planes for the Korean War.

I am proud of my grandpa because he made fighter planes in a center and testing area in Quonset Point. Now in the Quonset Point testing and building center they hold air shows. It was important for my grandfather to build planes because he made them for the harsh Korean War.

He was in the service for twenty-five years. He retired in the position of a devoted Chief Petty Officer. While in the service, he was out to sea for nine months at a time. He visited many ports, including Japan, Singapore, and California. He made a large amount of slide pictures of places he had been.

My grandfather and grandmother got married in 1957 and divorced in 1975. In the middle they had seven children; Alan, Vance, Janet, Miriam, Linda, Lory, and Jacquelyn. My grandpa retired in 1966.

Now you can see the boat my grandfather was on when you ride a tour train in Newport, Rhode Island. It is past the Newport Naval Base. When I saw that boat, I felt proud because I am one of the grandchildren of a brave navy officer.

Savannah Dority
Age: 10

Hello, my name is Joe and this is my dog, Spot. Say hello Spot. "Ruff Ruff!"

I will start telling you a story about a magical place full of adventure and danger that I had visited. It all started when I was moving to our new house in Connecticut. I was whining in the backseat because we had to move and I did not want to.

"Come on why do we have to move?"

"My job got transferred!" yelled my dad.

"Yeah," said my snotty eighteen-year-old brother, "Don't be a wimp." Whack, my brother punched me.

"Ouch!" I screamed at the top of my lungs.

Dad shouted, "Boys if I hear one more sound out of either one of you, that person can walk to Connecticut. Do I make myself clear?"

"Yes," we said.

Spot was sticking his head out the window with his tongue flapping in the breeze, globs of drool dripping from it. I placed my head against his chest; I could feel him panting heavily. I knew that this would be a long year.

Once we got there, we unpacked and picked our rooms. I got the worst room in the whole house. It had rotten old wood, slime coming through cracks in the wall, a smashed window, and cobwebs all around.

However, my troubles did not end there. Five or six days after school started, my teacher made me stand up and introduce myself to the class. At lunchtime, it got worse. This five-foot-two person came and took my lunch. "Hey give it back!" I shouted as I struggled to get my lunch back.

In a low voice, he said, "I'll never give it to you, shrimp!" He and his gang took me outside and tied me to the tetherball pole. They each took turns punching me until I was bleeding. All I could hear was laughter in the background. I stayed outside until a teacher came and brought me to the nurse. Once inside she helped me clean off the dried blood. After that, they put me in the principal's office. He asked who the boys were that beat me up. I was not much help because I was new there. After all that, the school called my dad to pick me up. Once my dad got there they told him that it would be better off if I stayed out of school for one more week. I thought my problems could not get worse but I was wrong.

In the week off from school, my brother tortured me; he too had the week off. After an hour, I could not stand it anymore! I ran outside. It was dark, foggy, and misty which made it hard for me to breathe and see. I quickly and quietly got Spot and ran. As we ran, I could feel the dew slide right between my toes. At 1 a.m. we just passed the Connecticut border. We were now in Rhode Island, but it was raining hard so we went under a bridge where there was a big hole on one side and we squeezed in and went to sleep.

The next day we woke up early. I realized we were not in the state of Rhode Island anymore but we were in a magical land. There were unicorns grazing in a field and pigs flying above. Everything turned quiet; suddenly a dragon from the forest appeared and started to burn everything in sight. Slowly he turned his head and looked right at me. I tried to move but I was frozen in fear. Spot had the right idea. He ran out of there as fast as his legs would carry him. Then the dragon leaned back his head. I closed my eyes, I did not want to see. After a little bit, I opened my eyes. There, in a blue robe and a blue hat with stars and long beard, was a wizard and the dragon was gone. I looked at the wizard with amazement. He turned and looked at me with a sparkle in his eye.

Then with a low booming voice, he said, "Who are you and how did you end up here?"

"My name is Joe and this is my dog Spot and we were just sleeping in a hole in the bridge then we woke up and now we're in the cave."

"So you are from a different world," he said with wisdom in his voice.

"Yes," I whimpered. Then a tear ran down the side of my cheek.

"Why are you crying?" he said in a soft voice.

"Because I'm never going to get back home and see my family again and there is nothing I can do about it!" I shouted through my tears.

"Actually, there is a way," he said with a shine in his eye.

"Really," I said jumping up and down.

"But it will be a long and dangerous journey!" I was so desperate I did not even care. All I wanted to do was get home and see my dad and my snotty brother.

"I'll do anything!"

"Well then, here is a map of the whole valley." Poof, with a blink of an eye I had a map right in my shaky hands. "Now listen, if you want to get back home you must climb the rocky mountain and pass through Poison Tooth's cave. Then you must defeat the dragon, take his golden orb, and bring it to the top of the volcano. This is the portal to your world and your wish to go home. Here is the dragon slayer's sword; you will need this to kill the dragon. Be careful," he said.

"I'll try. Thank you for everything." Spot howled. He was already down in the meadow. Well in a split second, we were off. It took us three and a half hours to reach the rocky mountain. Once there we sat down to take a break. CRACK went a stick from my right side. I drew my sword and prepared for a battle. From out of the bush came a giant spider. It had glowing green eyes, long hairy legs, and teeth that were so sharp they could cut thought metal. I stood there in amazement as I watched those hairy legs come slowly towards me. I drew my sword, I swung, and before I knew it the beast's head was at my feet.

I was in shock. "How did I do that?" I asked Spot. He turned his head to the side and panted heavily. Then we got going and soon we were over the mountain. We stopped for a drink and I reached for the map and looked for the next mark. It was Poison Tooth's cave.

I shook at the thought of it. However, I knew it was the only way home. I stood up, sucked in my chest, and ran off hoping that the snake would not be home. When we got there, it was empty. We walked knowing that we would have to reach the other side of the cave, and then a rock came falling down.

"What is that Spot?" He sniffed the air and whimpered. I looked over my shoulder and there I saw Poison Tooth behind me. My heart raced as I sprinted away! Once out, I looked back and saw the snake lying on the ground. He had smashed his head into the top of the cave. He was dizzy and dazed. I laughed at the funny scene, which made me less scared for a moment. I realized that the danger was not over yet and would get worse before it got better. I still needed to fight the dragon if I ever wanted to see home again. We continued on our journey. At dusk, we reached the volcano. There were skulls and bones in all directions where I looked. I drew my sword, ran into the mouth of the volcano, and saw the fire-blazing red dragon asleep in front of me. I thought, oh great this is my chance! I saw the golden orb clutched in the sleeping dragon's right claw. If I could be as quiet as a mouse and sneak up on him, I would be able to get the orb. I tiptoed toward the dragon. Crack! Crunch! I shattered a skull. The dragon awoke. He was furious. Just then, Spot started to bark loudly. This startled the dragon. I drew my sword and jumped into the air swinging it as fast as I could and stabbed the dragon in his black heart. He was dead! I grabbed the orb and Spot, ran to the top of the volcano, and thought about home and in seconds, we woke up under the bridge. I sighed in relief and realized this had all been a dream. I got up to walk home and noticed a golden shiny object; it was the orb!

Matthew O'Connell
Age: 11

THE ROSE

It all started with a young woman. She was the most beautiful and sweet maiden in the land. Every man that lay his eyes upon her was instantly in love. She had long, flowing, brown hair, eyes as blue as the river, and lips as red as the most beautiful flower; her name was Rose. Although every man was in love with her, she loved no mortal man. The only one that she loved was Arthemedos, the god of flowers. He was one of the most handsome gods of all. He had many different types of flowers breezing through his hair, but mostly her favorite flowers. Rose spent all of her free time up on the flowery green hill near her house. She was always picking these beautiful flowers, which had no name and were of a deep red with a smooth, green stem. As she picked, Rose gazed up to the heavens at Arthemedos, and the mortal men gazed up the hill at her.

Then one day, Arthemedos came to her in a dream and said, "To win my heart you must pick seven of those flowers that you love so much and lay them on the top of a cliff." When she woke up, she went straight to her hill only to find that the flowers were not there. Suddenly, a mortal man came to her side and said, "I know the flowers that you love so much; they are now growing in a bush down by the river. I will take you there." She was so grateful for his kindness that she experienced feelings toward him that she felt for no other mortal; she had fallen in love with him. When they got to the bush of flowers, they picked them together. After she had picked seven, she remembered the dream and with that she threw the flowers into the water. Rose did not know, however, that the flowers had floated away only to have landed on a very high cliff. As Arthemedos had said he would, he fell in love with her because he saw the flowers as an answer to the dream. He watched her at the riverbank every day, but was very displeased that she was with a mortal man and knew that she would only love him again if this mortal man, whose name turned out to be Lianos, was killed. So he told the god, Zeus, his story and asked him to strike Lianos with a lightning bolt. Zeus refused.

One day while he was watching Lianos and Rose picking the flowers and laughing together, he thought of a plan. The next day as Rose and Lianos were picking roses, Lianos started choking and couldn't breathe. The next thing Rose knew, he was dead. Arthemedos had poisoned that one flower. Rose immediately left the river and would not go back. After a while, Arthemedos appeared to her and took her back to the riverbank where they picked flowers together and laughed. Rose fell in love with him again and they got married. They were both happy together, but neither of them knew that when Lianos "died," he was actually morphed into the water.

So, one day when Arthemedos and Rose were by the riverbank, Lianos expanded the water and sucked Rose in with a great strength. She tried to fight it, but could not. Arthemedos was amazed and realized he had used the poison that made people the opposite of themselves, so now Lianos was ugly and vicious. After Rose's death, Arthemedos mourned for her. In her honor, he called the flower that she loved the rose. However, from then on, all roses had thorns so they wouldn't be helpless like she was. It is also sometimes said that Rose did not really die; she was just forced to live in the water with Lianos, as his wife.

Cara Fontaine
Age: 14

THE BRAVE TIGER

One day, a tiger named Sunflower went off to play with her best friend named Rajah, who was a cheetah. Sunflower's mother said, "Don't go to the bottom of the cliff. There are some dangerous things down there. Trust me."

Rajah was a daredevil! When Sunflower and Rajah were near the park, Rajah took a right and pulled Sunflower with her. They stopped at the cliff. Rajah fell off the cliff and got lost.

Sunflower jumped down and got chased by mean wolves. Rajah found Sunflower and helped her. Then Rajah got chased by more hungry wolves. So, Sunflower scratched and bit the wolves until they ran away. Sunflower helped Rajah. One wolf bit Rajah as hard as it could. Rajah fell down. Sunflower fought as hard as she could and the wolves ran away again.

Sunflower took Rajah to the vet. The vet said, "She will be fine." So, they went home and told her mom the story. They promised never to go on the cliff again.

Alexandra Soqui
Age: 8

HOW IVY CAME TO BE

Once upon a time, there was a young girl named Irvilla who hated men, and didn't want anything to do with them. She was a follower of Artemis.

One day, she was taking an early morning walk through the woods near the base of Mount Olympus. Just as she saw a wild boar and started chasing it, a man called out to her, "Over here! Come over here!" She could tell it was a man's voice, so she ran; she ran as hard as she could. The shockingly fast man followed her, chasing her through the woods shouting, "It's okay! Come over here!"

"No! Go away!" Ivrilla shouted at the top of her lungs. She ran into a cave to escape. Suddenly, a long, loud, deep roar came out of the back of the cave, seeming to get closer and closer as she listened.

"Whoa! Watch out for that bear!" cried the man as he swung toward her, grabbing her and pulling her out of the cave.

"Ummm . . . thanks," she mumbled toward the man who had saved her life from the roaring bear.

"No problem," he replied smiling. "I'm Aquis."

"Oh, I'm Ivrilla." Suddenly, she felt a strange feeling for this man; it was love. Under Hera's watchful eye, they were married. For twelve years, they lived happily together wandering the forest.

One day, Aquis went off to the market, as he did every month. As Ivrilla went off on her routine walk, something happened up on Mount Olympus. Hera found out that, once again, Zeus had been being unfaithful. Because Hera was mad, she wasn't watching over Ivrilla and Aquis's marriage. So, a young man named Stelantha saw her taking a break on a smooth, round rock. He came up next to her and started talking to her. She, out of reflex, jumped up and started sprinting away. Faster and faster she ran, father and farther she went, running away.

"Wait," he called, "I'm Stelantha, and I don't want to hurt you. Come back!"

But Ivrilla paid no attention. She ran on, slowly getting more tired than she had ever felt before. Surprisingly fast, Stelantha continued chasing after her. Days went by, and Ivrilla gradually became slower and slower.

Ivrilla cried to the gods up on Mount Olympus for help. Hera, suddenly reminded of her job, knew that there was no way to drive Stelantha away from her, so she turned Ivrilla into ivy.

Days later, Aquis came back and saw Ivrilla not at home. He went out looking for her and saw a lonely man staring at a tree. Aquis walked up to him and looked at the tree and saw some wilting ivy steadily creeping up the tree trunk. Suddenly, through a miracle from Aphrodite, the goddess of love, Aquis knew the whole story. With great rage, he leapt toward Stelantha and killed him, his blood making the soil a rich growing spot for Ivrilla. Aquis stood over the ivy, his tears of sadness forever watering Ivrilla, who is still creeping away from Stelantha, but now, toward her lover,

Aquis. Now, in the rich soil, and with Aquis's tears, the ivy will grow and thrive in that spot forever. To this day, Aquis is still watering Ivrilla's leaves, and she is still constantly creeping toward Aquis.

Emily Daigle
Age: 14

OCEAN FRIENDS

Once upon a time there was a dolphin named Zach. Zach had a dolphin friend named Alex. Zach had another friend Max. Max was a killer whale.

One day, Zach, Alex, and Max wanted to go on an adventure. They started in a place called Atlantis. They found treasure, danger, and a few other friends, too. One time they found eels; lots of them, too. They escaped, though.

On the second day of their adventure, they went to the coast of England and met five sharks. Four sharks were great whites, but one was a whale shark. The great whites wanted to eat them. The whale shark didn't because most types of whales have skinny throats.

All of a sudden, Max's mother scared the sharks off with the pod of other killer whales. Did you know that killer whales are the only whales that don't eat krill?

Max's mom said that they shouldn't be traveling alone. Zach, Alex, Max, and Max's mom went back to Atlantis. That was the end of their adventure.

Emmalee Martin
Age: 9

HOW CATS CAME TO BE

A god named Justifimous had just finished creating his world, his great masterpiece. He had created some animals, people, and other things he thought were essential for the growth of his masterpiece and to make it the greatest place compared to any place other gods had created in the past. The god was always competing against his brother, Darevus, and Darevus always tried to bring him down. After Justifimous created this magnificent world, he told his brother how wonderful it was compared to what his looked like. However, Justifimous did not get the answer he wanted. Darevus told him it was good, but that the one that Justifimous created still did not match up to his own. He told Justifimous that he had worked on his creation and had made the one thing Justifimous did not have in his, the cat. Justifimous got angry and stormed out. He had thought he had beaten his brother this one time, but he had not.

Once Justifimous got back to his kingdom, he tried to think of ways to create a cat that was better than Darevus'. He thought of a few different ways, but then he disagreed with doing them. For instance, he thought that he could take some of his fine animals and change them into an animal that walks on four paws, meows, has a medium or long tail, and different lengths of fur. However, he got upset with his idea because he did not want to get rid of any of the wonderful animals he created. Justifimous wanted to keep all of the animals he had and still get the new that he could not figure out how to create.

Day after day, after day went by and Justifimous still did not know what to do. He thought of some more ideas, but again, none of them were going to work the way he wanted them to. Justifimous even thought he would go and ask Darevus for help or even just a hint to get him on his way. He tried this one, though, and it did not go so well. Darevus just laughed in his face and said, "No one will ever create a world as magnificent as mine!" After saying this, Darevus cast Justifies out of his kingdom and would not let him back in until he had created the cat.

Again, days went by and Justifimous still did not have a clue on how he could make this cat. Until one day, Justifimous had a vision of what was to come. He envisioned the cat and saw many different types of it. Then Justifimous knew what he could do. Justifimous decided that he could take all the people that disobeyed him and did not respect him and cast them all to the ground to walk on their four paws for the rest of their life. Justifimous tried this idea, but it did not turn out as well as he had planned. All the so-called cats looked all the same and did not look anything like what he had envisioned. Better yet, they did not look anything like what Darevus had created either.

After the idea failed, Justifimous had cast the disobedient and disrespectful people back to the way they were. Once he had done that, he locked himself in a dark, empty room with no one but himself inside. He thought that this way he would be able to think of a way to create exactly what he envisioned. Justifimous stayed in this room for months, maybe years, and still did not know what do. By this time, his wife, Protenta, and his children, Watedon and Stronimes, had gotten really worried for him. They wished he would just stop and tried to get him to. Justifimous just told them that he would not let his brother and evil win this contest-like thing. He needed to create this cat. Then, he shut the door of the room on them and prayed to the higher gods for help.

A goddess who was higher in rank than Justifimous and Darevus heard the cry for help. Her name was Sequinity. She and her husband, Ugnatimous, were the king and queen of all the gods, living and dead. She decided that she would send Justifimous a dream that would show him the way and help him create the cats he envisioned. That, too, was of her doing and now she knew it was time for it to happen. Sequinity was waiting for Justifimous to realize that the competition was between good and evil and not just between his brother and him, for the better world was the one that the gods would choose to be the everlasting, the one to never be destroyed. The one animal the god really favored was the cat, which made it more difficult for the two, and they had to make sure that they had at least one species of cat in their masterpiece to make the higher gods happy. It was to be a sacred and diverse item in their works of art.

So one night, Sequinity sent him a dream. It showed Justifimous he had the right idea of casting the disobedient to walk on four paws, but it involved more than just doing that. He had to take his strength and put more into it like he had with the other animals. All that Justifimous had to do now was decorate them in his own way with the different color and lengths of fur, different-sized bodies and tails, different sounds to come from each, and whatever else Justifimous wanted to do with them They were his creation, and he needed to make them the way he wanted to and unique.

The next morning after Justifimous had awakened from the dream, he went straight to work with his creativity on the making of the cats. He worked and worked for three years. Then the many cats he had envisioned were right there in front of him. He had created them all different and exceptional. His hard work to make them paid off. Justifimous went to Darevus to show him the wonderful creation, and Darevus got mad that his brother had actually beaten him, for he did not know how to create them all that way. At that moment, Sequinity and Ugnatimous appeared. The king and queen of all the gods looked at both of the worlds that had been created. The two decided that they would think about it and tell the brothers their decision the next day.

Well, the next day came. The king and queen met with both of the brothers. The gods decided that both worlds would stay everlasting. The two brothers were confused and asked how that could be. The gods answered them by saying that one would be the world of peace and obedience and the other full of evil and regret. However, the world of peace and obedience is not the perfect world that Justifimous created, for there will be some evil in it, though not as much as the world that Darevus had created. The decision of which would be good and evil of the two perfect worlds had been told through the way it was said. Once the gods had declared their decision, Justifimous and Darevus knew that the outcome was final.

The two actually were happy with the decision and agreed entirely that it was the fair way to handle it. Both had what they wanted for their worlds and each contained what they had created to begin with. This is how cats of different types came to be.

Iole Heikkinen
Age: 14

149

THE BULLY PLAN

Ann-Lynn stood as still as could be, not breathing, not moving. Her eyes looking straight ahead. Following the fright that had just happened. Following the long strides of Nina. Following the long strides of the bully. But more importantly, her bully.

It happened. It happened in her own classroom. It hadn't been physical. She hadn't even touched her. But it had hurt. It had hurt bad—more than anything that had happened to her before. Thoughts raced through Ann-Lynn's head. She tried with all her might to decide what to do. Slowly, she walked to a slot between the rolling TV and the cabinet against the wall.

It took five minutes before Kammy realized Ann-Lynn was in the corner. She ran to get Caitlin and Lyric. Together they walked over to Ann-Lynn. "What's wrong?" they asked Ann-Lynn. But she didn't answer. She had a good reason not to. Because Nina had walked up behind them, but no one saw her though. She pointed to Ann-Lynn, and ran a sharp finger over her lips as if to say, "Shut it or else." Nina turned and walked briskly away. Ann-Lynn motioned for her friends to come closer to her. In a hushed voice, Ann-Lynn told them what had happened.

"I was over by the mailboxes, doing my classroom job, when Nina came over to me. We weren't very good friends, but I always thought she was kinda my friend in a way. She said she wanted to tell me something. She said it in a cheerful way. I asked if something was wrong. She casually answered not really.

'Let's talk over here,' she said as she pointed to the door.

But as I turned around, I heard her mutter something. When we were at the door, her smile turned to a sharp frown.

In a mean voice she said, 'Can I tell you something? All your friends hate you. And the reason they do is because you're fat, ugly, and a little baby.'

Gaining up my courage, I asked, 'Who is that?'

Nina responded, 'Me, and I just know they hate you, and I hate you too! You know what? You don't belong! You don't belong at all. You're dirt and there's no way you're going to tell, or else. Got it?'

'Got it,' I said.

After her story, Lyric said, "That's awful. We must do something! So, what do we do?"

"I have a plan," said Kammy. "You said we couldn't tell the teacher. What if we have Nina tell the teacher herself?" Kammy continued. "Okay, this is what we do. We must make a trap. A trap Nina can't get out of. It's going to be hard, very hard, extremely hard. Do you think we can do it?"

"We can totally do it," said Ann-Lynn. "I just have one question. Why would a popular girl like Nina stoop so low as to bully?"

"I don't know. I just don't know," said Caitlin. "So what's the plan, Kammy?"

"The plan is this." Kammy leaned over and in a hushed voice, she relayed her genius plan. "Do you think it's a good plan," asked Kammy.

"It's a great plan. Let's do it!" said Ann-Lynn.

Stage One: The Army

"Face it. We can't do this alone," said Kammy. "We need an army. An army of kids who have either seen her, heard her, or just want to carry out the plan."

"Okay. Come on. Let's get an army," said Caitlin.

Ten Minutes Later . . .

"We have eight more people. That makes twelve. That's a good army," said Kammy. They now had their army.

Stage Two: The Distraction

"We won't be able to tell the teacher if we don't distract Nina," said Kammy. She then told Evan, Dylan, and Lyric to go talk to Nina. "Pretend you hate me. Talk about that," said Ann-Lynn. "Just keep her distracted until we tell you," she ordered.

Stage Three: The Report

"Ann-Lynn, Caitlin, come with me," said Kammy. They walked up to the teacher who stood just a few feet away. "Okay, Ann-Lynn," explained Kammy, "you have the most important part—telling."

"No. No," cried Ann Lynn.

"It's okay," said Kammy. "We're right here."

"Okay, here I go," said Ann Lynn. "Mrs. Pritchett, I was by the mailboxes and Nina called me names." And she told her story.

Stage Four: The Jigs Up

Just as she was saying it, Shelby came up and said, "I heard her. It was mean, really mean."

"Well, let's talk to Nina," said Mrs. Pritchett.

"Nina, do you have something to tell me?" questioned Mrs. Pritchett.

"Like what I heard when you were talking to Ann-Lynn," said Shelby.

"Fine. Fine. I confess and I'll tell you why I did it," said Nina.

Stage Five: The Confession

Later, Nina spoke to everyone who was involved. "I did it for a terrible reason," explained Nina. "It was wrong and I'll take whatever the punishment might be. You might think it's strange that I only pick on Ann-Lynn. But I only picked on her once. It's because, well, I was jealous because Ann-Lynn has so many friends. I'm sorry. I just wish I could be her friend, too."

"Perhaps someday," said Mrs. Pritchett, "you'll show Ann-Lynn how good of a friend you can be. But for now, you need to apologize to Ann-Lynn."

"Yes, I will," said Nina. "It's a good way to start."

Castine M. King
Age: 10

151

THE MISSION

Chapter One

"Timber!!!" Carter announced as the tree he chopped nearly crushed my leg.

"Whose side are you on?" I asked, jumping to my feet.

"Sorry," Carter said.

I heard Noah yawn from inside the tent. "What's going on out there," Noah asked yawning again.

"Nothing," we said in unity.

I decided to pick up my goal sheet and saw that I had a swordsmanship test at noon; it was 11:20 a.m. "I'm going to be late," I yelled, picking up my sword.

A few hours after my test, I saw somebody out of the corner of my eye. He had a spear and he was coming my way.

Chapter Two: Captured

I started to sprint through the forest. I saw three more people coming near me ready to attack. I started to run, but I hit a tree that knocked me out.

"I thought Jesse was supposed to be back by now," Noah groaned.

"Help!" a shrill came from the forest.

"What was that?" Carter asked falling off his hammock.

"I don't know, let's find out," Noah said walking into the woods.

"Let me go, you evil little . . ."

"Be quiet!" said a guard cutting me off in mid-sentence.

I heard footsteps in the distance, a steady clicking. I just remembered I had my sword in my belt. I yanked it out and knocked the guards out. Next step: run.

On the way out I saw a large machine that had a yellow glow coming out of it. I would have stayed to look but I saw three guards coming after me with loaded laser blasters. I started to run, but I heard a clicking. Who is that? I wondered to myself.

Chapter Three

When I was out and safe I told the others about what I had seen.

"What did it look like?" Noah blurted.

"I don't know!" I said, before Noah decided to say anything else.

"We should sneak around the base tonight," Carter said confidently.

"Why tonight?" I asked, yawning.

"Good point. I'm tired," Noah said.

"We'll go tomorrow," I said.

I woke up to find Carter missing. It was three o'clock in the morning.

"Noah!" I yelled.

"I didn't do it!" Noah dove off his bed and onto the floor.

"We have to save Carter before he is killed," I said.

Carter was three-fourths of the way to the palace when he saw a long, pointy thing whiz right by his face. He had no clue what it was. Another flew by his face and he dove into the next one. He started to fall to the ground, but got back up and ran. He tripped and fell into a large pit. It had lights that led into a deep cave. He started to go into the cave when a guard saw him and called security. A garrison of troops started to storm the area.

Carter made it out safely, but he got an arrow stuck in his leg. When Carter got out, he saw a large explosion in the night sky. Carter returned just as I was about to leave. We tried to turn on the TV, but it did not turn on.

Chapter Four: Operation Stealth

When we all woke up we started to plan our attack on the palace. We knew the large device would soon strike again, but what would it fire at? Our operation was called OPERATION STEALTH. We all started to look for warriors in the woods. We had no luck until we found Austin and his gang of freedom fighters. It took us awhile to convince him, but we got him to join the team. His people were well-trained and willing to fight for their freedom. The battle plan was set; the mission started in five hours.

6 p.m.

As we split up, we wished each other good luck and walked off.

We spotted each other in the main hangar bay and I sent the signal. Noah lit a string of about twenty firecrackers and threw them into the hangar. The distraction worked too. The firecrackers landed on a guard's shoulder. In a matter of seconds, a loud BAM filled the hangar with noise. Austin and his freedom fighters were slashing the cameras when out of nowhere, a laser hit Austin's leg. He fell to the ground. For me it was like the world had stopped. The alarm started to sound. I grabbed Austin on my back and started to run.

Austin was just about twenty-one yards away when the whole facility exploded and a large cloud of fire lit the night sky.

6:55 a.m Day Two

In a hospital one mile away, Austin came out with a cast around his leg and started to say something, but was cut off by a message.

"Looks like it's back into the action. A call came in and it looks like another device has been built and . . ."

"What happened?" Carter asked.

"I don't know, let's go find out."

To Be Continued . . .

Jesse MacDonald
Age: 11

153

HOW THE DOVE CAME TO BE

"Hey, stop it!" giggled Dovella as her best friend, Perfia, chased her around the pond.

"Rahhh!" yelled Perfia. The two kids collapsed on the lush green grass laughing so hard their sides hurt. Dovella and Perfia grew up together all their lives. Dovella was the daughter of Zeus and Hera, but she lived with mortals. When the time was right, she would discover her powers and live on Mount Olympus to be with her own kind. Perfia, on the other hand, was a mortal. Everyone knew that one day Dovella and Perfia would marry.

Ten Years Later

Dovella and Perfia had fallen in love. Shortly after their first kiss together, Dovella found out who she really was. When she was told she would be sent to live on Mount Olympus, Dovella burst into tears.

"How could you do this to me? You know I'm in love with Perfia!" she cried. No sooner had those words left her lips, she thought about how she was going to tell Perfia.

Dovella asked Perfia to meet her by the pond; it was the first place they met and the place they would say good-bye. She said she had something important to tell him. When Perfia arrived, Dovella took one look at him and burst into tears the second time that day. Perfia took her into his arms and asked her what was wrong. "I'm, I'm a goddess, anndd I I have tooo leeaavveee youu," she choked out. Perfia had never looked so surprised in his life. He looked at Dovella and said nothing.

"Do you really have to go?" he asked.

"Yes!" cried Dovella bursting into tears again.

"Shhhh, it's going to be OK," Perfia said, comforting her. But deep down inside they both knew it wasn't.

Two Years Later

Dovella watched Perfia every day from Mount Olympus. She saw him meet another woman, give her flowers and whisper sweet messages in her ear. Dovella desperately wanted to go back to Earth and see Perfia again. Hera watched her daughter become more depressed each day. Finally, she confronted Dovella and asked her what was wrong. Taking a deep breath, Dovella told Hera her story. Hera felt a pang of sorrow for her. She told Dovella that she would give her the power to transform herself into a bird and visit Perfia whenever she wanted to. Dovella's face lit up, and she smiled for the first time in two years.

Every day, Dovella visited Perfia. She tried to look like a normal white bird when she noticed someone looking her way. On the day of Perfia and his fiancée's wedding, Dovella cried. She barely made it through the wedding, and when night came, she perched herself on Perfia's window sill, looking at him and his new wife sleep peacefully. A few moments later, Perfia heard Dovella cry. He looked out his window and saw her. At first he thought it was just another bird, but when she came closer to him and gently nipped him, he knew it was Dovella. Perfia couldn't believe that it was really her. Dovella, knowing that he knew it was her, gave one last nod and flew away. Perfia had no idea what kind of beautiful white bird Dovella was, so he named it dove.

Amy Richard
Age: 14

MY DOG GRUB IS FOUR YEARS OLD

I have a dog named Grub. She is four years old. She is my favorite dog that I ever had. My dog Grub is a baby girl. When she was a baby baby she was really slow. She got stitches and she is a lot better now. She has five toys that are mostly the size of her bed. She tripped off the couch and she tripped over the rug.

Grub and I play soccer together. We like playing. She is the best kicker in my family. Grub was playing soccer and she looked like she laid an egg because she sat on the ball. Grub was playing one day and she hit it off her head. Then it landed in the tree. My dad had to climb on the ladder to try to get it. The ball didn't come down, so the ball is still there.

Grub can almost run after a car. She protects my family. This morning she jumped up on the couch and she fell asleep, but we had to go. Last Saturday she fell asleep on my bed. She had a bad dream and she started to shiver. When she woke up she went on her dog bed, which is on the floor in my room. She saw her toy she pounced on it. She rolled on it and fell on it. Two weeks ago she went into my room, which my mom doesn't like. She went on my bed when I just made it. She is just a wonderful dog. She has a scar from when she got the stitches.

Taylor Williams
Age: 12

THE JOURNEY OF THE FUDGSICLE WARRIORS

Once upon a time there were two brave warriors named Fudgena and Fudgrich who lived in the town of Fudgsicles. They were the only warriors in the whole country. Then, one day, over one hundred tough-looking warriors came from the town of Hostage. Fudgena and Fudgrich went everywhere together and had to be careful where they stepped because the Hostage warriors put video cameras and trap doors everywhere to catch them. Whenever they went outside they often traveled in groups. Even the people in the groups could be warriors from Hostage.

So Fudgena and Fudgrich had to be super careful. Their house was a piece of crude work and it looked like no one ever lived there, let alone that someone lived there now! It looked like it came from the prehistoric times made by cavemen. The inside was no better. The kitchen had a mini fridge and a stove, but that's about it. The living room had one blanket that served as a rug and a rock, which was supposed to be a couch. The one bedroom they had only had one twin-sized bed, so Fudgena and Fudgrich had to take turns sleeping on the bed and sleeping on the couch. They lived in that dreadful home so that the Hostage warriors couldn't find them. They felt bad about leaving their families and friends, but they had no choice. The Hostage warriors had probably threatened their families to tell them where they were and when their parents refused to tell, they were probably hurt very badly.

So the warriors of the town of Fudgsicles had to keep one eye open when they slept. If the Hostage warriors found out where they were living, what would happen to the town, but most of all, THEM! This very question ran through their heads almost every night, but that night was the night their lives were going to change (of course they had no idea what was coming at them and being stolen right under their noses). When they woke up they were unpleasantly surprised that they were not in their old, crude house anymore. They were in a castle, but it looked rather evil with a rather drab color of black on the wall and what looked like a throne for a king was made of all black metal (which stood for evil). The symbol on the top of the throne was a floating ghost crown, but even though it was small, it was still horrifying to look at it. There was another throne on the side of it, and it was the size for a queen. This throne was the exact opposite of the first one though. It was pink with ribbons and frills on it. The symbol for this throne was a beautiful bouquet of roses and daises. It was the most beautiful thing in the world. But then Fudgrich remembered that the king of Hostage was the most evil man in the world and the queen of Hostage was the happiest woman in the world. They were in the town of Hostage!

The queen knelt down at the foot of their beds and whispered to the two of them, "I had my warriors catch you and bring you here. I wanted nice children in the house so that I could show the king that nice people aren't as bad as he thinks they are. But you best be off so the king won't see you." It suddenly occurred to the two of them that the most evil man in the world and the happiest woman in the world got married. How could that possibly happen?

The next day, the king saw Fudgena and Fudgrich and sent them to the dungeon. He said that the bars were indestructible and that they could never get out. One day, Fudgrich had a plan. He told the king that all the soldiers were going to Fudgsicles because he was mean to them. Fudgrich also said that if the king didn't let the two of them go, he would not tell them where a group of his missing warriors were (Fudgrich had seen them in his hometown of Fudgsicles recently). King Hostage agreed to his plan, and Fudgena made him promise to be nicer. The king reluctantly agreed to this.

So Fudgena and Fudgrich ran out of Hostage and back to Fudgsicles. It was a scary journey, but they managed to make it back alive. Everyone knew that they were captured, so when they returned everyone was delighted to see them. They were treated like royalty for the rest of their lives and they were never hunted ever again!

Everyone was shocked when Fudgena and Fudgrich went back to Hostage with some of their warriors. They were happy when they returned. The whole town chipped in enough money to let Fudgena and Fudgrich live in a formal house with a lot of rooms and a spectacular view of the whole town. It was the nicest house in the whole city and was built just for them. They felt so honored and this time they were in an actual castle, but without the happiness overload, and without the evil (which was now also an overload of happiness.) It was the perfect house for them and a month later, they decided they would get married.

When the wedding day finally came, everyone in town showed up, even the king and queen of Hostage were there! It was the most romantic day in world history. The gown that Fudgena wore was white and was very pretty. The tux Fudgrich wore was black and had a red rose pinned to it.

After that day, no one ever forgot the important journey that Fudgena and Fudgrich had. Now they are old grandparents telling this very story to their grandchildren. When their grandchildren are grandparents, they promised that they would tell this story to their grandchildren. This story will be turned to a legend and the town of Fudgsicles is now the most famous town in the whole world.

Kathryn A. Merritt
Age: 10

THE SAVIOR KITTEN

"Dancing lights across the sky
that twinkle and sing to me.
They make me wish that I could fly
over and beyond the sea.
In the darkness, they watch us.
On their journey, they travel far.
Just listen—hush.
They sing "Twinkle, Twinkle, Little Star.""

"Oh, please, Mother! One more song!"
"You need to go—now! Please, sweetheart, you cannot stay."
"But, Mother," whimpered a small voice, "what if I never see you again?"
"It is for the best, Dear. We will see each other again . . . someday."
Finally, the boy let go of his mother. She placed him in a seat in the dark car, wiped away his tears, and left the train. She did not turn back to look at him . . .

***

The train zoomed through the night, flying over the tracks to somewhere far away. A tiny boy huddled against the window of the train car as it bumped over the tracks. He was very tired, but could not sleep. He was very upset, but could not cry. He just listened to the roar of the train, an occasional squeak of metal, people murmuring, and the frightening booms that came from outside. He glanced at his backpack. It had food and water in it, but he could not eat or drink. He was far too exasperated and didn't know when he would obtain more food. He had some money in it, but most of it was spent in order to buy a ticket to get him over the border into France.

Why had his life come to this? An innocent boy, separated from his mother because they hadn't enough money to buy a second ticket. His father was long gone. His happy childhood turned to a life of running away. He didn't know what he would do when the train stopped its journey. He became very upset as terrible questions yanked at his heart. Where was he to go? Would the Nazis find him? When would he see his mother again—if ever? Many more unanswerable questions filled the boy's head. If only the war had not started and caused this great pain that slowly ensnared the world . . . Suddenly, a great crash came from outside, and light briefly entered the train car. People gasped. The boy crouched in the musty seat. Was it another Ally who had gone down?

But when the flash occurred, the boy noticed his backpack slumped beneath the seat in front of him—it had jumped. He cautiously opened it and something leapt onto his lap. In the darkness, the boy could not tell what the object was, so he extended a finger and touched it. Instantly, the boy was comforted, and he lay his entire hand on the warm body. It was as soft as a young goose's down. It had a long, skinny tail, and it mewed delicately. He lifted the gray kitten to his face, and its eyes glittered with excitement. Although he didn't know where this bundle came from, a moment of blessings was bestowed upon the boy as he traveled through the war-torn country. The boy petted his new friend and they curled close together. He was finally able to sleep.

***

She watched with watery eyes, and bit her lip to squelch her cry of anguish. Soon the train could no longer be heard, and dark clouds covered the sky. An icy breeze whipped at her sides. She turned away, a crystal tear falling. The woman wandered, dazed, back to the tiny house, where her boy no longer lived. The door creaked as it always did when she opened it. His toys were sprawled across the living room floor as they always were. But for the first time, she picked them all up, putting them in a box. Then she put the box in the back of her closet, and closed the door on her former life. She scuttled about the house, drawing the draperies, closing the kitchen cabinets, neatly folding the blankets, fluffing the pillows, and then locked the door. It looked like a doll house—everything precisely placed by a little girl, but now the girl had grown up and left.

The woman, her face wrinkled with misery, sat in her favorite rocking chair, and stared at nothingness. She thought about her life, and the terrible things that had happened to her. Where were her good memories kept? There were only a very few of them. Darkness began to approach. Nevertheless, no lights were turned on. She sat in the gloom, just thinking. When would she see her son again—if ever? Many more unanswerable questions filled her head.

A while later, when it was pitch black outside, she got up. Something was wrong. Moments later, talking came from outside. She quietly dropped to the floor and crawled to the window. She carefully pulled back a corner of the drapery and peered out. Several men with dim lanterns were prowling the streets—raiding the houses—doing their job as Nazis. The monsters banged on her door, shouting insults in German. The woman froze clutching the velvet, eyes wide. The Nazis burst through into her house, into her life.

The Nazis killed her, but she had seen the Lord and He sent her to Earth again . . .

Suddenly, she heard a great crash, and there was a flash of light. She was in a dark bag, which she unconsciously leapt out of and landed on a tiny figure. Her boy was looking at her, as happy as she'd ever seen him. As she tried to speak; not words, but a meow, was produced. Unable to express her joy enough, her eyes glittered with excitement—she was reunited with her son! He petted her, and she purred with delight. She curled into a ball on her son's lap, licked a gray paw, and they both fell asleep.

***

Early in the morning, before the sun had spread its rays, the train lurched to a stop with a bloodcurdling screech. The boy and the kitten awoke. Instantly, the boy dreaded the worst: the Nazis had stopped the train. The companions hunched low in the seat, and stayed motionless. The boy began to sing his favorite song in order to give the kitten some comfort. "Twinkle, twinkle, little star, how I wonder what you are . . ." Just then, several shrieks came from outside, while men with thick German accents shouted and shook the train. The boy held his kitten closer as a tear fell. He continued his soft singing, his voice beginning to waver. "Up above the world so high, like a diamond in the sky . . ." Finally, the car door was ripped open, and men in army attire trampled in, ordering everyone out. The boy was thrown from the car as the kitten was grabbed by its scruff, tossed into a mud puddle, and disappeared. But the boy could not cry when he was forced into the line of people standing beside the train. He simply finished the song. "Twinkle, twinkle, little star, how I wonder what you are."

A German voice shattered the fog that clung to the dark ground. "Don't bother to save them. They're not worth it. Kill them all!"

***

And so, many blameless people were killed that gray, early morning. The Nazis continued to Paris, where the French and Germans signed an armistice in 1940. Due to this, most of France was given up to Germany. The Nazis went on to perform more atrocities all across Europe, but the stars above kept watch, and Germany was eventually brought to their knees.

***

Angels in Heaven sang that day when the Germans surrendered. Two in particular—mother and son—cried out and thanked their Lord for reuniting them in Heaven. They surpassed the fear of death to gain a greater prize: eternal life, rather than a despondent life separated from one another. And this was what could be heard all across the globe:

> "Twinkle, twinkle, little star,
> how I wonder what you are.
> Up above the world so high,
> like a diamond in the sky.
> Twinkle, twinkle, little star,
> how I wonder what you are."

Katy Sternberger
Age: 15

160

"You'll love the adventure and I promise it'll be one-hundred percent safe and relaxing! Together we can discover the mighty world around us," announced Mousey as he spoke to Mrs. Mousey. He wasn't quite sure what the adventure would hold, but he was about to discover it would actually be quite dangerous.

"I can't. Grandma Mousey is too busy to mouse-sit, nobody else can help me with the children," she replied.

"There has to be a way. I'm begging you, please."

"I'm sorry," she sobbed as she came up to hug Mousey, "you will just have to go without me this time."

"Oh well," mumbled Mousey as he scampered away. "Bye!" hollered Mousey as he pushed the heavy wire cage cover off with a thud.

"Good luck," shrieked Mrs. Mousey.

"I'm free!" he shrieked as he tiptoed quietly across his owner Joey's huge room.

The furry little creature skidded to a stop when he reached the stairs. They looked as steep as a mountain. Oh no, he thought, how am I going to get down these stairs? Mousey thought and thought for what seemed like forever. Then he got a great idea. He leapt onto the rail and slid down into the living room. When he got to the bottom he saw a monstrous-looking truck in front of him. It had huge wheels, a flatbed, and a reddish-orange fire blare with Ford F150 in the middle. Mousey loved the truck and decided to escape and explore in it.

The escapee zoomed out of the open back door in his shiny, black truck like a wild maniac. Staring at Joey's amazing yard , he shivered with excitement! As Mousey cruised slowly around the strange and mysterious yard, he stared at the tiny, gray, whistling birds flying high in the beautiful sky. A huge, bright sun and lots of puffy, white clouds looked like humongous clumps of ice cream floating in the sky. Tall, thick pine trees soared high above him. The trees looking like huge, green eagles that were going to swoop down and grab him. They gave Mousey the goose bumps just looking at them. The fresh smell of flowers wafted into his nose. Loud, buzzing bees quickly circled the flowers collecting more and more honey. The sound of a noisy, gray chipmunk chomping on a hard acorn nearly made Mousey jump out of his seat. Joey's yard sure is full of surprises, he thought. Suddenly, a huge dark figure appeared out of the darkness. "Probably just a large squirrel or bird," said Mousey. Green, short-sleeved shirt, long arms and legs, and a head with shiny, dark brown hair. It glowed in the bright, yellowish-orange sun, topped off with a devilish-looking grin. Mousey knew it was Joey.

He quickly put the truck to speed two and tried to speed away, but he saw a gigantic, brown pit approaching. He was stuck in a mud hole. "Oh no!" Mousey shrieked. Joey was getting closer and closer. Just as Joey was about to get him, he got an idea. Mousey put the engine into speed three and zoomed right out of the mud hole.

"Ha, ha, you can't catch me!" laughed Mousey.

"Oh yeah, you zoomed right into my trap!" exclaimed Joey. Mousey stopped his truck and nervously peered around the yard.

"W-what t-trap?" shivered Mousey.

"This trap!" replied Joey.

Suddenly Jaime, Joey's six-year-old little sister, jumped out from behind a small bush stopping Mousey dead in his tracks. Jaime's hair shimmered in the sun, blinding Mousey for a moment. Looking up, Mousey saw Jaime frantically running toward him. Mousey put the motor into speed three and zoomed away. Oh no, there was another huge, brown pit approaching. Mousey slammed on the brakes but it was too late. Mud was spraying all over the place and Mousey could hear the engine revving. He was stuck in another mud hole! Thinking quickly, Mousey put the motor into speed three, but the truck wouldn't budge. "Ahhhhh!" cried Mousey. Jaime was about to get him and he was trapped. This time Mousey was really in trouble!

Suddenly, the mud hole began to sink underground just as Jaime was about to get him. Mousey was shocked! As he sank Jaime's face looked very worried and confused. She ran to Joey and told him, "Mousey is going to discover our secret hideout, we have to do something!"

"Don't worry," Joey said. "The security will take care of him."

"Good point," agreed Jaime.

Meanwhile, Mousey continued to go down the mud-hole elevator. This place is very deep, thought Mousey. He wondered what Joey and Jaime meant about there being a secret hideout under here? Lots of terrible thoughts popped into his head. What if there's a torture chamber down here. What if there's a thing that scans for intruders without you noticing, then traps you inside a cage. What if there is security. All these terrible thoughts bubbled around in his head, as he approached the hideout. Suddenly, the elevator boomed to a stop "This must be what they meant," squeaked Mousey. "It sure is creepy down here," he shivered, as he peered around the narrow tunnel.

Dim lights barely lit the hallway. Next to Mousey was a ledge with fancy-looking desks and a huge screen. Mousey jumped when he heard Joey and Jaime's voices. He turned around to see them. "We see you discovered our secret tunnel," they both announced. "We love you, Mousey, but you came too far. Laser beams on!" they shouted. Before Mousey knew it, laser beams were aiming at him. He dodged them all just in time, but they chased him all the way to a door with a star on it. Mousey had no choice except to enter the door, or else the laser beams would get him. As soon as Mousey entered, a huge boulder fell down and almost got him. That didn't make a difference because the ground shook more and more. Soon the ground was violently moving up and down like huge waves and then it began to crack until his car flipped over. This is an earthquake! Mousey realized the car couldn't move so Mousey had no choice but to leave it behind. When he escaped, he had no luck and found himself hanging off the edge of a cliff. Mousey struggled to pull himself up, but couldn't. He was feeling hopeless. Mousey closed his eyes and thought I'm not going to make it. I lost my truck and I'm hanging off the edge of a cliff. Mrs. Mousey must be so worried about me. I better just close my eyes and wait for the ending, thought Mousey.

As Mousey closed his eyes, he saw an emergency button. Mousey was so happy he was about to cry. He pushed the button and a string popped out. His dangers weren't over yet, though. Mousey knew that while he was swinging, the tunnel could collapse and he would be buried under there forever. He grabbed the rope, almost fell, but then grabbed on again. Boy, my hands are sweaty and this rope is very rough. After Mousey got a good grip, he peered into the distance and saw a bright light. No matter how much his hands hurt, he kept hanging on. By the time Mousey got to the light, his hand felt like baseball players had used his hand for batting practice, but it was worth making it to safety. As Mousey slid slowly down the rough rope, he peered up and saw a huge trampoline. At first Mousey thought it might be another trick, but then he remembered that the tunnel could collapse any second. So he climbed onto it and jumped. When he opened his eyes he was back inside his cage!

Wooh! What an adventure, thought Mousey. I better go find Mrs. Mousey and the babies. Mousey dotted around the humongous cage looking for his family. He finally found them in their kitchen box splitting a large berry. Tears were drooping down their eyes and Mrs. Mousey was hugging all six of their babies. They looked very worried, especially Mrs. Mousey. He ran over to greet her to let her know what happened and he was safe. As soon as Mousey entered, the whole family threw their arms around him for what seemed like forever. Mousey called over all his relatives. Soon, a huge crowd anxiously gathered around him in a large circle ready to hear his exciting story. The whole crowd oohed and aahed at every event. All his family and relatives couldn't believe he had even survived this wild adventure. Mousey hoped his next adventure would be more fun than dangerous. To this day, Mousey and his family still talk about Mousey's unbelievable adventure you just heard.

Joey Santoro
Age: 10

I am the prince of the jungle. I am a good hunter. I like my stripes. No one can beat me. No one is better looking.

William Cousineau
Age: 7

RAVEN'S DISCOVERY

Off in the woods of Wisconsin, on top of a mountain peak, there was a thirteen-year-old, dark brown-eyed, straight black-haired Native American girl who thought searching for things and making discoveries was interesting. That girl's name is Raven and the best thing about this story is that her life changes forever. How do I know, you may ask? Well, that answer is easy, because I am Raven and this was the most exciting discovery of my life!

Maybe I should tell you a little bit more about my family. I have a younger brother named Sparrow, who is eight years old. He has dark brown eyes and light brown hair. I also have a mother, Brown Deer, and a father, Hawk, and most importantly my grandfather, the tribe's leader.

When Grandfather came to visit, he rode in on his white and brown-spotted Mustang, while I was setting up my tent. "My beautiful granddaughter, Raven," he said to me. "How nice to see someone working hard." My discovery began with a fire at our campsite. Another tribe was burning ours down. I'm the one who always protects Penny, my copper mare, so I ran to save her. When I got to the stable, Penny wasn't there! Looking for her, I frantically called to her hoping she would come to me. Penny was standing by my tent, so I mounted her and we were off.

"Sparrow!" I exclaimed.

"Help!" he shouted. I looked in the direction Sparrow's voice came from. The other tribe was capturing him.

"Hold on," I yelled. "I'm coming! Mom," I said nervously, while throwing water over a burning bush, "I have to go find Sparrow."

"Take some food and blankets," she said. When everything was packed, I set off in the other tribe's tracks.

"Giddy up," I shouted!

Crack! What was that? I thought. Thunk! "Penny?" I called. "Where are you?"

"Pbbbb!" Penny called back. The wood in my hands fell to the forest floor.

"Penny," I said, the color draining from my face. "What did you do?" I asked inquisitively.

Running over to her side, I saw what looked like the beginning of a river of blood.

"Poor thing," I murmured. "It'll be okay," I said in a slow, soothing tone. I took a carrot from my bag. "Here. I'll be right back." I grabbed a pail that was lying on its side by a tree and ran down to the pond. The fish were swimming so close I decided to catch some. With the water in one hand and my catch in the other, I started off for Penny.

After Penny and I finished supper, I decided to patch up Penny's cut. Shhh! "Here you go." I said, wrapping the part of my dress that I just ripped off around Penny's ankle. "All better. The only thing is I can't ride you when you're in this condition." She whinnied and I knew she'd be okay for a day or two, until she could walk herself home.

"Ouch!" I yelled. "Darn twigs!" I have been walking for what seems like days.

"Whaaa!"

"Hello?" I called. The noise sounded like a tiny baby crying. As quietly as possible, I tiptoed around the nearest oak tree. What I saw surprised me. It resembled a china doll, but when it opened its mouth, I realized what I was looking at was a Native American baby girl. As I approached her, she stopped crying. Crouching down, I gazed into the infant's eyes and saw an amazing resemblance of me! Surprisingly, the baby reached up and put her hand on my cheek. In our tribe, this means that we are glad that you are here. I was so taken back by this friendly gesture that I had to pick her up and cradle her. I'd never been so happy to see someone look like me!

Later that night, I decided to name the baby Fawn. Putting Fawn down, I built a campsite where we could sleep. Feeling tired, I gently rocked her to sleep, while thinking about how much longer could Sparrow last with the other tribe. When Fawn finally dozed off, I snuggled close to her and fell asleep as well.

"Raven?" a voice called quizzically. Startled, I reluctantly opened my eyes. As the image came into view, I saw a sight that I thought I would never see again.

"Sparrow!" I shouted.

"Whaaaa." I had woken the baby up.

"Who's that?" Sparrow asked, as I started rocking Fawn.

"It's a baby girl I found under an oak tree and I named her Fawn."

"Let's get going," Sparrow said, as we started on our route back home.

At around twelve o'clock noon, we were almost home. Sparrow had told me a little earlier that he was getting firewood for the other tribe when he spotted me. He also said that they had only taken him to do work for them. "Raven? Did you know Fawn looks like you?"

"As a matter of fact, I did notice that. In my opinion, I think that we are related!" I said triumphantly.

"Pbbbb!" a non-human voice called. When we rounded the next corner, I saw where the odd voice had come from.

"Penny!" I called, delighted to see her at last. "Let's see that cut of yours." It looked nearly all better, but I didn't take the risk of riding her. "Well, let's get going. We have to be home before dark."

As we got closer to the campsite, I saw a beautiful crackling fire. A rather depressed-looking man sat by it. "Father?" I asked, hoping this man wasn't a stranger. "Is it really you?"

"It is I, Father!" Father jumped up and embraced me in the world's tightest hug. "You don't know how much I've missed you!" he said.

"I think I do! Look at what I found in the forest."

"Rose?" he said, staring at Fawn.

"Do you know her?" I asked.

He was about to answer when Mother appeared and interrupted him. "My baby!" she said, sounding tearful and happy at the same time.

Then she glanced over my shoulder and saw Sparrow. While she did this, I saw a tear fall down her face. "Hawk," she said quizzically, "is that Rose?"

The suspense was killing me and I finally burst. "Who's Rose?"
I was practically screaming now.
"Calm down," my mom said in a soothing tone. "Rose is the baby in your arms; she's your sister."
The next day came rather quickly. The night before, Mother and I had straightened things out. What I found out was that about two months ago, while I was a trip with Sparrow, my mother had a third child. While we were on that trip, there had been another fire at my tribe's campsite. The other tribe had taken the infant, so all the men set out looking for the baby, but never found her. My mother was very depressed until we found Rose. Sparrow said that he did not mind being an older brother. After working things out, we were overjoyed to have Rose back. So this morning, I woke up to the sound of a baby crying. The weird thing is, I didn't mind it at all. I'm going to like taking care of Rose. I love my younger siblings! I am so glad that I discovered Rose!

Rebecca Hannah Glick
Age: 10

WHY DOES THE TURTLE HAVE A SHELL?

One day, Bear said, "Turtle, why do you have a shell?"
"I don't know," said Turtle. So he went to China.
He meets a wise guy who tells him, "You want to know why you have a shell? Your shell is for keeping you warm." The wise man falls asleep. Turtle goes to other places to ask why he has a shell, so he goes to Africa.
"It is so you can go slow."
He did not want to know that so he goes to Maine and he meets Mason. He said, "You have a shell for many reasons. But most importantly, you have a shell for protection."

Mason Henley
Age: 8

POISON IVY

Jealousy has more power than the wisest sorceress. Jealousy is a monster that consumes its victims and leaves them with nothing but their ruined lives. This monster knows no limits and follows no rules. It destroys families, tears apart friendships, and breaks hearts. Jealousy is what poisoned Ivy.

Ivy was envied by all for her radiant beauty. She moved with grace, spoke with elegance, and was considered to be more ravishing than Aphrodite, Goddess of Beauty. Ivy's flowing locks of auburn hair were always wreathed by daisies, and no one could resist her emerald-green eyes. Ivy could have chosen to live a life of luxury. Her love for her family and her friends hindered her from pursuing the life that she deserved. One friend in particular was key in Ivy's decision to stay.

Jalousie was the opposite of Ivy. She was awkward and clumsy, stumbled over her words, and could pass for Hephaestus. Her oily black hair hung around her face, and her cold, gray eyes always seemed to be looking through you. In her life of darkness and pain, she had one light, Ivy. Ivy and Jalousie had been close friends since the day they met, though no one ever knew why.

There was a river that ran through the quiet woods adjacent to the village of Trahison. Ivy and Jalousie spent many hours of their childhood splashing along the banks, skipping stones, and picking flowers. The two girls would lie in the grass and gaze at the clouds. It was on a day like this that Jalousie's luck changed.

"Ivy, do you ever wish for anything?" Jalousie propped herself up on her shoulders and looked at Ivy. "You know that you could have anything you wanted."

Ivy rolled over onto her side and gazed at her friend. "Jalousie, I've told you time and time again. The only thing I want is to lie in this field with you forever. My deepest desire is to gaze at these clouds and lose all my worries. I just wish to be happy and be with you," Ivy smiled. "And of course, I want you to be happy."

Jalousie shrugged. "I suppose you're right. Happiness is the best thing." She rolled onto her back and shielded her eyes from the sun to get a better look at the clouds. The girls lay in peace for several more minutes, until a cry broke the silence.

"Oh, Jalousie, I think that came from the river!" Ivy sprang to her feet and ran down to the bank. "Jalousie, look. Someone is trapped under the rock! You stay here. I'll run to the village and get help!" Ivy turned and ran, leaving Jalousie with the woman and the rock. Jalousie stared after Ivy.

"Ivy, wait. What do I do? Ivy!" Ivy did not respond, but the woman under the rock did.

"Child, come here and help me. Come here."

Jalousie slowly turned to face the woman. Her left foot was trapped under water, and she was clinging to a rock. Her weak appearance made Jalousie approach her.

"Good, Child. Now move that rock so I can be free."

Jalousie reluctantly stepped into the water. She rolled up her sleeves, plunged her arms into the icy water, and pried the rock off the woman's ankle.

"Thank you, Child. Now let me repay you for your services."

In the conversation that followed, the woman revealed herself to be the powerful sorceress, Sorcellerie. She told Jalousie that, for saving her life, she would grant her one wish. When Jalousie heard her reward, she thought of everything from beauty to riches. Overwhelmed by the sudden, generous gift, Jalousie asked Sorcellerie for some time to consider her possibilities.

"I'm not sure what to wish for now, but I will tell you as soon as I know."

"All right, Child," Sorcellerie murmured quietly. "When you know what you want, Sorcellerie will find you." Without another word, Sorcellerie turned away from Jalousie and walked away.

Fifteen years had passed since the day at the river and Jalousie still had not used her wish. She often thought to wish for money or her husband, but these seemed too selfish. She considered using her wish to please Ivy, until the day her best friend announced her plan to marry.

Tresor was the son of the village priest, and was as handsome as Ivy was beautiful. He often visited Jalousie's family farm to pick up eggs for his father. Jalousie adored Tresor, and eagerly awaited his visits. When Ivy announced that she and Tresor were to be married, Jalousie's heart broke. She feigned happiness for her friend, but a deep hatred began to grow inside her.

Jalousie collapsed on her bed and began to sob. "Why Ivy, why?"

A soft voice came out of the shadows in the corner. "I think someone is ready to make her wish now."

Without hesitation, Jalousie turned to Sorcellerie. "Make her ugly," she snarled. "Make Tresor hate her."

Sorcellerie sighed. She had been afraid of this. "If you wish child, if you wish."

On her wedding day, Ivy was more radiant than usual. Her hair was braided and adorned with an ornate wreath of roses. Ivy did not care about her hair, or her dress, or anything at all. She only wanted to marry Tresor.

Sorcellerie sat unnoticed in the audience. She removed a small maroon pouch from her robes and poured its powder onto the floor. As she did, Jalousie's voice came out of thin air. "Make her ugly. Make Tresor hate her."

Sorcellerie slid the pouch into her pocket and exited the room. She really regretted what she had just done.

When Ivy began her walk down the isle, no one smiled or oohed and aahed. Instead, her entrance was met with gasps. Ivy was covered from head to toe by a rash. Even Tresor was disgusted by his bride's appearance. When she stood next to him, he did not look at her face. He just turned and walked off the altar. Ivy was humiliated. She lay on her bed sobbing. She could not understand what had happened to her.

Then, a voice said, "Don't cry, Child. Sorcellerie can make this up to you. You can make one wish, and I will grant it."

Without hesitation, Ivy, turned to Sorcellerie. "I want to spend the rest of my life in the field by the river. And I want to spend it with Jalousie."

Sorcellerie sighed. If she only knew.

"Your wish is my command."

Sorcellerie removed another small pouch from her pocket and sprinkled the dust on the floor. As she did this, Ivy's wish was repeated. Sorcellerie murmured something under her breath, and then a blinding flash of light filled the room, and Ivy disappeared.

Weeks later, Tresor walked through the field near the river. No thoughts of Ivy crossed his mind, nor had they since her appearance at their wedding. He was looking forward to a pleasant swim in the river.

Tresor sat on a rock and began to remove his sandals. As he did so, he noticed a rash forming on his ankles. The rash looked just like Ivy's on her wedding day. As he looked closer, he noticed it had spread to midway up his calf. In a panic, Tresor ran from the rock back towards the village to see the doctor.

Sorcellerie emerged from the shadows, smiling at her handy work. She had granted Ivy's wishes, but had added her own personal touch. Ivy and Jalousie were together, but not in the way Ivy had intended. She appeared in the form of a three-leafed plant, but Jalousie was a poison covering her leaves. Jalousie had been nothing but a poison in Ivy's life, so Sorcellerie made her what she truly was.

Poison ivy, the plant we admire from afar, is the embodiment of Sorellerie's cunning, Jalousie's jealousy, and Ivy's forgiving nature.

Lauren Fecteau
Age: 14

THE SWARM

All of a sudden a snap. What was that? The gemsbok looked up from the grass it was grazing on. The swarm was coming. That must mean there's a hunter on the way. It had to get out of there and fast unless it wanted to be butchered and sold! As the gemsbok began running, it took a vast leap over a log and when it got over the log, it encountered the hunter.

As the hunter took aim he felt a tremendous pain in the back of his hairy neck. Then another, and another. The hunter knew he must shoot very quickly, so again he took aim and this time he jolted from an alarmingly awful sting to his back and let a bullet fly. This shot missed and the gemsbok narrowly escaped. This wouldn't be the last time these two would meet and the hunter wasn't one to ever give up.

The gemsbok sadly knew the hunter would continue tracking him so he had to really confuse the hunter. The gemsbok found a round path and cleverly walked around it five times in a row. Then he leapt as far as he possibly could. He landed in a slow-flowing stream approximately twenty feet away. The hunter would be stuck there for a while. Now the gemsbok bounded away a few miles and lied down for the cold night.

When the hunter came to a path, he saw, to his joy, gemsbok tracks, so he followed them. After a while, he realized he was going in a meaningless circle, so he sneakily turned around and walked the other way thinking the gemsbok was following this path the way he had been going. So, he thought that if he turned around, he would surely have dinner for a long time! Of course, he was horribly wrong. He didn't think a dumb old gemsbok would be able to trick him . . . it did.

As the gemsbok awoke, it heard something far off in the distance. It was a human shouting. It must be the hunter getting rabidly angry about being outwitted by an animal. He knew the hunter would take a long while to cross the stream, but the gemsbok heard another recognized sound . . . it was the swarm. But it couldn't be the swarm because it only came when there was a hunter nearby and it was approaching far faster than any human being could possibly run. The gemsbok decided to stand its ground. The bushes began to rustle and out of them came an angry, spotted leopard. He tried to leap away, but his leg got savagely snapped by the ultra-powerful jaws of the spotted leopard. The swarm once again saved the gemsbok by stinging the spotted leopard directly in its glowing green eyes.

The spotted leopard had been stung in its eyes by those extremely fierce, buzzing insects. She couldn't keep her grip because of the agonizing pain in her eyes. As the spotted leopard let go of the leg, it let out a ground-shaking roar. She ran away and decided to look for some other helpless thing to prey on that wouldn't have the swarm to protect it.

The hunter heard a terrifying sound. All of a sudden, out of the blue, he heard a deep, ear-piercing roar. He was about to instinctively turn and run, but he remembered the look of that thick, silky hide of the gemsbok and decided to press on as long as he could.

The gemsbok was in such shock he could barely even walk. He didn't like this because it meant he needed to rest if he wanted any hope of surviving. He knew if he stopped he had the danger from the hunter. He had to move a little further to find a water source to cleanse his wound. As he was walking, he once again, amazingly, heard the swarm! How could another potential danger be coming!? Or was it a danger at all? It might be after something else. He had to keep moving because every second he was losing blood and energy. As the gemsbok was walking, thankfully, the swarm's continued buzz was fading away. Now he heard the sound of a rush. It must be some kind of water source. As he grew nearer he realized it was a slow-moving, gentle stream. He approached it and found the water. The gemsbok waded into the water and that somewhat stopped the bleeding. Now he had to rest to regain some energy.

The hunter was terrified as he proceeded through the forest. He wasn't in any danger, but whenever he heard the sound of a hooting owl he would almost fall from astonishment. When he found a trail of blood on the ground he was happy, sad, and scared at the same time. Happy because the gemsbok he was tracking might be wounded and easier to track and kill. Sad because that blaring roar could have been a predator taking down and defending its kill. And scared because if there was a predator it could come after him. He decided that he would settle there for the night and make the big decision tomorrow.

When the gemsbok roused, it noticed a difference from when he fell asleep. He couldn't quite pick it out. There! There is a tree with its roots exposed! It must have been a big creature to uproot a tree! He learned a lesson and that was to never sleep by a water source because many animals will pass by it while you are asleep. The gemsbok was lucky it wasn't a hungry carnivore. The wound on his leg was much better and no longer bleeding. The leg was very stiff, though, so it felt awkward as the gemsbok walked, resulting in an occasional stumble. The gemsbok had lost valuable space between him and the hunter. He chose to hook around back so he was behind the hunter and went the other way.

The hunter decided to turn around and go back because he didn't think it was worth possibly risking his life just for a little hunt. The hunt didn't mean much anyway because his family still had a few weeks worth of food left and didn't necessarily need the food. He began to head back.

The gemsbok was almost back to the path when it had a new feeling . . . hunger. The gemsbok hadn't eaten anything in the last few days so when he got to the path, he grazed on some grass. Then he heard a twig snap. Turning its head to see what made the sound, there in the open, he saw the bulky hunter. He bucked and ran for the trees. There was only one problem: they were around seventy-nine yards away! He took off at full speed and was almost there when he felt only pain.

After the gunshot, the hunter began to hear a faint buzz. What was that? he wondered. He didn't mind because he had made the kill . . . or had he? As he approached the gemsbok, it suddenly twitched and got up. It took one huge leap into the forest, and, as the hunter got ready to shoot again, he felt a dreadful, tormenting pain on his forehead. He let out a yelp and ran in the other direction. The swarm had, for the third time, saved the gemsbok!

The swarm followed the hunter for nearly a mile! They drove him to the road where an unsuspecting driver stopped and the hunter frantically scrambled into the heavy-duty pickup truck.

The gemsbok was having trouble even walking through the woods. He didn't know what to do next. Well, he did, but he didn't know how. Somehow, he needed to make it to the stream before nightfall or a leopard would find him by the bloody path. He needed to follow that path to get to the stream again. When the gemsbok emerged from the woods, to his contentment, he didn't see the treacherous hunter anywhere. He began to walk down the path, but he was getting weaker by the minute. The gemsbok began to awkwardly stumble and eventually he started to completely fall down once in a while.

Nighttime approached and the gemsbok heard something. It was the stream! He couldn't believe he had made it to the delicate stream. Once again he waded into it and came back out. If he could get away from here he might incredibly survive. The gemsbok was still having trouble walking, but it had gotten better. He started to walk wherever he saw somewhat of a path. There was a meadow ahead and he needed food remarkably bad! He had made it to the meadow and began to eat ravenously. After what seemed like a decade, the gemsbok laid down and went into a final rest.

Jeffrey G. Pepin
Age: 11